On Canaan's Side

by the same author

fiction
THE SECRET SCRIPTURE
A LONG LONG WAY
ANNIE DUNNE
THE WHEREABOUTS OF ENEAS MCNULTY

plays
THE STEWARD OF CHRISTENDOM
SEBASTIAN BARRY: PLAYS I
OUR LADY OF SLIGO
WHISTLING PSYCHE
THE PRIDE OF PARNELL STREET
DALLAS SWEETMAN
TALES OF BALLYCUMBER

poems
THE WATER-COLOURIST
FANNY HAWKE GOES TO THE MAINLAND FOR EVER
THE PINKENING BOY

On Canaan's Side

A novel

by SEBASTIAN BARRY

ff

faber and faber

First published in 2011
by Faber and Faber Limited
Bloomsbury House
74–77 Great Russell Street
London WC1B 3DA

Typeset by Faber and Faber Limited
Printed in the UK by CPI Mackays, Chatham

A CIP record for this book
is available from the British Library

ISBN 978–0–571–22653–5

The paper this book is printed on is certified independently in
accordance with the rules of the FSC. It is ancient-forest
friendly. The printer holds chain of custody

FSC
Mixed Sources
Product group from well-managed
forests and other controlled sources

Cert no. SGS-COC-004311
www.fsc.org
©1996 Forest Stewardship Council

2 4 6 8 10 9 7 5 3 1

For Dermot and Bernie

Livin' on Canaan's side, Egypt behind
Crossed over Jordan wide, gladness to find.

AMERICAN HYMN

PART ONE

First Day without Bill

Bill is gone.

What is the sound of an eighty-nine-year-old heart breaking? It might not be much more than silence, and certainly a small slight sound.

When I was four I owned a porcelain doll given me by a strange agency. My mother's sister, who lived down in Wicklow, had kept it from her own childhood and that of her sister, and gave it to me as a sort of keepsake of my mother. At four such a doll may be precious for other reasons, not least her beauty. I can still see the painted face, calm and oriental, and the blue silk dress she wore. My father much to my puzzlement was worried by such a gift. It troubled him in a way I had no means to understand. He said it was too much for a little girl, even though the same little girl he himself loved with a complete worship.

One Sunday about a year after I was first given it, I insisted on bringing it to mass with me, despite the long and detailed protestations of my father, who was religious in the sense he hoped there was an afterlife. He bet all his heart on that. Somehow a doll was not a fitting mass-goer in his estimation.

As I carried her in stubbornly to the pro-cathedral in Marlborough Street, by some accident, possibly the great atmosphere there of seriousness, she started to fall from my arms. To this day I am not certain, not entirely, that I didn't let her go on some peculiar impulse. But if I did, I immediately regretted it. The ground of the cathedral was flagged and hard. Her beautiful dress could not save her, and her perfect face hit the stone and smashed worse than an egg. My heart broke for her in the same instance, so that the sound of her destruction became in my childish memory the sound of my heart breaking. And even though it was a babyish fancy, I do wonder now if it might not be a sound like that an eighty-nine-year-old heart makes, coming asunder from grief – a small, slight sound.

But the feeling of it is like a landscape engulfed in flood-water in the pitch darkness, and everything, hearth and byre, animal and human, terrified and threatened. It is as if someone, some great agency, some CIA of the heavens, knew well the little mechanism that I am, and how it is wrapped and fixed, and has the booklet or manual to undo me, and cog by cog and wire by wire is doing so, with no intention ever to put me back together again, and indifferent to the fact that all my pieces are being thrown down and lost. I am so terrified by grief that there is solace in nothing. I carry in my skull a sort of molten sphere instead of a brain, and I am burning there, with horror, and misery.

God forgive me. God help me. I must settle myself. I must. Please, God, help me. Do You see me? I am sitting here at my kitchen table, with its red Formica. The kitchen is gleaming. I have made tea. I scalded the pot, even in my distraction. One spoon for me and one for the pot. I let it brew, as always, waited, as always, the yellow light in the window facing the sea as solid-looking as an old bronze shield. In my grey dress of heavy linen, that I regretted buying the moment I paid out the money for it in Main Street

years ago, and still regret, though it is warm in this struggling weather. I will drink the tea. I will drink the tea.

Bill is gone.

The legend of my mother was that she died in giving birth
to me. I broke free, my father said, like a pheasant from
cover, noisily. His own father had been steward of Humewood estate in Wicklow, so he knew what a pheasant looked
like, breaking from cover. My mother died just as the need
for candlelight failed, at the first instance of the dawn. It
was in Dalkey village, not far from the sea.

For many years that was just a story to me. But when I
was pregnant with my own child, it suddenly became vivid,
and as if it was present time. I sensed her in that cramped
delivery room in Cleveland as I strained to get him out. I
never had any true thought of my mother till then, and yet
in those moments I do not think any human being was ever
closer to another. When the baby was laid on my breast at
last, me panting like an animal, and that matchless happiness surged through me, I cried for her, and the worth and
weight of those tears was more to me than a kingdom.

When I was shown the Catholic catechism at four, in the
little infants' school attached to the Castle, and the very
first question was posed, *Who made the World?*, I knew in
my heart that the teacher Mrs O'Toole erred in providing
the answer *God*. She stood before us and read out the question and answer in her wren-sized voice. And I might have
been inclined to believe her, because she was impressive to
me at four in her skirt as grey as a seal in Dublin Zoo, and
she had been very kind to me as I came in, and had given

me an apple. But the world, as I thought she ought to have known, was made by my father, James Patrick Dunne, not quite at that time, but later to be, chief superintendent of the Dublin Metropolitan Police.

The legend of my father was that he had led the charge against Larkin's men in Sackville Street. When Larkin came over O'Connell Bridge in a fake beard and moustache, and walked up through the marble corridors of the Imperial Hotel, and out onto a balcony, and began to give a speech to the hundreds of workers gathered below, which had been forbidden by edict, my father and the other officers ordered the waiting constables forward, with batons drawn.

When I first was told this story as a child, on the very evening it happened, I misunderstood, and thought my father had done something heroic. I added in my imagination a white horse, upon which he rode with ceremonial sword drawn. I saw him rush forward like in a proper cavalry charge. I gasped at his chivalry and courage.

It was only years later I understood that he had advanced on foot, and that three of the working men had been killed.

Old matters. And not much to do with the grief of the present except it gives me my bearings. Now I'll draw breath and start properly.

When I came back in from the funeral my friend Mr Dillinger had come into the hallway while I was out and left flowers but not waited for me. They were very costly flowers, and he had put a little note against them, and written,

'To my dear friend Mrs Bere, in the time of her great loss.' It touched me, truly. I am sure if Mr Nolan was still alive he also would have crept in. But it would not have been welcome. Maybe if I didn't know what I know now, maybe if Mr Nolan's death had not occurred when it did, I might have gone on imagining him my closest friend in life. It is so strange that his death and the death of my grandson Bill have happened so close together in time. All things come in threes, no doubt this is true. The third death will be my own. I am eighty-nine years old and will end my life very shortly. How can I live without Bill?

I cannot do such a terrible thing without explanation. But who do I explain to? Mr Dillinger? Mrs Wolohan? Myself? I cannot depart without some effort to account for this despair. I am not generally despairing, and I hope I have exhibited little enough of it as a living, breathing woman. It has not been my style at all. So I will not entertain it for long now. I feel it, so deeply I fear it troubles my very pancreas, that strange blue organ that has killed Mr Nolan, but I do not intend to feel it much longer. As long as it takes to speak into the shadows of the past, into the blue ether of the future, so long will it be, I hope and pray. Then I will find some quiet method to dispatch myself.

I have not been immune to all the lovely sights of this world that I have been granted, whether some corner of Dublin as a child, some little unprized courtyard in the castle that seemed to me like a dusty paradise, or in these later times those long-limbed creaturely fogs that walk in against the Hamptons like armies, whether attacking or defeated, whether going out or returning home is hard to say.

I hope and pray Mr Nolan wends the long downward

road to hell, with the fields beginning to burn about him, and the sunlight to take on a worrying, ragged hue, the vistas to alter and seem strange to him – not the wide tobacco fields and blithe, wooded hills of home after all, for he was born and raised in Tennessee, despite his Irish name, and, like every dying son of a place, he may have imagined himself wending homeward naturally in death. And though in essence I loved him while he was alive, and for many many years we were friends, it will only be just and right now that the devil takes his hand and leads him in among the smoking meadows.

The devil, I am beginning to suspect, and great grief it is causing me, has a greater sense of justice than the other man.

'Only the unfaithful can be truly faithful, only the losers can truly win' – this was said to me once by my grandson Bill, with his usual sparkle, before he went to the desert war. He had already been divorced, aged nineteen, and already believed himself to have lost in life. Or Life, with a capital L, as he called it. The war took the last sparkle out of him. He returned from the burning desert like a man that had seen one of the devil's miracles. Some mere weeks later he was out with his friends, maybe doing a little of that drinking he liked. Next day he was found by a cleaner lady in the toilets of his old high school, of all places. He had climbed in there on some impulse known only to himself. He had killed himself on a Saturday night, for the reason I am sure that only the janitor would discover him on Sunday, and not the great tide of children on Monday. He had hanged himself on his tie from the door hook.

Why am I alive when he is dead? Why did Death take him?

Nothing else on earth would have set me to writing. I hate writing, I hate pens and paper and all that fussiness. I have done well enough without it too, I think. Oh, I am lying to myself. I have *feared* writing, being scarcely able to write my name until I was eight. The nuns in North Great George's Street were not kind about that. But books have saved me sometimes, that is the truth – my Samaritans. Cookery books when I was learning my trade, oh, years ago, though in these later years I sometimes still find myself dipping back into my tattered *White House Cook Book*, right enough, to remind myself of some elusive detail. There is no good cook that has not found errors even in their favourite cookbook, and marked them in the margins, like an old book maybe in the lost library of Alexandria. I will read the paper on Sunday sometimes, in a certain mood, from stem to stern. Burn through it like a growing flame. I quite like the Bible in a rarer mood. The Bible is like a particular music, you cannot always catch the tune of it. My grandson Bill also liked the Bible, he specialised in unpicking the book of Revelation. He said that was what it was like, the desert, Kuwait, burning burning, like the lake of fire. *He who is not written in the book of life will be cast into the lake of fire.*

I like stories that other people will tell you, straight from the mouth – or the *gob* as we used to say in Ireland. Easygoing tales, off the cuff, humorous. Not the heavy-hearted tales of history.

And I have had enough history for a lifetime from my

own life itself, not to mention the life of my employer, Mrs Wolohan.

That is an Irish name of course, but as there is no W in the Irish language I must suppose the letter was added in America, many years ago, in another generation. Because one thing I have noticed about words in America, they don't stay still. Like the people themselves. Only the birds of America seem to stick, birds whose natures and colours so intrigued and confused me when first I came. Hereabouts, these days, the seaside sparrow, the clapper rail, the grackle, and the piping plover, and the thirteen species of warbler that grace these shores. I myself have been about a bit, all told. The first town I hit was New Haven, a thousand thousand moons ago, as one might say. With my beloved Tadg. Oh, that was a wild story enough. But I will try and write about it tomorrow. I am cold, even though the heat of early summer is adequate. I am cold because I cannot find my heart.

Second Day without Bill

Not content with leaving the flowers yesterday, Mr Dillinger brought himself back today. The actual flowers I had
put not very beautifully in an old milk-jug, but for all that
they shone brightly on the kitchen table. He touched the
blue petals absent-mindedly, as if he only half-remembered
they were something to do with him.

Mr Dillinger has discretion, I am sure he knows when he
is not wanted. But the difficulty with him will always be it
is hard not to be glad to see him. He is one of those perhaps
rare men that bear the face of an emperor, rather craggy, and
what I imagine as noble, not being entirely sure what that
might be. He has the looks to go with his reputation, which
is as a wonderful writer. He is one of the very closest of Mrs
Wolohan's friends.

Even in his late sixties, his manner gives no hint of age.
He is very long and lean, so he didn't so much sit in one of
my parlour chairs, designed for lesser mortals, as lean himself against it somewhat, like a ladder someone had propped
there. Such is the nature of his mind that his head is always
in clouds of a sort, and he speaks what is uppermost there,
what is most important and urgent to him at that moment,
and has not much small talk, something he shares with
Mrs Wolohan. But she never had much need of it, with
me. We went on like clockwork, in the days of my actual
employment. I cooked the same round of things for her, and
Wednesday lunch was the same thing more or less every

Wednesday, except when the pressure of the seasons was on me, and some items might be scarce. My days in Cleveland had been well spent, and my dear friend there Cassie Blake, who showed me the first oyster I ever saw, and many other mysteries, left her mark on me for ever, so that I just cannot say I was a bad cook. Which is just as well. Mrs Wolohan may have put great store on my being Irish when she first engaged me, or inherited me from her mother, but it would never have been enough for an employment.

Mr Dillinger has no small talk, but he does have talk. 'I think I should bring you with me next time I am going to North Dakota,' he said, as if the tail-end of a vast train of thought, as long and mysterious as the great freight trains that wind down through America. 'When I was very sad myself, when my wife passed, I found great solace there, among the Sioux.'

Of course I did not for a moment think he meant it, about bringing me with him. But there was its own kind of solace in his odd playfulness.

He began to talk about other things. Like an old-fashioned Irishman of my father's generation, he did not want to get at the main topic directly, but to creep up on it. Now he was telling me a story about his family during the Hitler years. Mr Dillinger's father had been quite wealthy, he said, and far from fleeing Germany with a cardboard suitcase, had made the journey hopping from five-star hotel to five-star hotel, all the way down through Europe, as far as Gibraltar, where he managed to book a first-class passage for his family to America. But his wife, Mr Dillinger's mother, at the last moment refused to go, and later died in Dachau, with two of her daughters. Mr Dillinger visited Dachau years

12

later, when it was a sort of museum. Mr Dillinger did not look at everything with the eyes of a tourist, he said with a beautiful solemnity, but with eyes made of the same stuff as his mother and sisters. There had been a huge photograph, he said, he remembered that, in an exhibition hall, of a woman running, staring back in terror, her arms flying, her breasts cut off. I jumped in my chair when he said that. I felt it in my own breasts, somehow. Terrible, very terrible.

'It is not always possible to know exactly what you are looking at,' said Mr Dillinger, his body visibly shaking.

Then he said nothing.

'I apologise,' he said. 'Please forgive me.'

'For what?' I said. 'I am very sorry what happened to your mother and sisters.'

'I came to try and say some words about Bill,' he said, his head down.

'There's no need,' I said.

Because of course there are no words of consolation, not really.

Then he seemed to shake his head at the next thing he thought to say, and the next, and so continued to say nothing.

I sat very quietly. I didn't want to cry in front of him for one thing. Tears have a better character cried alone. Pity can sometimes be more wolf than dog. I wonder if I were to have an X-ray at the little hospital, would the machine see my grief? Is it like a rust, a rheum about the heart?

At last he bestirred himself, and his face broke out into a warm smile. His blue eyes lifted their lids, those very eyes he had mentioned.

'Mrs Bere, perhaps I have taken up too much of your time?'

He rose nimbly from the chair, eliciting from it a half-musical squeak, and stared down at me. He seemed to be waiting for an answer, but my throat was stuffed with silence. Then he nodded his head, bent down towards me, and patted my arm very briefly. Then he went silently into the hall and away out into the dusty brightness of the day. The light of the Hamptons, with the lustre of a pearl.

Discretion.

When he was gone I took down the book he had given me years before. I had never read it, as indeed he had predicted the day he gave it to me. He had been coming up my lane, he had said, after a long walk by the sea, the beach in a great shroud of fog, just the way he liked it. He had seen a little wren going in and out of a hole in the old roadway wall. Stretching away from it, he said, was the vast potato field. Stretching the other way, the great series of dunes and salt-water canals. Above this tiny bird was the colossal, clearing sky of the Hamptons, the fog being dispersed by the huge engines of the sunlight. This, he had thought, was a bird that didn't know how small it was, that existed in an epic land-scape, and believed itself to have the dimensions of a hero. This was a bird, he thought, that only read epics. And for some reason, best known to himself, whether he associated me with that bird, I don't know, or because I merely lived next to it, that very same afternoon he had decided to bring me a gift, a red-leather-bound volume of Pope's Homer.

'You may read it, or not read it, that is not part of our contract.'

The contract he referred to, I believe, was the contract of friendship.

I smoothed the beautiful leather under my hand:

Achilles' wrath, to Greece the direful spring
Of woes unnumber'd, heavenly goddess, sing!

The light sat on the myriad cobbles of the parade ground as if there were a bright penny balanced on each one. I was standing with my sisters and brothers in a shock of vaguely made-up dresses and a slight stab at male grandeur. Our mother was dead my whole life and there was only my father's hand and eye to manage these dark matters. It was I think the day my father was made chief superintendent, and we had moved that morning into our new quarters in Dublin Castle, because we were to be denizens of that place. It was a lovely square flower-pink house and I was still so young that I had spent the morning showing my dolls the rooms. But I don't quite know what age I was. My brother Willie seems young enough too in my mind's eye, so it was certainly before the Great War. But all that, whenever it was, before and after, was nothing to the emotion that filled me at the sight of my father in his new dress uniform. There was no guesswork in that. The commissioner, dressed as my father said 'in a London suit of the finest sort', had come over from said London and was formally bestowing on my father, my own father, the signs and formulas of his new condition. I know now he was to lead the B division of the Dublin Metropolitan Police, and had risen now as high as he could ever expect, after thirty years in the police. No Wicklow sunrise over Keadeen Mountain, where our cousins and aunts and uncles still lived, could have matched the brightness, the shavenness and utmost delight in his face.

It was the same look I saw every evening I came home from school, and I ran into his arms, and he kissed me, and said, 'if I didn't have your kiss I might never come home', but magnified a thousand times. His large frame that would have thrown any tug-of-war team into despair at the sight of it, if it were coming to oppose them, was bound up in a black uniform with rushing darts of what looked like silver to me on the cuffs, but may only have been glistening white braid. His hat had a white feather that streamed in the solemn castle wind. His height made the commissioner, splendid enough but in his mere civilian suit, look sketchy and oddly fearful, as if my father might somehow engulf him on a whim of strength. The commissioner spoke for a few moments, and all the ranked constables and sergeants, themselves as black as burnt sticks, every one of them six foot tall and more, made a strange murmur of approval, as sweet to my father as the rush of the salt sea on the Shelly Banks was to me. The small delicate tide of friendship, shoaling against my father's bursting face, bursting with pride and certainty.

'A day for Cissie, a day for Cissie to see,' he had said to me, as he dressed me a few hours previously. This mysterious and unknown Cissie was my mother, whom my father rarely invoked. But it was the sort of day when a widower misses the excited eyes of his lost wife watching him. My father, who had learned much arcane expertise as a father, scorning at every turn any maiden aunt offered to him from Wicklow, smoothed out the sash on my dress with his big cold hand, and went round behind me and hunkered down, first tugging at the top of his trouser legs to prevent creases and stretching – one of the thousand possibilities in his life he said 'would never do' – and with just the right amount of care and the right amount of speed, tied my bow.

'There,' he said. 'No king's child could be better kitted out, and no king could be better pleased with his daughter.'

Then he took me in his arms, myself a little silken girl, and squeezed me so that just for a moment the small cage of my chest was without a breath, and glad I was to be breathless, and he put his large moist mouth to my cheek and kissed me with enormous precision. I did not need to be told what the delicate tip of an elephant's trunk felt like, as it ate its stale loaves in the Dublin zoo, because I was sure and certain it felt like my father's mouth.

'There now, there now, and wouldn't she have delighted to see you, Lilly, wouldn't she though? She would.'

This little conversation with himself, though seemingly addressed to me, needed no answer since he had just supplied it himself.

Now we were out on the parade ground and our father had been taken from us, so that things could be said to him, and his men beam their approval at him. But soon we would go home to our new house, and my sisters Annie and Maud would stoke up the challenging new range, and we might have God knows what, tea, and I knew in the dripppress Annie already had a bowl of bun-mix curing, and she would set that out dollop by dollop into paper cups, and they wouldn't be long plumping out in the range.

So far so good, so far so good, but then I come in my head to the strange souring of that memory, and I am wondering to this day if I really did see what I think I saw. Not having clapped eyes on Annie or Maud for a whole long lifetime, and indeed both of them dead, Maud a long long time, I could not ever ask them. I wonder is it mentioned or described in any annal of the Dublin police, I suppose not, because who is there left on the earth to read of the doings of the DMP? I can imagine all the books, all the daybooks and the night sergeant's ledgers, the infinite and infinitely growing sheaves of reports and court-papers and the like, put into some cellar like the very coffins of vampires, and left there for the million pages to soften and melt together, so that not even the eyes of angels could turn them.

We returned to our splendid house. What I would make of it now with my grown old eyes I do not know, but its big front door, its five high windows, excited me because it looked like a place where lovely things would happen, my sisters spoil me, while my brother tramped in and out, glowering and happy in the same breath, and my father continue to master the tying of sashes and the complimenting of daughters. The photographer, who had already done his work on the parade ground, had followed us over, and my father was to be photographed standing now in the frame of his front door, and while the photographer adjusted his dials and prepared to throw the black cloth over his head, my father stood there, fidgeting, I thought, which I knew was a minor crime in this life, and looking to me differently from on the parade ground, there was an odd look in his face, not fear, but something close to it, a little traipsing leak of anxiety that I had never detected before. He was thinking his thoughts and what they were no child was ever to know I suppose.

Big as he was, and he was a man that ate four pounds of meat a day, the door was three times his width. It was open, and I could see the black darkness within, and it amused me that the last sunlight of that day might quite soon inch its way along our red-bricked wall and peer ever so briefly into the house, like a person with a candle. The sun currently sat on the extravagant roofs of the chapel royal, where all the flags of the Viceroys hung, but not a place we would go into much, as Catholics. There was a little clasp of soldiers coming up from the Little Ship Street gates, they had just changed the guard there I am sure, and they were moving along smartly enough, but at the same time chatting and laughing, their guns carefully laid to their shoulders. Now and then the laughter grew, and the youthful noise clattered along the cobbled way, and climbed the low wall into the stable yards, making I was sure the lovely horses stir in their solitudes.

My father stood on the top step. Now the photographer was ready.

'A few minutes, sir, now, do not stir yourself. Now, sir, a good smile for me, sir, please.'

And my father, much to my surprise, obliged this person, a rangy long fellow in a suit with shiny leather patches on his knees and elbows, no doubt related to his work, with as much kneeling and leaning involved as the life of a nun or a cornerboy, and, his boots planted firmly, his feather stilled now in the lee of the house, the little raggle-taggle of soldiers just passing, beamed out a smile as good as the Wicklow lighthouse when at last it turns in its great arc towards you. What use was the lighthouse's light to those on land, I never knew, giving light to heather and fields, but really desiring to put that moon path of silver light along the tundras and swells of the Wicklow sea. What use was the lighthouse's light?, I was thinking, a child's thought, and curious that I remember it, but that is partly because as I write I see it again, I am that girl again, Lilly Dunne herself, before everything, in my full reign as it were as a little girl, Queen Lilly herself, and my father is my father again, though dust he is now. I do not even know precisely where that resplendent man is buried, God forgive me, and when he died I was not told of the fact, or did not receive news of it, for seven years, for seven years my father lay dead in an unknown yard, and still he lies there, but at this moment, this long-fled moment in that long-fled life, with his uncharacteristically unsure face, beaming his smile, the photographer under his cloth, the soldiers passing respectfully enough, but not entirely so, because this was mere police business, and they were soldiers, mighty soldiers, in the shadows of the hall I saw something. And just at that second the last finger of sunlight that I had been anticipating touched into the hall also, and gave a grave little light there, as if a deep well with a last glistening coin of water far below, and there loomed up from the shadows into the explaining sunlight a long brown creature, at first on all fours, and then when it saw my father's back, reared up, and most foully roared out, roared out like a great steam engine emitting steam, making my father spin round in adroit terror on his substantial feet, and stand there entirely frozen, the soldiers also frozen, but then in a moment one of them rushed forward and levelled his rifle, and fired it just by my right ear, an enormous and bewildering sound that I had never, in my years as a policeman's daughter, heard, the celestial effort it requires to force a lump of lead from a barrel, and in the instant of the bullet a sudden poppy of blood appeared on the bear's face, just above the nose, and in the same instant I saw that from the huge soft nose, through a hole in it, a hole that shouldn't have been there it seemed to me, hung a few feet of chain, jangling about, and the bear, because it was a bear, reared up further, in violent pain, his last pain on this earth, and fell full length out onto the top of the granite steps, hitting the stone with a soft bang, whoof, and my father seemed to bend at the knees just slightly, as if poised to leap away now, and throw himself to safety among us, but strangely he didn't leap, he seemed to fix there with bended knees, gazing and gazing at the dead bear, and it was a child's eye that saw it, and I hoped, I hoped and prayed no one else did, but the beautiful creases and the excellent material of his dress trousers began to darken at the crotch now with piss.

Quite changed and different we sat all together that evening in our new parlour, children in unnatural but seemingly unbreakable silence, eating a sombre tea, Annie's bun-mix undisturbed in the drip-press, and Annie looking every few seconds at her father, in his nightdress and dressing-gown, his serious-looking slippers like the bellies of seals, Maud, who took small things badly, now crying small tears in a corner, all our things still unpacked in tea-cases, left where the recruits had put them that morning, all the tune gone out of the whistle of life, on that day of days, long awaited, long worked for by my father, his long beat as a policeman, Dalkey, Store Street, Kingstown and now the Castle, all our dwellings along the way, most especially Polly Villa in Dalkey where my head first cleared and I knew I was alive, and loved, all the story of those places, chapter by chapter, leading to this moment of the strangest humiliation.

At length, as a bell somewhere in the castle buildings marked some forgotten hour, making the many stone stat-

21

ues briefly jump, and I jumped with them, a man in the uniform of an inspector came in to us, and spoke quietly to my father, who this once did not get up, and did not seem to have any orders to give back. My father only nodded his head, quietly receiving whatever information he was being given, and the inspector nodded his head, and said something I didn't catch, but knew from the tone that it was a pleasantry, and how relieved I was to see my father's face lift up to him, and offer a halfpence of laughter back. Then he laughed a little more, and then Annie began to laugh, and the inspector laughed, maybe greatly chuffed to have his remark so universally well received. But I did not laugh, because I saw still in my father's eyes those tiny hunting dogs of sorrow, moving across that dark terrain.

Next morning early at breakfast my father was recovered enough to tell us what the inspector had whispered to him. Some men unknown had come in by the gate and steps that led down into the police headquarters at the back of our house, though how the gate had been unlocked inside was a mystery, unless it was by a friendly hand, again unknown, and had led in by the chain in his nose a dancing bear, belonging to some travelling huckster, now identified, who had wept at the news of the death of his stolen bear, though whether because of the loss of his livelihood in hard times or from affection for the bear my father could not say, but at any rate they had led the bear stealthily in, and down the mossy steps, and into our house from the rear, and let the animal loose into the hall to cause grief to my father in his moment of great triumph.

'You may take some comfort, Jim,' he had said, 'from the fact that the teeth of a dancing bear are knocked out when he's a cub, and his claws are drawn from his paws – though a blow from one of them might have made you stand up straight right enough.'

And it was only many weeks later that these men were found, and identified as members of the new civilian army, the citizen army of Larkin himself, who my father had arrested in Sackville Street some while before in the great agitation and turmoil of the Lock-out. And I do not think, though at the head of his profession now as he was, did he ever quite get away from that moment, nor ever quite clear the new motes and hounds of sorrow from his eyes.

Third Day without Bill

Mrs Wolohan very kindly telephoned me this morning but was obliged to leave a message on the machine, which I know she dislikes. I went out early, having experienced a strong desire suddenly to stand and look at the sea. It is a long long walk down the sea lane, and getting longer, it felt like. But I was very content to reach the shore and gaze upon it. There is such solace in the mere sight of the water. It clothes us delicately in its blowing salt and scent, gossamer items that medicate the poor soul. Oh yes I am thinking the human soul is a very slight thing, and not much evolution has gone into it I fear. It is a vague slight notion with not even a proper niche in the body. And yet is the only thing we have that God will measure.

Having stood there, and having thought these useless thoughts, I traipsed back the way I had come, at least teasing a little heat into my bones from the exertion. Then I came into my wooden hallway and saw the light flashing on the answering machine. And it was Mrs Wolohan's welcome voice. 'Oh, Lilly,' she began, as she always does, with everyone, Oh Henry, Oh Whosoever she has rung, 'I am just ringing to let you know I am thinking of you. I will come over later with strawberries. They are really lovely strawberries and I will bring them over in a little while. I just have to do something with the dog.' Then she hung up. Very abruptly some might say, but not I, who know her so well, or flatter myself that I do. I know *my* Mrs Wolohan, and I have no argument with her. Years ago when I married Joe Kinderman, and I asked the priest in Cleveland, Catholic of course, if there might be an objection to me marrying someone of origins so vague he didn't know his own religion – Joe *thought or said* he was Jewish, but Joe was not Jewish – and not against taking the religion of his new wife, the priest, Fr Scully, said the prospect was 'unobjectionable'. And I think that is a fine word, and I have often applied it in life, as a sort of high compliment.

Mrs Wolohan. Unobjectionable. Who nursed her husband through his great illness, and buried him at last in the certitude that she had gone the last yard for him. Now there is no one on earth more lonesome than she, I do think, despite her wealth and her infinite busyness. Her capacity for survival is infinite, and you might supply a church with the stations of her life, and draw tears from the observation of it. She has allowed me to live here for twenty years, an expense I am sure she did not entirely agree to undertake, when she said she 'found a little house' for me. She said recently, when I mentioned this, that 'the quality of your baking' made it an absolute duty and necessity. She said it with her usual lightness, and she delighted me in the saying, even though it is of course twenty years since I baked for her with all the old passion of my kitchen self of those days. There is a way right enough to make a fairy cake that is not just about the simplicity of making them. A child of five can make them. But then, another ingredient can slip in all unexpected and the cook herself unaware – a sense of her own mother's baking, or in my case, the fearsome, fiery activity around the pot oven in the yard of an Irish cottage, when you see your aunty hovering with a tray of raw cakes, trying to get them under the lid of the pot-oven before the rain pelting down melts them, and all the care needed to make sure that not a speck of the blackened lid touched them. Something of that great dance may have got into me, right enough, I hope so. It is not for me to say.

Her husband, a man actually of similar energy, but not applied to mere cakes, deserved her devotion. He did deserve it, and doubly so, because she thought he did. I cannot claim much expertise myself on the topic of husbands. But I cooked his breakfast for him from 1955 to 1970, when he was at home, which is no small thing, if you were to imagine all those pancakes piled up in some strange heaven in an aromatic pillar.

Unobjectionable. Maybe it is servile in a former servant – for what else was I, in the little dictionary of life? – to admire her former mistress. To love her, and to feel brightened by her voice on – I noticed – a slightly grimy answering machine. It is queer the items in a house that never receive proper ministrations.

Mrs Wolohan is like a landscape to me, a whole country. Or that pleasing lighthouse on the last spit of land, where the beach has become stony, more like the Atlantic where it gnaws away at Ireland. Even if her idea of 'a little while' might not result in her actual appearance. But I was able to sit down here at the kitchen table, the Formica beaming the sun on into the hallway behind me, like a great flat stone of light bounced on the sea.

And be thinking, remembering. Trying to. All difficult dark stuff, stories stuffed away, like old socks into old pillowcases. Not quite knowing the weight of truth in them much any more. And things that I have let be a long time,

in the interests of happiness, or at least that daily contentment that I was once I do believe mistress of. The pleasure in something cooked right, just the small and strangely
infinite pleasure to be had from seeing, from witnessing, a
tray of freshly baked biscuits. Like I had just completed the
Parthenon, or carved Jefferson into a rockface, or maybe
the contentment, felt in the very sinews, of the bear when
he digs a salmon out of the water with his paw. Mightily
healing, deeply, and what else could we have come here for,
except to sense these tiny victories? Not the big victories
that crush and kill the victor. Not wars and civil ructions,
but the saving grace of a Hollandaise sauce that has escaped
all the possibilities of culinary disaster and is being spread
like a yellow prayer on a plump cod steak – victoriously.

I am thinking of these things even as I am about to go.
Mother sauces. The infinite delicacy of the bain-marie
saucepot. 'Heat is how the pot thinks, Lilly. It is like my
grandma singing a lullaby, not too loud so you keep sleep
away, not too soft and baby can't hear the words. Try and
hear the heat, Lilly. Hear the pot thinking. You hear it, you
hear it? It's there. You will. And when you do, you'll be able
to do any sauce in the world.' And her big arms showing
me, oh yes. Arms that could punch out your lights, but
never used for such. Dear Cassie Blake, who gave me these
guns and bullets for the long fight of life. And was herself
shipwrecked on the rocks of life in the upshot.

I am dwelling on things I love, even if a measure of tragedy is stitched into everything, if you follow the thread long
enough.

The one thread maybe, from Bill to my brother Willie,
all the way back, through how many wars is that, it must be

at least three? No, it is four. Four killing wars, with all those sons milled into them, and daughters these times too. And I have felt all that, for those that went out for the good of America, for the love of her. Oh, and I knew what safety and haven was America to me, so how could I not understand that something had to be given up for her? Something so close in to me, it was really part of me. Oh, Bill.

He used to like to look at the photos in the corridor, going down to my bedroom. It's not bright there, because it has no window of its own, but you can see them plain enough, even in daylight. There's a picture of Willie in his uniform. Bill used to gaze at that when he was very small, he spotted it quite early, because, truth to tell, he had a look of Willie, and he didn't just grow into his own face, but eventually into Willie's. Willie went out to the Great War as they called it, he was only a boy, just like Bill in the desert, and he was very happy to go, and when he was a few years in it, I don't know if he ever came home, even when he did on furlough. Something of him was lost in France, buried into the ditches they dug there, so that he would appear in our house in the castle right enough, but dressed in shadows, disguised by the thin dust of terror he carried on him maybe. But he was a sweet boy, I do remember that, or let me say, that is how I remember him, as sweet. What his true nature was I will leave to God, but I have a sense still that I loved him, I mean to say, I feel that love still. Even as I sit here, I don't know what I am, I suppose like any grieving person, I am broken-hearted, but even so, in the centre of that, in the heart of things, sort of beyond reach, I can hear my love for Willie still abiding, like the heat in the bain-marie. The thing put away most carefully in a drawer can sometimes be the very thing beyond finding. It is beyond finding, right enough – but it is still there.

Willie fought for three long years. He was nine months first in training down in Cork. I must have been twelve when he left, a child. When he didn't come back finally, I was a young woman. Willie not coming back . . . There were thousands, millions, of boys in that war, that didn't come back to their households. Parents grew old in the little aftermath of letters. Nice letters written conscientiously by their officers, lads themselves sometimes. Platitudinous, how could they be otherwise, with boys killed every day in trenches? Even unimaginable and murderous news has a formula, maybe it has to have, I mean, maybe it is better so. You have your marching orders then. You lose a child, a brother, whatever it might be, and you die in the aftermath, so you are walking about, breathing and thinking, but you are not alive.

I am not alive. It is almost a comfort to me that although I will take my life, I am already dead when I do so. It seems less of a sin. Because I know it is a great sin. It is a sin that we were told as girls had no remedy, one of those, with hell to follow, for certain. I suppose it might be so. I don't know.

My poor father got three communications about Willie. The first from his line officer, formal and distressing. That came to him among all his official post as an officer himself of the DMP. A letter, he said, that burned his hand as he read it. He came away from his offices at teatime, his big face flushed with terror, I saw it as he entered into our sitting-room, as if he had exchanged his own face for a lantern. He could have used his face to beam a light to Baltinglas. My sisters Annie and Maud were fussing about at the table, and I must confess barking at me to assist them, an eternal struggle I am sure, and my father in his big clothes and his burning face stepped in. He took the helmet off his bald pate. I caught the strange mood a few moments before Annie and Maud, and stood in the centre of the room, my bold mockery of my sisters stilled in my throat. I felt like a dog that has been reprimanded but cannot work out his misdeed. My father looked into the middle distance. I think he looked into it for the rest of his life.

Then Annie at least caught up. She conscientiously put down the great platter she was bearing.

'What is it, Papa?' she said.

'Terrible . . .' said my father, but could offer no further words at that moment. He drew out a letter from his coat, with the elephant and pineapple on it of the Dublin Fusiliers. Not that we saw that then. But we examined that letter for flaws and lies many times in the days after, with no success.

'He has been killed in Picardy,' said my father. He gained his old bentwood chair and sat gently into it. He was a huge man, and the chair was spindly enough, and perhaps he loved it for that.

There was a great clatter as Maud's less lucky plate went down onto the floor and smashed enthusiastically into a dozen parts. No one even looked at her.

'Aye,' said my father, though we had said nothing, 'in Picardy. A little village called St-Court. I wonder where that is? Yes, yes.'

And he sighed out with the last sigh in all the world.

Annie just stood. I got a fright when I saw her face. She

was often cross, Annie, and rarely smiling, but I had never seen this look. And seeing the look seemed to bring the same feeling into me, and my father's words found a nest in my breast. I heaved up great sobs, feeling also in my sixteen years a great embarrassment. I had never read any manual of grief certainly, and did not know if it were to be hidden or not. And anyway it could not be suppressed.

'Poor blessed boy,' he said, very vaguely, quietly. 'Do you remember when he was home last and I cleaned him in the tub, and you three banished to the kitchen, and the terrible muck on him and the fleas and the lice, and the ringworm on his skin? Bless me. Do you remember that? And Annie, you teasing us at the door, saying you were going to come in, and Lilly laughing her head off. Poor blessed boy. And no meat on him at all, and when I put the big towel round him, I thought I would lose him in the folds, there was that little of him. But he was strong, he was strong in spite of that. That was Willie. And he was a good boy.'

There was not much done in the house that evening except grieving. The grief at first sat in us, and then leaked out into the chairs, and at last into the very walls and sat in the mortar. I will be bound it is still there, if there were only someone with the heart to sense it, someone there that knew Willie Dunne, a lost name in the history of the world.

The second letter or communication came later, a few months after that dread news. Like all the families of Ireland, of England, France, Russia, Germany, the whole wide world, we did our best to rub two sticks of life together to make a small fire to live by. My father, as the person who had after all created Willie I suppose, mourned him most deeply, most terribly. He had no remnant of him except his soldier's smallbook, in which he had written his father's name as his executor, and given our quarters in Dublin Castle as his home place, a battered volume of a strange Russian novel, and the little figure of a horse Willie had picked up somewhere. These items were sent back to my father by Willie's unit. Annie was given the little horse, myself the Dostoevsky book, and my father kept the smallbook, a quite pristine object considering what it had been through, and I imagined Willie keeping it wrapped in a scrap of tarpaulin maybe, warmed by the heat of his chest. My father in turn kept the volume against his chest, in one of the inner pockets of his uniform, of which there were many, warming the pages in turn with the furnace of his own body. We, three quite grown-up girls already I am sure, especially in our own opinion, genuinely did grow up in that aftermath. One of the strange consequences of her sorrow was Annie lightened in an unexpected way, and was much nicer and gentler to me, so that mixed in with the treacle-heavy sorrow of that time is a little vein of goodness, because she had in other times a tongue that would shave your beard for you.

What arrived now for my father was a letter from Willie's sergeant. This letter, which probably does not exist now, thrown out on the scrapheap of things as families and all their small stories pass away, became as precious to my father as the smallbook, and was tipped into it. It is so strange to me that I still remember phrases in the letter, maybe because the sergeant, Christopher Moran, in the great effort of writing to my father, who he knew to be a policeman, fell into a queer kind of officialese. It was his 'solemn pleasure' to write to him, the letter said. But it gave an astounding account, astounding to us simply because it was uttered, and given freely, of Willie's simple death in Picardy. How he had heard a German soldier singing, and had sung back to him across no man's land, only to receive the bullet of a sniper.

'Just like Willie,' my father said, in equal simplicity. 'Always singing.'

I knew even at sixteen that Willie after three years of war had been hollowed out by horror and extinction, and my father maybe knew that too, so that the solace of the sergeant's letter, describing Willie dying in a moment of generosity and ease, did not have a measure.

Poor Willie. There is hardly anyone alive that remembers him besides myself and Bill. I am sure there is no one but me, Annie and Maud are dead, my father is long long dead, and of course Bill is dead. Bill that gazed on his great-uncle's photograph in an American house, and knowing almost nothing about him, smiled at him across the many decades, and maybe, now I think of it, took something of a tune from him in joining the army.

Then came Tadg Bere to see my father. Willie had three memorialists, and the third was Tadg.

Tadg Bere. He looked like he had swum the Channel and the salt had scoured him out, his face was that clean. Which was an achievement, considering he had sat in trenches for years. Trench dirt didn't always wash out, I am sure. A beautiful rinsed-looking boy, or so I thought as he sat with my father, giving him his own memories of Willie, as a friend and fellow private in the platoon. He had stayed on in the army and spent some months with the South Irish Horse in Cologne on traffic duty, since his own regiment had been destroyed in the war, only itching, as he told my father, to be able to come to Dublin and speak to Willie's people, as he thought Willie would have liked. It was then I really understood that Willie had been valued in the army, loved indeed I suppose. This boy we knew nothing about, except that he was from Cork city, and heading home directly after talking to us, had been part of Willie's world, unknown, dark and frightening, but with friendship in it. I don't know why that struck me in particular. I turned it over and over in my head.

My father for his part sat quietly as Tadg Bere spoke, only nodding his head now and then, and sometimes shaking it. By now, I suppose somewhere in 1919 it must have been, my father was about to retire, and go home to Wicklow. There were those new murders everywhere in Dublin, dozens of Royal Irish Constabulary men had been done away with, in ambush, in pubs, in beds. My father had reached sixty-five just as all the world he knew had gone on fire, big flames, dark smoke and all.

'The thing about Willie was,' Tadg Bere was saying, 'it wasn't just you could be depending on him, you knew he was keeping a weather eye out for you, like you might a brother. So I was always thinking, that was a sorta compliment to his family, that they had reared him up in that frame of mind. And what I am wanting to say to you, and have wanted ever since that day we buried him, the poor lad, and stuck his rifle over the grave, and his helmet on top of that, me and the sergeant and Willie's best pal Joe Kielty, that was kilt after also, ever since that day, over by St-Court so it was, and the war nearly over in those parts, and the bloody old Hun excusing my French driven back, was, was

. . .' And here Tadg drew breath, and for some reason looked over the bare boards and our little Turkish carpet in the centre, to me, and smiled, and in that smile, I swear to God, I read something of the future, like a proclamation. 'Was, by Jesus, Chief Superintendent, by Jesus, he loved you all. We knew of Annie and Maud and yourself, and little Lilly there, and he never tired of telling us how good and pretty you were, Miss Dunne, so he didn't. And I thought I had better come to ye some day and just be telling you that.'

'And we are immensely grateful,' said my father at last, heaving his voice out of the dark cavern of his breast up into the room. 'We are. How tremendously kind of you to stop on your way home, and I am sure your family is longing to see you, and so grateful themselves that the war spared you. That the war spared you.'

Then Tadg Bere stood up, feeling it was time to go and he had done what he had come to do.

'There was no one like Willie,' he said. 'That's a fact.'

'Now, Lilly,' said my father, rising also, and taking Tadg's hand in a handshake, 'you be walking this lad down to the gates. And look about you, Tadg, as you go through the town to the station. These are different times, and there are some will not like to see your uniform. We had a great procession just recent, you know, the victory parade, and thousands came out to remember, and thank you lads, but there are others now, tucked away in the crowds that don't like to see khaki. They do not.'

'Well and, sir, I can surely look after myself. Thank you, sir.'

I crossed the cobbled square beside him, feeling a bit strange suddenly, to be with a stranger, in my old summer dress. And I wished I had taken a cardigan with me, because it was autumn now and cold, and a huge lid of dark grey cloud sat over the city. And a boy like Tadg, who had gone into the army at eighteen, and was coming out the other end at twenty-two or so, like Willie would have done, he had probably not been with the female species for a long time, unless I suppose those wild women that serve soldiers in broken towns. Not to say that there weren't regiments of such women all up Montgomery and Marlborough Streets, because of the barracks, in that very city of Dublin, there were. But I did not think he knew much of talking to ordinary girleens like me, and he said almost nothing to me. But just as we reached the sentries at the Dame Street gates, those humorous lads let us say, who would not let me pass without some quip, Tadg surprised me. He stopped in the lee of the old granite gates, as if he had known me all his life, and spoke quietly and calmly.

'Willie spoke of you so often,' he said. 'And he worried about you so. When the rebels rose those few years ago here, he worried all the more. I used to see him sitting there in trenches, like a lobster boiling, fretting and fuming and worrying. So I came particular to see you, and to say, if there is ever anything you need me to do, I will do it. And if you will let me say, now I am seeing you, I know everything he did say about you was true, and I am only so glad that I met you, indeed and I am.'

And he held out his hand to me for shaking. I was dumb-struck. No one had ever made such a speech to me. In fact I wonder was it the first time I was ever spoken to as a grown woman, not a girl. And I suppose I was a girl still all the same. But I felt a heat flush all the way up my body, and I am sure a red rose of heat blushed up into my neck and face, I could feel it anyhow.

'If I write you a letter, will you answer it? I am sorry to be so odd to be talking like this. But I live in Cork city, and to be sure, I will be back in Germany a while longer. Then I don't know what I will do. I didn't like to say to the Super, but my ould man is in the Irish Volunteers, and he don't like me much in the army at all, so I don't know if I can go back to Cork when I am finished with this uniform. So I may come to Dublin instead and see what work there might be. I am told there is little enough work anywhere.'

I only nodded my head, he had given me such a fright.

'You're saying yes then to a letter?'

I reached into myself for an answer, come on, Lilly, come on, Lilly, speak.

'I am,' I said, and it was a great victory that I did, worthy of a parade I thought.

Then with a salute to the sentries off he went down the lane to Dame Street and away. As he turned the corner, he looked back, and seeing me still there shivering in my dress, looked surprised enough, and waved a hand, and waved again. And my own hand went up in a slight wave, the sentries gazing on all this and laughing, laughing.

I was deep in the memory of Tadg Bere when I heard a car draw up at my gate and thought I knew the engine. Here was Mrs Wolohan now after all. She came in my door as she always did, and why not, since it was her own house really that she had lent me after I retired? There had been no onus on her at all to do anything for me. It was such a nice sort of a cottage, she might have rented it out to the summer people for a tidy sum. But she hadn't. Twenty-odd years I have been installed here, so she might have wearied of her generosity. But no.

'Well, well, you are all shipshape here,' she said, coming into the kitchen. She had a bundle of something wet wrapped in a cloth, which I supposed was the promised strawberries, which she ferried over to the sink. She was as neat as a starched pillow in her white trousers and light blue shirt. She is sixty years old and I suppose could with justice be ground down by all the sorrows of her life, but somehow she has learned how to wriggle free. There have been many brambles in her path, but she has ducked around them. Perhaps in truth that is a recent victory. For some of the years I tended her, she was so sad that her silence became habitual, she rarely sallied forth into the world. But now these new days after her husband's death, and when the first deep grief of that has abated, have brought her onto fresh ground. There is a crispness to her, and to her talk, like someone had brought her basket of conversation and rinsed it all out, and washed it, and starched it; and an old wittiness that had been hers when she was young has returned. She likes to tease, never more so than when other people might have offered sincere platitudes, as now after Bill's funeral. But her teasing was more welcome to me. I could not now be consoled, so I preferred her sharpness, and anyhow, I had been reared with a similar tongue, that had resided in my sister Annie's mouth.

'I think I will have to get you to do something about that hair,' she said. 'You will come into town with me next week, and Gerard will do something with it. Our good friend Ger-*ard*,' she said, mocking the foreign pronunciation, 'whose real name I understand is Chuck, but never mind.'

'Do you think anyone cares what an eighty-nine-year-old person does with her hair?' I said.

'Never more important. When I am eighty-nine I will be having a makeover every few weeks. No one will be able to credit my beauty. It will be astounding.'

So we were laughing then.

After a cup of tea, I walked out with her to the front porch.

'Is everything good here?' she said. I feared we were to have the funeral conversation after all, and my heart sank. I had been so grateful to her for not saying anything, knowing full well it was uppermost on her mind. She who had waded through the fires of grief many times had usually infinite discretion. So my face dropped a little I am sure.

'This is where I will miss poor Mr Nolan,' she said. 'I think that damn gutter is leaning somewhat. It was the snow last winter I'll be bound.'

'I suppose it is a bit more crooked than it was,' I said, gratefully, though the mention of Mr Nolan disturbed me. Of course I had not attended his funeral. Nor I am sure had Mrs Wolohan, who did not like funerals, as a general rule, but had certainly liked Mr Nolan.

'I know nothing about gutters, but I believe that gutter is lying the wrong way. You will have the summer rains in your sitting-room.'

And having pronounced this certainty, she got into her car and drove off, leaving me staring up at the offending gutter. Summer rains. Maybe so. I did not think I would live to find out.

Fourth Day without Bill

A troubled night. There was a great storm that loomed in
from the Atlantic. I kept falling into a half-sleep and the
storm had no trouble following me there. Woods fell to it,
it felt like, and seas reared up, galloping through my addled
thoughts. I woke again and again, startled, not knowing if
I were young or old, in America or Ireland. That's what
comes of raking through old coals. Dredging up the past.

Yet I will confess there is a certain pleasure in this. I
scratch away at the Formica table, coming down the pages
of this account book with my pencil. I seem to see everyone
and everything as I write. I am able in some strange way to
greet my father again. I would like to say to him, Papa, I do
not know where you are buried, I am so sorry.

Pleasure, of a sort. It is always at the back of my mind
the things I have read since about the time of the war of
independence, the capture of rebels, and they being held
somewhere in the castle, and I fear tortured, and I wonder
did my father engage in that? He was in charge of B division, which was mostly a patrolling division. G division was
the detectives and they did not all have savoury characters. I
do not know how much such histories are weighted against
the losers, in this case men like my father, loyal to kings and
the dead queen, but I am sure there was evil and cruelty on
both sides. I am not so great a fool as to imagine otherwise.
I could not even if I wished, given Tadg's part in that story.
But even if my father were the cruellest, bloodiest, darkest

man in history, which he was not, my simpler heart, the bit of myself that perhaps invented him as a child, created in my mind an idea of him, fabulously adding to it as I grew older, misses him greatly, and would be more than enchanted to see him again. So in dreams he is a welcome piece of human flotsam floating by, and I cannot fear or criticise him. I will not make excuses for him, but also I will not deny him.

Perhaps in that moment, as Ireland stirred like a great creature in the sea, and altered her position, we should all have been taken out and shot, as a sort of kindness, a neatness.

Now I am laughing in my kitchen, but who is to hear that laughter? There are many forms of freedom, and this is one of them, to be so old I can lay claim to those I loved, without my own mind qualifying, erasing, hiding. My father was chief superintendent of police under the old dispensation. He was the enemy of the new Ireland, or whatever Ireland is now, even if I do not know what that country might be. He is not to be included in the book of life, but cast into the lake of fire, his name should not be mentioned because it is a useless name with a useless story. But all I had from him was kindness. Perhaps the children of that lad in Russia, Stalin's chief of police, would say the same. What was his name? To my eyes, reading about him, a monster. Is that what my father was, a monster? How will I ever know? Can I ask St Peter?

How I feared when first I worked for Mrs Wolohan's mother that she would cast me out if she discovered who I came from. Of course like her daughter she was an Irish-American, who loved Ireland, and the idea of Irish freedom, which for her was heroic and inspiring. As it was indeed, I am sure, unless you were on the wrong side of it. And I did feel obliged to touch on that a little, because I did not want her to think me something other than I was. When I went to work for Mrs Wolohan herself I said a little more about it. Of course what she liked first about myself, and later Mr Nolan, was that we were Irish, pure and simple, even if Mr Nolan had never been to Ireland, but was third-generation, like herself indeed. But she showed no great surprise, no disapproval. She was *interested* in it. I remember her sitting me down and asking me questions. She was intrigued my father was a policeman of the old British regime. Her whole being lit up with *interest*, the hallmark of her personality. That is a person truly democratic in her thoughts. That is a merciful person. Because she knew who I was, I gradually came to see myself better. When a criminal gets out of prison, he looks for work, but must be upfront about his prison term. Whoever takes that man knows all about him, and if he is lucky enough to find such a person, he might well find a strange and unexpected happiness working for them. That is what I felt somehow, with Mrs Wolohan. Not so much on probation as given a new lease, a new term among the living and the just. And she did that it seemed to me with her whole heart.

Tadg Bere wrote me his letter. It was a short letter, the work of a soldier. Soon he turned up in Dublin again, and wooed me. My father liked him well enough. There was little work for anyone in those times, but least of all for ex-soldiers, with the dark colour of the trenches in their eyes. So Tadg took a chance and when they were looking for men for a new auxiliary police force, he joined them. Most of the men in that force were survivors of the war also. They were set up to try and deal with the turmoil of rebellion in the country. But something of the despair of the war was in them. In the first days, Tadg was happy, aflame, even inspired. My father certainly had assisted him in his application. He was proud to be working, at something akin to soldiering, and something that would allow him to serve his country. He felt he was making a new beginning. He did not believe in any new Ireland, he devoutly loved the old one. The new force paid decently, but was otherwise poorly funded and put together in great haste. They barely had uniforms, and in the beginning wore bits and bobs of various forces, half army and half police, which is why they were dubbed the Black and Tans.

It is like a dirty phrase. A curse. An expletive. Well I know it.

My father was down in Wicklow now setting himself up in the old house. His brother had been farming the land all this while, in Kelshabeg above Kiltegan, and working as the steward on the Humewood estate, as his father, that is, my father's father also, had done before him. It was a small cottage set into the hillside for shelter, and what shelter it did ultimately give him I do not know. At any rate he was spring-cleaning it, scraping off the old damp and white-washing the walls inside and out, and he got a thatcher to repair the old roof, and a mason to put manners back on the ruined byre and henhouse. He aimed to be a retired man in the comfort of his old homestead, where seven generations of his family had been reared, and have a certain style to himself as a former officer high up in the police, with a pony and trap and, he hoped, one of his daughters to do for him.

A noble ambition I am sure in its way. In any other country but Ireland, who may give freedom to her sons and daughters quicker than a future. But he carefully limed his walls and set his new geraniums on the sills, bought his Rhode Island Reds and his bantam cock, his pig, his pony and his milking-cow. Maud was to be married and I was also, so it was Annie that was with him, scouring out and searing and poking and polishing. Poor Annie with her polio back was not likely to find a husband, so he was secure enough in his helpmate. He bought two Jack Russell terriers to terrorise the rats. Myself and Maud were lodged with our first cousins in Townsend Street, where they had a huckster's shop, and every fortnight we went down on the Wicklow bus.

Old Kelshabeg. The home place, despite the fact I had spent all my childhood in Dublin. A great fume of white heather on the hillside in the spring, it sometimes wouldn't even wait for the snow to go, but show its million small flowers in the drifts, like a second snow itself. Annie so proud to have put order on the place, the flagstones in the kitchen shining, the plates on the dresser shining back to the flagstones, the wide fire with its stack of reddening turf, the companionable cricket in the hearthstone, the water in the rainbarrel to plash your astonished face in the mornings, the devious hens trying always to come into the house and live a human life, the helpful pig eating everything in the yards including all the spoils of the 'quiet spot' where a person would quietly do their business, and wipe their backside after with a moist dock leaf, a better thing than any piece of paper.

We walked up the long green road, Maud and myself, in our best travelling attire, and in our cloth bags some more sensible country clothes, old grey dresses and white and blue polka-dot over-dresses. There were a hundred sorts of clean clinging muck to come at you on an Irish farm. A few stooping men digging over a quarter-acre, shovelful by shovelful, the land too steep and poor for a plough, lifted themselves and straightened their backs as we passed, no doubt glad of the relief in their obligement to greet us, as essentially local people passing. The English words gone muddy and lovely in their mouths.

'That's it, that's it, there's the two beauties passing,' and this despite the fact that Maud did not consider herself a beauty, but she was indeed a beauty, with a thick hank of black hair tied in a bit of ribbon more cousin to string than fashion. 'Are you going up to the father? You are? God bless ye.'

And up we did go, and it was the last house on the hill of Keadeen was our cottage, where nature ran out of patience with humanity, and struck out wild and pagan on the mountain proper, all heather and streams and sloughs. I am writing of these things, and as I do, as I sit here in my American clothes, clothed in my American self, all this long lost, long done with, all those people swept away, in the normal manner of the world, those stooping men, Maud, my father, the blessed hen and pony and pig, the whole sacred shebang, in a way we never give credence to while we breathe in and out as young women, as I sit here, an old person, a relic, even a grateful relic, for what I was given, if not for what was taken away, my sere heart calls back to it. I think again of the strange fact, plainly accepted, that that very heather would be sent up on the Wicklow train in sprigs in springtime, so that my father could set a bit of it on his mantelpiece in the castle, a piece of home, a badge, a sort of poem really, a song, and we as little children would smell it, pull on its scent with our noses gratefully. And I am remembering other things, the bell-flowers on the ditches that we could burst between thumb and index finger, I suppose it was digitalis, friend to the heart attack victim, and the blackthorn blossom in April, a greyish white, and the mayblossom itself in May, a different white, a whiter white, and the gorse as yellow as a blackbird's bill in May also, with its own smell, the smell as near as bedamn to the smell of a baby's mouth after drinking its mother's milk, I do believe. And the rooks rowing in the old high trees above Kelshabeg, such fractious birds, yet married to the one bird all their life, like good Catholics, and the wren in its tiny kingdoms in the earthen banks, and the woodpigeon offering its one remark over and over, and when there were storms out in the Wicklow sea, we heard the seagulls bickering and badgering on the winds, and in the dense copses the badgers themselves in the night-time, choosing among roots, and the fox both feared and admired, the red renegade, coming down to test our henhouse for weaknesses in the dark, and the nightingales and in stormy spring the fresh arrowheads of the house martins and the sparrows, could even God tell the difference between? And Maud and me, before any of our life took darkness to it, she content in her artist she had met in St Stephen's Green, myself content in my ex-soldier, going along without a thought for tiredness, it did not exist, and when we got to the cottage there was the bucket at the door to pull a drink out of, and a stew stewing on the hearth, and bread perfected in the pot-oven out on the yard, and then tea to kill the thirst, the best drink for thirst, and then bright early in the morning to get up with the sun and set to all the tasks, the hens, the dairy, the butterchurn, the dry sheets harvested from the fuchsia bushes, whatever was needed, and when the tinkers came up the path, to hold down the latch against them if our father was up the land, and not let them in the yard, them with their wild fumes of hair and not caring a damn what they did, and all the sort of turmoil of music everywhere, didn't even sunlight have a sound?, and the rooks, and the wrens, and the robin singing his desperate song, and my father singing *There was an old woman*, and the infinite, kind, searching mercy of the turf in the evening, our legs thrust out to it, the funny wood-thin legs of girls, and not caring in that moment about the chilblains we were sure to engender. I am writing it, I am writing it, and I spill it all out on my lap like very money, like riches, beyond the dreams of avarice.

It was after just such a day that my father came in all changed and dark himself. It was a short spring evening, but bright, with a small rain sparkling down on the packstones of the yard. He made a darkness in the room as he came in through the half-door. He put Maud and Annie out of the room, and sat me down on the stone perch by the fire, and took the old dark chair for himself. His face was bleakened by a sort of terror.

'Big news,' he said, 'big news. I was over on Keadeen gap looking for that damn ewe that doesn't know any better than to be wandering, when two men I know slightly came to me. I thought for a moment they meant to do me harm, as I know for a certifiable fact they are in the Baltinglas brigade. So you might think they wished harm on an old policeman. And I am sure there are those that wish me harm, and wouldn't mind shooting me.'

'I hope that is not true, Papa,' I said.

'It may be true, and it may not be true. But this is what they told me. It was something quite other than I had been expecting. It was about Tadg and yourself.'

'How so, Tadg?'

'They were coming to me out of old association, in that their father worked for my father, and the like, and they had a strong wish, a strong wish to let me know . . . To tip me off, I suppose, is the term I am looking for. Lilly, Lilly, it is terrible serious, it is a terrible serious matter. And you are to go back to Dublin this very evening and find Tadg and you are immediately to . . . And I will write an order for the bank in Sackville Street, and they will give you money, and . . .'

'What, Papa, what do you mean?'

'I don't know what I mean. I am trying to gather my thoughts. Oh, Lilly, Lilly,' he said, 'my own daughter. And maybe it is my fault. Maybe this bad thing is all my fault, and if it is I was not meaning it at all.'

'But what, Papa?' I said, very unhappy and alarmed, because his face was so unhappy and alarmed.

'There's a death sentence put on Tadg, and he's to be hunted and killed straight away. That's just for certain. There isn't a Tan that isn't on a death list, I am told, but the order for Tadg was made in Baltinglas, after that ambush recent in Glenmalure, you see, a little crowd of IRA men lying in wait for a lorry of Tans, and Tadg in the damn lorry among them, and the thing set for a certain time, it's a lorry that brings bread and victuals to the men in the Aughavannagh barracks, regular as anything, but there was a terrible preparedness in the Tans, there was no surprise at all, and four of the IRA boys were killed. And they were boys here from the mountainside. And one of the survivors recognised Tadg, because he has been down here visiting like any normal man, and doing a bit of drinking in Kiltegan, hasn't he? And they were looking at the names after, and linking names with names, and they know you are engaged to Tadg, and since they know who he is, and since they know he was there that day in the lorry, and are desperate to avenge their comrades, they start to wonder, did Lilly Dunne hear something spoken in the fields, the way she is so friendly, and go telling her beau, and anyway, isn't her father an ould policeman, so she'd be likely to do that, and be snooping about, and anyway, doesn't she deserve worse than hanging for going about with a Tan, and now Lilly, all their tying-up and thinking has led to this, that Tadg Bere is to be killed immediately, but also, you yourself, Lilly, are to be hunted, and they only told me that, they said, out of old association, to give you a head start so to speak, so that in effect you could flee your fate, as they put it, and they were very nervous telling me, because it could be death to them in turn to do so, and it was gospel they were saying.'

Such a sensation of utter terror descended on me. If my father had told me that wild wolves were to drag me off and eat me in the dark night I could not have been more terrified.

'But, Papa, it's not true. Tadg never tells me anything, and I didn't even know he ever was in Wicklow on a lorry, and I never heard anything said in the fields, or anywhere.'

'True or not true does not come into it, child. You know, I will bring you up to Dublin myself. They might be mustering now somewhere local, coming to get you. Throw your few dresses in your bag, and we must catch that evening bus.'

It was curious then to be sitting knee to knee on the Wicklow bus as it threw itself up and down the hills beyond Kiltegan.

'This is a terrible difficult matter,' my father said, keeping his voice low, so that the ould biddies and the working men and the flowery heads of children would not hear him. 'We are going to have to be mighty clever people to get through this,' he said. 'Mighty clever,' he said again, as if he was not quite sure we were such a sort.

'I am very frightened, Papa. What is going to happen? What will Tadg do with the death sentence against him?'

I don't fully know what I thought about Tadg up to that point. There's no point talking about love, what's sure as sure is no human person knows what that is. A youngster uses the word as if it has no mystery, like it is a factual matter, like a nun says the word 'God'. That clean look to him, a sort of scrubbed appearance, and the lovely liquorice-looking eyes he had, with pupils the size of farthings, and the feeling I had about that, could hardly be deemed love. It wasn't till I sat in that bus, now weeping with terror, my bare leg banging against my father's, I do remember that so vividly, and him thinking thinking at my side, that I realised that, if I didn't *love* Tadg, I was certainly not willing to be torn away from him, by his death or my death. I had had a secret plan, unknown even to myself, to attach myself to him, and those black eyes. And this huge emergency did bring it home to me that I set a great value on him. His friendship with Willie was bound into his bones like the tendrils of a plant. His delight in his new job had delighted me. His curious Corkonian courtesy, the fact that when we were close to each other, at the music-hall say where he liked to bring me to see the mad clog-dances and hear the sentimental songs, and we were both melting with desire for each other, he was never so still as then, as if he were thinking about that desire, and was so hugely interested in it, that he was devoted to the purpose of forming a great philosophy about it! Not to be jumping my bones, as he might legitimately have done, since we were betrothed to each other. But his delicate, simple heart, that he had carried through slaughters more terrible than he had words to say during the war, and which he was now carrying into fresh scenes of turmoil and despair as a policeman of a kind, paid a sort of queer homage to our desire. We were Catholic people, of an ancient vanished category, and though we were eager to jump into each other's knickers, we weren't planning to do so till our wedding night. The fire that that engenders in a person has to be experienced to be believed. You are sitting with your beau and your private parts are melting. You need to eat well and drink a lot of water to survive it.

When we got to Dublin, Tadg was just as certain as my father that we had to go. It wasn't just his name, he said, but mine, and while he might fight off assailants himself, he could not in all practicality protect me. And he said that indeed he had been on the lorry in Glenmalure, protecting in the normal way the delivery of supplies to the barracks, and it was terrible bad luck that he had been recognised, and he would never have credited it, and the man seeing him knowing me too, and my father, it was a horrible coming together of things, he said, and he said my father was right, there would be no safety for us now anywhere in Ireland, and go we must, and straight away.

That very night I stood in our sitting-room in the castle, and embraced my father. He said not a word. He bestowed on me the tickets he had given big money for, two large long tickets with the name of the ship, the destination New Haven Connecticut on it, and our names written in a clear, flowing ink, like you might on a census. A little effort made to be clear. So that that particular person would be taken on that particular boat, taken out of that particular life into another particular life.

My father walked me down to the gates and helped me onto the horse-cab that would bring Tadg and me to the North Wall. He put his left hand over his face, how strange I remember that, and his right hand on my hand where it rested on my lap. He stood there for a few moments, breathing strangely through his fingers. He took back his hand and waved on the jarveyman. He took his left hand from his face. He said not a word.

On the damp cab, as we moved through the muddled lights of Dame Street, Tadg put his arm around me. He was wearing a rough set of civvies and didn't look much more than a labouring man. Although we intended to be married correctly in America, we were really married in that moment, when my heart was so heavy that without his presence, without his arms, I would have perished of fear and loss.

Now I will lay up this writing for today, and wipe off the Formica table, set the chair carefully against it, make some tea, and go to my bed. The sea-light has crossed the potato fields to me, and touched the darkening room with the scent of salt, which, as an animal of this place, just as much I hope as the sparrows and the plovers, I take as my signal to seek my rest. Something presses on my crown, presses up against the soles of my feet, presses against my breast and my back. I suppose it is how a poor carrot feels in a pressure cooker – there is a huge stillness everywhere, a sharpness in the air, a sort of tingling, that puts a wave in my hair, which if it were the hurricane season might make me suspect a hurricane, although it is a feature of this district that hurricanes most often reach us only as echoes of their great Atlantic selves, in the form of benign downpour. My head is burning.

Fifth Day without Bill

Mr Eugenides, who owns the drugstore at the corner of Main Street, came out onto the sidewalk after me, when he saw me passing and not coming into his shop, as I would most likely normally have done. Although I am beginning to forget what normal was, when I used to be almost another Mrs Bere, going about her business, secure in her love of Bill, even when he was far away in the desert, and I worried so about him in the long nights. I would hear our own sea fretting in the distance, across the wide reedbeds and the sleeping marsh birds, and wonder what was happening to him in that place of sealess sand, and try to work out on the complicated wristwatch he had given me what time it was in the Middle East, or Arabia as I used to think of it.

Mr Eugenides came out, with his short steps, because he is a very small Greek man of very large character.

'Mrs Bere, come back into me, I have a certain delicacy for you, which will be delighting you. I tell you, my friend.'

So I was obliged to follow him, out of the half-hearted sunlight, into the deep cave of his store. In the seventies he used to have a counter, with swivel seats and soda fountains, but he had done away with all that, though I always noted the round marks on the lino where the metal chairs used to be bolted, and besides his few isles of medicines and the like, he imported certain goods from his home place Trikala in the region of Thessaly. But he was rather old now, and not ambitious for a new line, and these items were really for himself and friends, to allay his extreme homesickness. He would have big metal tins of olives in olive oil, and eggplants Greek-style, and a tray now and then of baklava, although I wasn't sure if that wasn't made by his cousins in Queens, of which he seemed to have legions. As always, as I stepped in, a low music was playing, the plangent and beautiful strains of 'the great Tsitsanis' as Mr Eugenides called him. The great Tsitsanis had also been a native of Trikala. 'We marvelled at the speed of his playing,' Mr Eugenides would say, as if that was the final test of great music. 'His hand flying like a sparrow over the strings of the bouzouki. It was great genius.'

And Mr Eugenides would stop, and cock an ear to the playing, and look at me, and nod his head, as if to say, 'don't you think?'

He had taught me some Greek, just for friendship and fun, and he liked to hear me say the phrases he had taught me, and when there was a Greek friend in the shop, he would get me to speak, and the friend might pretend amazement and delight.

'*Apo ti poli erchume, e sti corifi canella.*'

I would only have to say the first half, and he or his friend would finish the saying, because it was that sort of saying.

Amazement and delight were Mr Eugenides's bywords. When Bill was going into the army, just a couple of years ago, Mr Eugenides bought him a copy of Homer in translation, which Bill dutifully brought with him to the war.

In this way, Bill and I, on very separate occasions, received the same book, in different editions and translations, as a gift.

'There has never been a better book about these matters. Friendship, loyalty. The bricks and mortar of Greece, and of America.'

He had that extravagant patriotism of the immigrant. He had been just too young for the Second World War, in which his father had been killed, and too old of course for Vietnam.

'Now dear Mrs Bere, tell me I do a bad thing. Tell me I do not understand you. See, see . . . I offer you this, as a solace, in this great time. Your Bill has fought far away, you have laid him to rest. I have nothing to give you but this, which is the honey of my father's village.'

And he pointed, he more or less introduced me, to a little pot, humble and plain enough, with a very austere white label, and a big yellow bee on it, and some Greek writing.

'I wonder,' he said, 'what you would give me from Ireland, if I was suffering your suffering. I wonder.'

'I would give you the white heather from my father's hillside,' I said, trying not to cry like a child, and as soon as he noted my small distress, his left hand was on my shoulder, patting it – yes, I would bring him that white heather, I said, indeed I would, if such a thing had legs to travel, though I knew the little white pods would be blackened by the long journey from Kelshabeg to New York.

'Ah, ah,' he said, as if I had offered him the solution to an enormous problem, as if just by mentioning the heather, I had found at last the answer to the death of the earth and allied matters.

Now I sit at my table, and today there is not just tea and milk in my cup, but also a spoon of Greek honey.

Greece, America, Arabia, Ireland. Home places. Nowhere on earth not a home place. The calf returns to where it got the milk. Nowhere is a foreign place. Everywhere a home

57

place for someone, and therefore for us all.

A few weeks back Mr Dillinger was here, just across from me, sitting in Bill's old chair. He was talking nicely as usual, with his blue eyes sunk into his long, lined face keeping a good guard over me, to see how I was liking his talk. Because he would stop immediately if he thought he was tiring me. No man I ever knew is less of a fool than he.

'What is the greatest discovery in our lifetime? Moon rockets? Maybe penicillin? In my view, Mrs Bere, it is DNA.'

'Deeny what?' I said.

'Three letters, Mrs Bere, D-N-A. Don't ask me what they stand for. The DNA of every modern person goes back to one, or maybe three women in Africa. The good news is, we are all the same family. The bad news is, we are all the same family.' This was his little joke. 'The point is, all these wars, all these teems of history, all this hatred of difference, and fear of the other, has been a long, elaborate, useless, heartbreaking nonsense. America is not a melting pot of different races, it is where the great family shows its many faces. The Arab is the Jew, the Englishman is the Irishman, the German is the Frenchman, it is a wonderful catastrophe, no? It is the most important thing we have been told in our lifetime.'

Which might explain the strange feeling I had standing on the deck of our ship as it approached New Haven. There was a scent, the scent of America, that came off the land, so suggestive, so subtle, there was something in it that claimed my heart. Even before we got there, I was experiencing a sort of nostalgia for the land, I do not know how other to describe it. As if I had been there before, had left it, and was returning after a long voyage. We were drooping with fatigue, after the days of the voyage, because Tadg had felt seasick as we left the arms of the Great South Wall, and the sickness had never left him. The crossing was a torment for him, and my mind had turned round and round sleeplessly the images of my sisters and my father. We had kept to a tiny cramped corner of the ship as Tadg, even in his sickness, feared every man on deck, that he might have been placed on board to kill us. And indeed he barely looked now at the small city looming nearer, but I saw his eyes dart about, trying to judge the relaxedness or preparedness of other passengers, as if any man there in his belted overcoat might not have nesting in his clothes a cold metal gun.

As if to honour both the seasickness and the fear, Tadg had not shaved on the voyage, and had grown a reasonably successful reddish beard, which he allowed me to trim roughly to a point with a borrowed scissors, so he looked less like a poor balladeer in a Dublin street.

We were in the sort of situation that can show you pretty quick, and painfully, that you are travelling with a person that in effect you do not know.

Neither of us were now what we had been. My father in great haste had put together some letters for us on his official paper, and gave our names as Timothy and Grainne Cullen, brother and sister, should we need them, but just to muddle everything, he had put our real names on the ship's passenger list, in case using aliases would make our naturalisation eventually in America more difficult. But at least we would be able to travel for the moment in America as people other than what we were, and give our names that were not our names, until things might seem to die down, and we might marry at last as who we were, and give our real names at last to the minister. Like normal human beings. Without sentences of death on their heads.

But Timothy Cullen, or Tadg Bere, I hardly knew who he was, either way.

Perhaps in Ireland, right up to the moment we had to go, he had been Tadg. Perhaps it was fear altered him, like one of those small earthquakes under farms that alter the watercourse and make a well dry up, though there is no visible sign of alteration in the landscape. Now that I was grappling with an unknown Tadg, I was panicking in my thought that I had never really known him, had allowed myself to become engaged to a man because he had known my beloved brother, and had written me a gentle letter, he a boy who had survived years of unrestrained carnage. As if the love I had for Willie was strangely transferable, and while maybe even a real love, was a blind one, an unhearing one, an unseeing one.

Fear is a force like a seasickness, could you call it a life-sickness, a terrible nausea caused by dread, creeping dread, that seems to withdraw a little in dreams while you sleep, but then, just a few moments after waking, rushes back close to you, and begins again to gnaw at your simple requirement for human peace. Gnawing, gnawing, with long ratlike teeth. No one can live through that without changing. A small measure of my terror was I was now moving through America with this stranger.

I had the oddest sense as we sat on the train to New York that America was being built in great haste all in front of us, being invented for us as we went. I had only ever seen America in newspapers and the little film reels at the music-hall in Dame Street – where Maud my sister used secretly to take me – maybe that was why, and it seemed to me now an endless series of pictures, water towers, great coastal installations of unknown kinds, a multitude and an infinity of backyards and houses, the broken hems of the towns and small cities we passed through, another sort of shock to me, the poorness of it, although I suppose railway companies found it easiest to run their lines through the districts of the poor. I gulped the ham sandwich Tadg bought for me on the train, I gulped the strange dusty water, I gulped the air with its slight aftertaste of metal, gulp, gulp, gulp, like a fish in starved water.

My stranger was infinitely kind to me.

'We have the name of your cousin in New York, we can try him first. We'll find out where the best bet for work might be. We won't be long setting ourselves up, Lilly. You can be sure of that. I didn't get through the war only to be letting myself down here.'

The enormous 'here' rushed past the windows, its solid forms and darkening colours torn and blurred.

'We have each other,' he said. 'That will be our kingdom. We're not the first people to come to America anyhow. Jaysus, we're not.'

He said nothing for a bit, and then he said, maybe worrying about my silence:

'I'm only glad to be off that ship. Jaysus, I thought I'd never feel right again. Jaysus.'

'Thank God,' I said.

'Aye, aye,' he said, much cheered suddenly by two small words. 'We'll conquer this place. It will be no trouble to us. Hard work, Lilly, and Bob's your uncle.'

Another great carpet of erased night scenes and burning lamps sped by.

'You'll see,' he said. Then with a huge effort added: 'You'll see – sweetheart.'

His long face – suddenly moving into a sort of beauty, like a painted man, so that my heart stirred – was glowing now in the carriage. I thought we would be all right, just at that moment. I thought we would be. I didn't think I knew who he was, but I adjudged him honest and good-hearted. And terrified, like me.

Coming into the city was a new fright all its own. I stood on the familiar enough pavement outside the station, and glanced up, but my head hurt with the great swoosh of the buildings, I had to stare down at my feet, or I would have fainted. I had vertigo, at ground level.

I gripped Tadg's hand, like a veritable child, trusting in his greater strength.

You'd have been inclined to be trusting him, the way he took charge then when we entered deeper into the city, him clutching in his hand the piece of paper with my cousin's name writ on it in my father's black-inked policeman's hand. Like the whole world before us we were speechless at this place. We were salmon in dark deep water at the bottom of a great system of sunken rivers, that had carved so deep into the soil that the sky itself was only half-remembered. Would human deeds here be similarly darkened? I almost laughed at the memory of Dublin, with its low houses, their roofs tipped like deferential hats to the imperious rain. In the first while I couldn't understand how any human agency had built such a place. How were there ladders long enough to get bricks up so high? And every road in spate, with a flood of angry cabs, people shouting and calling, plunging along, horns raking through the noise, it was already a kind of assault, a terror you had to learn.

My father's little note said *Mick Cullen*, I think it was somewhere on the Lower East Side, or was it 8th Street it said?, I can't recall. We had been given two addresses, this one, and another in Chicago, which for all we knew might have been near or far. The first address in truth was ten years old; he was a brother of the famous coppicer on Humewood estate – famous to us anyhow – and was known to be living there in New York, running some sort of lumber business, my father had said, but there had been no letters to and fro for a long time, in the way of these things. Even though he and Mick Cullen shared a grandmother.

'You needn't stay long with him,' said my father, in that other life that already seemed a thousand years ago. 'Just till you get your bearings. The Cullens are all right.'

Canut Cullen had been able to harvest an acre of hazel rods in a day, and only his sons bringing him great jugs of buttermilk to keep him going. That was fame of a kind. True fame.

They may have been all right, these new American Cullens, but they weren't there, and no sign of them. We stood on the sidewalk like goms, holding the bit of paper, staring up at an old premises with a corrugated iron roof, and a long metal balcony up the side, and an air of dereliction so complete that even where someone had bolted doors and barred the way, perhaps Mick Cullen himself on some long vanished day, these things were sundered, and old

63

metal openings showed drear and bleak against the darkening sky.

We were so tired from the huge journey in the ship, but I think we had been buoyant enough till that moment. Tadg slowly put the piece of paper back in his pocket, and brought out the other one, with the Chicago address, like a cardplayer with a poor hand that was going to venture an even poorer card. Because the Chicago address was only the friend of a friend of a sort of a cousin. Tadg gave a laugh then in the cobbled street. It was going to be quite dark soon, except just as I thought that, the lamps started to light one by one, in a miraculous sequence. Were they singing, those lamps, did they make a tiny noise for themselves? It wasn't that I was a woman and scared, it was that I was a human being and scared. The future, the following day, was as dark as the high sky, and suddenly what I had lost bore in on me, my father, stern and strange as he was, and my sisters, one a hunched unmarriageable girl, and the other a nervous, touchy person soon to be a similar bride – funny how I suddenly saw them like that, whereas before they had just been my eternal sisters – even the loss of poor Willie, that in some way had brought me here to this desolate, angry street in New York, all pushed through me like a flooded mountain stream through previously secure whinbushes, pulling at their tremendous roots, assaulting their safety, and I quailed there, in the street, and shook, my travelling coat failing to keep me warm suddenly, my legs failing me. And that was another moment when Tadg might with profit have put his arms around me, but what was he himself? only a boy returned from the war, and odd deeds done in his home place, and all his ordinary dreams put aside by a death threat, standing there in New York with a girl he didn't know, and who didn't know him.

Scared as we were, we didn't feel easy enough to linger in New York without the protection of those we knew, or who were related to us – maybe something to do with that DNA Mr Dillinger told me about. I remember reading in a book of palmistry and dreams or some such years ago, I don't even know why I was reading it, it was a book belonging to Cassie Blake herself, who liked such things, books about the shape of the head and what you could tell from that, and books about dreams, and this book said that people liked train journeys because no one ever died on a train, and when you dream of trains it's a dream of eternal life. Maybe there is something in that, because we were strangely content to get back to the great station, with its main room the size of an Irish county, and put some of our few last dollars to the journey north to Chicago.

Sixth Day without Bill

And then to some degree God smiled on us, and forgave us.

My cousin in Chicago was by some way more distantly related than Mick Cullen in New York, but at least she was there, married to a man that worked along the shore of the lake, and though they hadn't two cents to spare, they did have a timber shack behind their few rooms, that was too cold in winter and too hot in summer for ordinary mortals, but we were not that. We thought the heavens were beaming down on us right enough, when Hannah Reilly, in her big American-looking apron, and her exhausted face, said we could nest there. And Tadg went out the next morning with her husband, and by another miracle, though jobs were not too scarce in that time, found some temporary work, I think it was clearing out land where they were putting in pilings for new buildings, and it was rough hard toil, but Tadg wasn't bothered by that.

Everything was wider than New York. They had pushed the great buildings further apart, built everything fatter and heavier-looking, in case the wind blew them away.

My father had put us in some difficulty with his hastily made plans, in that our official-looking letter had us as brother and sister, but there was no point offering this fiction to Hannah Reilly, because she knew who I was. But I couldn't give that name anywhere else, and when Hannah remembered, she called me Grainne. Tadg at least was able to be Tim Cullen for the taking up of the work, though we regretted my father's hasty choice of Cullen, which after all was a family name. So in the matter of getting married we were already in a sort of knot, since according to my father's official letter we were brother and sister, and clearly to Hannah we were not, and yet now sharing the little wooden room. And she was very anxious for us to put this right.

'Do you know, Lilly, we're respectable people, and even if you're in trouble, you know, at home, well, if you're to make a new start here, you need to be married.'

'We do,' I said. 'We'll just have to decide which names to choose for that.'

'Why did your father say you were brother and sister?'

'I don't know. It seemed like a good notion, in the great hurry of it all. But it was our real names anyhow on the ship's manifest, and we don't seem to be bothered much here. Maybe we can just go and be married as who we are.'

'I don't see why not,' said Hannah.

But Tadg didn't think that was very wise.

'We cannot do that,' he said, that evening. I had fried up some wondrous big sausages for him, and he was devouring them, even though they looked a little lonely on the plate, for want of potatoes. 'The new names are no good to us either. It would be a very poor thing to use them, and then someone thinking later we were brother and sister. And the old names might be the death of us. It's a third set of names we need, Lilly.'

'And can we do that in America?'

'There must be some way here of getting names officially and I am going to have to look into it.'

But he had little enough time to be doing that. At six in the morning he went down to his work, and in the cold evening he returned, and in a few weeks he grew thinner and darker. And stranger.

We had a narrow thin bed for ourselves and we lay on it side by side in the dark, with everything we had heaped up on us against the cold. The lake wind blew down from Canada and in through the slats of our room, and played about our faces and hands, and snuck into our layers of socks, and found out our vulnerable toes.

In our courtship we had kissed. It felt like a long time ago, sitting on the farthing seats in Stephen's Green in the traitorous sunshine of the Irish spring, holdings hands in the threadbare heat, or withdrawing into the shadows of one of the bandstands there, and trying our chances in each other's arms. And I had delighted in his kisses, and loved the big bloom of warmth in me they caused, and how in the summer such as it was, we started to be baked by our kissing, my breast sweating against his chest, in a far from disagreeable manner.

But here, in those first weeks, with the wind, and the sound of the lake massively beyond our window, a dirty gun-grey in the darkness, and Hannah and her husband snoring the other side of the wall, when we might have gone at each other like the first lovers on earth, we lay close together but as utterly apart as if a priest had put a curse on us.

And that I do think now was part of the terror, that though we were adrift in America – and for all we knew hunted, although Tadg *said* he was confident we might have slipped through – we were no longer united as we had been, but bizarrely sundered by the very threat of this intimacy.

For my part I mightn't have been so minded, because he was a lovely long man, but for that first while he was a person frozen, and fixed in an unknown intent. And maybe that was because, in some manner, with a death sentence on his head, he felt a little murdered already, at least his life greatly altered. He had not even had time to be in touch with his mother in Cork, and I don't think he liked to think of her there, knowing nothing of him, or why he had disappeared.

I don't think he liked that at all, and it was then I began to wonder, did he blame me to some degree for our predicament, or rather, I began to wonder, *was* I to blame? I had made his doings in Wicklow very personal by being from Wicklow myself. He had lost the anonymity of the policeman working far from his own district, as policemen always do. I had destroyed his namelessness, and put a name on something frightening in the landscape, a lorry passing through with guns and maybe laughter and certainly reckless, ruined hearts aboard, and then the ambush, and the local boys killed, and the seeming readiness of the Tans – my fault, my fault. I had said nothing to Tadg about anything, but it was still my fault. It was such matters, like a hopelessly knotted ball of wool, that kept us apart also in our apparent closeness, lying perforce arm to arm, the mere heat of his body so desirable in the cruel cold of that room, his red beard jutting from his face like a figure on a tomb in Christ Church Cathedral.

Even as I write this, I long to be back there and turn to him, and hold him, and prove to him that at least one saving grace of us as a creature might be that everything can be unknotted by a simple gesture.

That the darkness of a room can be solved by a single candle.

I wish, I wish, that we had not wasted so much of our time together.

But there was a loosening. Perhaps the few dollars and cents he was given for his work was little enough compared to his pay in the Tans, but it seemed to me a magical affair, because it guaranteed our ability to continue there, in what was beginning to feel like safety. My father had sent me a letter through a P.O. box number, giving me the precious details of Maud's wedding to her Matthew, and although his account was spare and perfunctory, as was his fashion, my imagination supplied what was missing, and at the heart of it I thought I saw Maud smiling her rare smile. I hoped she would make a habit of that smile, because it was a good one, if rare, and I hoped, while knowing nothing about such a possibility, being in the dark myself about all things, that she might be well beloved by her husband.

And as I read and reread the letter, I felt certain pangs of sadness too, and a homesick pain, and yes, jealousy.

But Tadg and myself were beginning to thaw out, and as Chicago loosened itself from winter and spring, we loosened.

'I'm going to say I like this place,' he said. 'I like it.'

It was easier for us there certainly, because there was no history. I realised slowly that as my father's daughter, unthinkingly, I had lived as a little girl and young woman through a certain kind of grievous history, where one thing is always being knocked against another thing. Where my father's respect for the King was knocked against Tadg's father being in the Irish Volunteers, where Willie's going to war was knocked against his dying, where even Wicklow life was knocked against Dublin life, the heather that came up to us on the bus knocked against its eventual blackening, its little darkened flowers saying, time passeth, time flyeth. Where the very fact of my being alive was knocked against the fact that my mother had died in giving me that life.

I just did not know yet what things knocked against other things here in America.

Tadg had begun not just to like Chicago. He had begun to use the word 'home' and he no longer meant Cork or Ireland, but that wretched wooden room where we still boarded, able now to give my cousin something approaching a rent. And slowly all the things about us widened into a sort of personal kingdom, the nervy lake that thought it was the sea, the accumulated buildings of the city that we began to use as our landmarks in conversation and in dreams.

And then something grand happened.

We were lying side by side one Sunday morning and with one accord, without real thought, with the simple instinct of ordinary human creatures, we turned to each other and gently kissed, then fiercely, like wakening beasts, and before we knew where we were, like a sudden walking storm down the lake that we had witnessed in the deeper weather, we seemed to go into a stormy gear, we clutched at each other, we got rid of our damned clothes, and clung, and he was in me then, and we were happy, happy, young, in that room by the water, and the poetry that is available to anyone was available to us at last, and we breathed each other in, and in those moments both knew we would marry each other after all, and not a word needed to be spoken about it.

A cold-minted yellow light I remember that Sunday then as Tadg and me strolled into the city, like people restored to life. Maybe in truth the warmth of early summer had taken a step back, as if unsure of itself. But we were walking arm in arm, jubilant, exultant, and barely noticed, and anyway did not care.

He was suddenly full of plans. It was as if he had awakened to being in America, abruptly made manifest to him as a place of safety, maybe infinite safety. As if he had suddenly remembered he was young, and though banished from his own country, might have come to America anyway, in the natural way of an Irish person, and now it was all laid out before him, before us, like a glittering Canaan.

I will never forget his happiness in that ordinary Chicago afternoon, and I give God thanks for it.

I give Him thanks, I give Him thanks.

We came up the wide steps of the Art Institute. One of Tadg's pals among the pilings was an Armenian man, who in his former existence as an Armenian in Armenia had studied painting at some academy, before his people had been dissolved like sugar in tea by the Turks. 'He said *lonesome* academy,' Tadg said, 'what do you think he meant by that? He has the most beautiful and interesting English. Or I suppose it is American.' But his mother, Tadg said, had been killed before his eyes. She had died as it happened in his arms. He was wielding spades and pickaxes now in America, there by the shore of Chicago, and he had no money for brushes and paints. But he had told Tadg about a wonderful building in the city, where for nothing at all, not two cents asked, you could see room after room of paintings, *windows of beauty*, he called them, said Tadg. Now Tadg was not a man for such things, ordinarily, and it was maybe partly out of liking for his small and passionate Armenian friend that he had decided to bring me there that Sunday, added to which might well have been the enormous optimism that somehow or other our lovemaking had created in us.

And into a great hall, which in itself seemed a marvel to us. It had a high roof and hordes of dark-suited men and women in bright dresses. They were passing in and out through the many doors, little rivers of blackness and brightness going along you might think because of the slope of the earth. And then, like tadpoles gnawing away at pond-weed, little stranded groups of them at particular pictures, gawping. And there were children doing their immortal traipsing, and here I spotted a pregnant stomach, and there I spotted a withered man, but in general as we entered we caught a strange note of gaiety and completion, as if this great building might be a hospital of sorts, but curing the unknown and *non-specific* maladies of the daily soul.

And we felt it. All other matters fled away. It constituted a moment of clear thought, such as you might get only three or four times in a life. When the sea-fog clears from the sea and the blue expanse is revealed like an explanation. I loved my father and my sisters and the memory of my brother, yet would most likely never see Ireland again. But there was this new ease with Tadg, this pleasant wandering, and surely now we would be married soon, and both of us glad that it would be so. I suddenly for that second, and maybe never so clearly again, knew who I was, or thought I did, and knew who Tadg was, my husband, and God forgive me, he seemed to me a resplendent husband, a shining man. In my so-called clarity I thought I was lucky. I felt lucky. And I must have been giggling away to myself like an eejit.

'What are you laughing at, Lilly?' said Tadg, not entirely approvingly.

Then he stopped by a particular painting. Just then there was no one else near us. He stopped, and I imagined in a crazy moment that everything stopped, his heart, his story, because he seemed to bunch himself up, he seemed to pause mightily. He began not just to look at the painting, but to gaze at it, gaze at it. I stood at his left elbow, looking at him, and looking at the painting.

'What is it, Tadg?' I said.

'Look at the painting,' he said, 'look at the blessed thing.'

It was a portrait of a man, young enough or not too old, it was hard to say, because it was to my eyes quite roughly painted. We were close up to it, and there was a label beside it, that said it was a self-portrait by the artist Van Gogh, with a date, and where he came from, and the name of a foreign town. I had never heard of such a person, and I do not know if Tadg had, but the name stuck in my brain, it printed there, Van Gogh, in the selfsame black letters of the notice. I smiled up at Tadg, not that he saw me, and put my hand on his sleeve, and said again, with an instinctive quietness, as if sensing an unusual mystery in him, he who was a haunted man, I said again:

'What is it, Tadg?'

'Do you not see, Lilly, do you not see?'

'What, Tadg?'

'It is a picture of myself.'

I looked again with renewed effort. I was startled. What did he mean? Maybe there was a resemblance. The face in the picture had a rough red beard just like Tadg's right enough. The strangely shifting lines of the painting, as if this Van Gogh had made his picture out of strings, one packed against the next, and of different colours, like from a darning bag of ends and oddments, made it difficult to decide. Whatever I thought of it, Tadg seemed to see his exact image. He was transfixed by it. He stared and stared.

Now over to my right, in the very corner of my eye, I started to pick up a movement. Again pure instinct, no actual thought crossed my mind. And I looked over that way, towards one of the entrances into the deeper galleries. A figure, one among many, had issued forth from the blackness, and what it was about him that had caught my eye I do not know, unless it was his long coat in that improved weather, although there were plenty of men in coats. He wore a black hat, but there was nothing unusual about a hat, it was the great heyday of hats and caps, indoors and out. Maybe the person, the darkness of him, the thinness, matched something in some dream I had dreamed, as Cassie Blake's book of dreams might claim. I do not know. I do know I followed his progress across the wide red marble floor, he was coming at the angle a trout does in its first strength after being hooked, when the fisher is exerting pressure, and the trout will not deign to come in a straight line. It was like this dark man found the floor at a bit of an angle, and was falling ever so slightly down that angle, and it was bringing him nearer and nearer to us.

I plucked at Tadg's sleeve.

'Tadg, Tadg,' I said. 'Tadg, love.'

'But Lilly,' he said. 'How could there be a picture of me in here?'

'I don't think it can hardly be of you, Tadg, look at the little notice, it is a picture from Holland or somewhere.'

'I was never in Holland,' said Tadg, as if offering an irrefutable fact that yet I might be about irrefutably to disprove. 'Was I, Lilly? I never was.'

The black-coated man was halfway across the floor to us. I don't know if I was frightened in that moment. But in the next moment, I thought he made an odd movement, a sort of fishing movement in the drape of his coat, for he did not have his arms in the sleeves, I saw that now, and maybe that was what had attracted my attention, one hand was acting like a brooch and was clutching the two sides of his coat at the breast, but the other hand was invisible, except for that dipping motion, except for that dip also of one leg, a little stooping gesture, as if fetching something, fetching something out.

'I have never seen such a thing, Lilly. I do not know what is going on. God bless us, Lilly.'

'Tadg, Tadg, I am frightened,' I said.

'No, no,' he said. 'No need. This is a wonder. It's not a frightening thing.'

'But Tadg, I am afraid of that man, there is a man coming over to us, I am afraid of him – greatly, greatly.'

'What, Lilly? I am sure they will not like me to touch it. But I feel I could reach out there and feel the warmth in this face. Do you see? Is it not breathing? And right here, right here, where I am standing, I can still sense the lad who made this, occupying this exact spot, his arm out, like this,' and he put out his hand and just tipped the paint, no doubt breaking some sacred rule – 'and don't you feel it, Lilly, the fierceness of him? I do feel it, my God, Lilly, my God, his face, and my face, these two faces, and his own is gone, and mine here in its place, and . . .'

'Please, please, Tadg, I beg you, come away, come away. There is a man coming over to us.'

'What?' Now his gaze broke at last from the painting, and he glanced down at my face. 'What man?' And I heard the little policeman tone in his voice, the little seriousness. And now the man was just four feet behind him, four feet beyond the back of his head, turned as it was to me, and I was in enormous panic, because I thought, what can Tadg do?, he cannot defend us. I clutched at his arm, pulling at him, wanting him to run, to run, away out into the free Chicago light.

Tadg at last turned his head fully about. He had looked for danger in a thousand places. We were weeks, months in America. I am sure there had been days he had crept along streets carefully, wondering were there enemies gathering against us, were there letters and words, and whisperings. He had sought no security from any police here, because he knew well that many were Irish and how could he judge their affiliations? It would be too dangerous to try and find out. Better to be quiet, careful, in our little room and his anonymous work. Yet now, in a clear instance of possible danger, he was almost at his ease, and I saw his face actually break into a smile, as if he expected the man, now just upon us, to greet him in some friendly fashion.

Before I could quite see what had happened, before I could untangle in my mind the various blacknesses, the black coat, the hat, the awful darkness of the face under the hat, not something that made *me* want to smile, there was a huge sound, a huge violent sound that filled every niche and door of the hall, that swelled and swelled at an infinite pace, that battered against me, that seemed for a moment to cancel out the space, like the atom bomb all those years later, one moment lives and buildings and breathing souls, next dust and oblivion and burning, and then the room righted itself, and though my ears were ringing with noise, ringing, I saw a queer blaze of whiteness and redness, as if quite unconnected to the noise, but not unconnected, because it was flames and noise issuing from a gun-barrel, existing just for a breathless instant, then gone, but never gone, never gone again, and the muddle of the gun in the man's hand, and some bullet bursting into my Tadg, into his side, where his heart lay hidden, so that his whole body went banging against the wall, just under the fatal portrait, like a lorry-man had thrown a sack of loose grain to the floor, he folded at the waist, and on his poor jacket all under the arm was a surprising hole, or maybe a bullet hole and a flower of blood, I didn't know, and in that fraction of time, in that clumsy merciless falling, I saw life pulled out of him, I saw the face grow ashen, grow dark, I threw myself at his body, I held his face, I kissed his face, I begged him to return to me, I begged him, I begged him, but he could not.

I expected my own bullet then in the moment following, the back of my head tensed to receive it, I wasn't sure if I had a terror of that, I just thought it would come, would come, but it did not.

Then indeed I seemed to cross over into another country. That Tadg-less country was not that first America, which his presence had made safe, a sanctuary, if an uncertain one. It was another America. Nothing could have prepared me for it. Some hidden drain of the world opened under me as I knelt beside him, and I was sucked down into its darkness. How do we survive? How are we not crushed? The pressure of sorrow is like being sent down to the core of the earth. So how are we not burned away?

I stood up. He was so dead the rest of the world seemed to have died with him. The walls looked ashen as his face, as if some fire had after all torn through the museum. Maybe it was my tears, though I do not remember crying. I was gawping, at this picture of sudden and ruinous death. Only the portrait of Van Gogh shone out just the same as before, still and indifferent, acquiring now a terrible notice beneath, of a person destroyed, the one face troubled and eternal, the other beneath twisted by a last surge of pain. The Sunday crowd, when it was adjudged that the murderer had fled, gathered near us, watching, watching. I think they thought I was a figure of some threat and danger too. No one maybe had seen the act of killing, or few. I am sure it was hard to tell what had happened. I cannot say I was full of thoughts myself. But right or wrong I did have one thought, that I could not stay there. I was anxious to be with Tadg. For some crazy reason my only other thought was the task of unclothing him, washing his body, and laying him in his grave. I wonder where he does lie. I should have gone long ago to look for him, he must be in the city records of Chicago. Here lies . . . who? Did they know his name? His pocket book might have had something to identify him, old tickets or the like.

I spun about to get away from there, and there was a multitude of people in my way, but I stretched out an arm, like a woman broadcasting seeds, and plunged forward, in among them and through them, reached the huge door all brightened by its harvest of sunlight, and went through that light as if it were solid also. Then I stopped, head down, staring at the huge pavers under my shoes. How could I leave him there? Was there something I needed to do, to say? The great pull of that strange inner civic being in all of us had stayed me. But as I looked down I saw the blood on my clothes, a continent of it, ragged and spread like an elephant's ear, infinitely clean and dark-looking, glistening, slippery. The very selfsame mark I had seen as a child on my aunt's apron, when she was bleeding the pig in Wicklow. The poor lonesome pig hung up by the trotters in the barn, and his throat slit, and all the black blood draining down into the bucket beneath, that the black puddings would be made of. Her lap so slippery with it that in that instant as a little girl I wanted to ask her if I could climb on her breast, and slide down the stain. And later that same day she was milking the cow, in a fresh apron, sun-dried on the bushes, and she turned the udder and skited me with milk, so that was a day of whiteness and blackness, and . . .

Mad thoughts. But this grief was a madness, mixed as it was with terror. That a man, a living breathing man, lucky so lucky himself to be alive, to have the gift of life, should stride across a great public room, and take my Tadg's life away. Unimaginable, even if it was the thing we had feared. No thought we had had about it, no conversation, no opinion offered since the death sentence, bore any relation to this. Because the ingredient we had missed was the actual enormous violence of it, the tearing out, the vigorous unstoppable intent, the distraction for Tadg of the portrait, me seeing the killer come, me trying to alert Tadg, and then the huge war of it, the suddenness, the completeness, the colossal ungenerosity of it, implacable eternal hatred of it, that they wouldn't let us go, forgive us our trespasses. That they wouldn't allow us to cross into Canaan, but would follow us over the river, and kill him on Canaan's side. The land of refuge itself.

I am sure I did not have all those thoughts. I am having them now.

I sort of gathered my soiled skirt and coat, and hitched them up somewhat, and started to run. Running away from something or running towards something, I did not know. From danger to safety, or from danger to danger, I did not know. I began to run, and soon streets took me that knew nothing of what had happened, with eyes and faces and hats and coats that knew nothing, though they may have wondered at the sight of a young woman scampering, with what looked like blood all down her front. That *was* blood. The blood of a man that, just as he was leaving me, had become beloved.

It is very late. When I looked up just now the security light came on and I thought there was someone crossing my little garden. A wind raked gently across the tiny shoots of the new potato plants in Yastrzemski's field, and beyond them the long, still dunes showed their whale backs in the darkness, and then the cooling sand, and then no doubt the sea. Mr Dillinger says in the twenties the Ku Klux Klan used to gather on the beach there and burn their crosses, not so much because of the black people, but the Polish . . .

I thought there was someone in the garden, but when I stood just now and looked out, my head quite dizzy from the past, it was just the flick, the blur, the flounce of a big dog fox. Just for a second he looked in at me as he passed. I was curiously grateful for his glance.

I am tired. I will go to my bed – my doss, as my father used to say. I am tired, but just for a few moments I have been in love with Tadg Bere again. How strange, how strange. We may be immune to typhoid, tetanus, chickenpox, diphtheria, but never memory. There is no inoculation against that.

Seventh Day without Bill

This is a day when the land is being absolutely thumped by rain. Millions and millions of little explosions in the fields, making the soil jump. The roots of things I am sure are delighted by it, if it doesn't actually kill them.

I walked over to the other side of the pond to see Dr Earnshaw, because, even if my stay on earth is to be short from here on, I had to do something about the constipation that is plaguing me. I had my umbrella, and my long plastic coat, but the wind was very disrespectful of me, and blew the rain against every bit of me, so that I arrived at the surgery drenched.

'Mrs Bere, did you fall in the pond?' the receptionist said, with her spiky blond hairdo. It is a wonder to me how caring and consoling she is, given the possible monotony of her job. But she apparently likes the world, her place in it is acceptable to her, and she seems to be happy to see her employer's patients. But this is a quality generally in a small American town. It is one of the graces of America.

'I did not, Mrs Pilat,' I said.

'Are you wet under the coat, Mrs Bere?'

'I am fine. I shook it out on the porch.'

Then I went in to Dr Earnshaw. He is one of the old Presbyterians of Bridgehampton, his family came up here hundreds of years ago. They must have been English settlers, and there is still a little touch of Englishness to him, I think. But he is very austere, and depressed-looking, and he never smiles. You can have confidence in a man like that, though, in the matter of doctoring.

He placed a thermometer under my tongue, which could only remind me of childhood, and my father looming solicitously at my ancient bedside, and he checked my blood pressure, he looked down my throat, and when I spoke to him of my constipation, he nodded in his sad way, but neutrally, and asked me to get up on the trolley. There he pulled down my skirt a few inches, and felt about my stomach, shaking his head all the while. You might think he was about to tell you the most distressing news.

'Perfect,' he said. 'Perfect. Let me write out a script for you. You are a little backed up there. Just a little. This will settle you.'

Then he sat down and wrote on his pad with his black ink pen.

'It's gentle stuff,' he said. 'Don't worry.'

'Thank you,' I said. 'It is just hard to sleep when I am all blocked up.'

'I quite agree. Of course.'

And handed me the piece of paper.

'You are all right otherwise, Mrs Bere?'

'I am fine.'

'I want you to know,' he said slowly, turning his body in the chair a little towards me, so as not to stir anything, frighten anything, the infinite small bird of our persistence, not to scare it out of the garden, 'we are very proud of your grandson. There was no onus on him to go. I gave him all his injections before he went out. I do believe no person ever went to war with so pure a motive, so clear a love of his country. What age was he when he came to live with you?'

'He was two, Dr Earnshaw.'

'He wasn't a big child, was he? Quite skinny in fact, but he couldn't care less what I did to him. I put what was virtually a horse needle into him, I remember very well, one time he had food poisoning. I had to get something into him quick, poor fellow. It is quite painful when it goes into the muscle. Not a flicker out of him. I remember that so well.'

I laughed. It was very true.

'We were obliged in my generation to go to Korea, that was my war, Mrs Bere. I was eighteen in 1950. Well! Considered a short war, but your William's war was even shorter. Months? I want you to know, Mrs Bere, that I am very proud to have known him. What can I say? Desperately proud. Truly.'

'He liked coming over to you as a young boy. He liked the lollipops.'

'Ah, the lollipops. Still an institution. I couldn't do my work without them.'

In the porch, Mrs Pilat helped me back into my coat, and vigorously shook out the umbrella. She was laughing, laughing, brightly laughing.

I set off along the sidewalk with my script.

Lord, we do not know to pray to you as we ought. That's from Romans. Bill liked to quote that. He would be talking about something, trying to express to me a thought, and not getting anywhere with the thought. And all he really meant by it was, *Do you know what I mean, Granma?*

It is God who acquits us. That is also Romans. I suppose when St Paul was writing his letter he would have had things in mind to say, and they were turned in a certain way because he was writing to Rome, where he was from himself. Lilly's Letter? But to who? As the days have gone on, sitting here, sometimes I have my father's face floating before my eyes, or behind my eyes, sometimes indeed Mr Dillinger, a bit incongruously, but oftentimes, more and more, the face of God the Father, beard and all, that I probably have from some painting in a book that I was shown in deepest childhood. I know I love God, because I love the world he has made. My sin is I do not want to linger in it without Bill. I don't think it is the devil put this sin in me. I am an interloper at the feast of life, I am eating food and drinking drink meant for him.

This choking up. One moment, fine enough, sorrowing, but fine, sort of. The next, a big bulge of grief in my throat, so that if I had to speak in that moment my voice would be high and squeaky. It feels foolish, because we are taught when we are small that tears are foolish. Grief is certainly comic at times. An eighty-nine-year-old crone choking up. I do not think that could be very graceful-looking. But I am at peace with that foolishness. I've put grace aside.

Running through Chicago in a bloodied dress, aged nineteen, and so frightened I knew I had peed down my legs, drenching my underclothes, all niceties well and truly cancelled, what a great conglomeration of gracelessness I was then also.

The honest daylight was also adding to my terror, the bareness of me out there in that elegant city, reduced by the observation of murder to something not quite human, and certainly not civilised. In my mind's eye I could see Annie and Maud, looking on me appalled. But my mind's eye was not full of much sense, in that time. I tore along, making for the more ragged part of the city where we lodged. I could vividly imagine the police automobiles drawing up at the Art Institute, I could imagine a hundred shadowy moiling things, and above all that dark man who had run out somewhere before me, for all I knew in the same direction, for all I knew aware of me now, and following after. And mostly I saw Tadg, folded like a huge roofer's angle against the splattered wall.

As I crossed the river again, the wind found out all the wetted parts of my body, and even heavily running as I was, I felt an intimation of some shocking pneumonia to be got from it. My eyes, which felt like they were made of metal now, little dishes with something burning in them, painful and alien, seemed to be losing their sight. The lovely buildings were blurred and vague, and I was having difficulty navigating my way along imperfectly known streets and ways. All the while those various wolves following me, the thought of the murderer, the vision of my Tadg, and no doubt the four beasts and the four-and-twenty elders of the apocalypse wanting to avenge themselves on me for a Godless and guilty person.

The truth was, good Hannah Reilly, with her clear, well-intentioned visage, had stepped a few steps away from me, because Tadg and I didn't seem as intent to be married as she would wish. As my father's cousin and mine she would never desert us, or ask that we go. But I knew she had the local priest to wrestle with, and unlike ourselves, who were hoping in every way to keep a low profile, she went off to mass every Sunday morning, in the church on the lake, and liked to increase her chances of a good spot in heaven with polishing the glimmering rooms of the rectory. So we were slowly becoming cousins to hide, and not to mention, especially as the nature of our flight from Ireland had only been sketched by my father. Though if Hannah had politics I don't know to this day what they were.

So I was obliged to enter her house in quietness, and reach my little wooden room, shut fast the door, and pant there on the bare boards, not in the least knowing what to do. I think it was the first time in my life I was actually alone, without prospect of seeing another soul who would want to assist me. I felt standing there as if my life had been indeed rescinded, as if indeed some strange cancellation had taken place in some hall of heaven, and I was now to be dispensed with in some ruthless dispensation. I wondered and wondered should I have stayed where I was, at Tadg's side? Would the American police not have helped me, in some way I could not articulate or fathom? I knew Tadg was gone, his sentence of death carried out it would seem, even across the four thousand miles of the Atlantic Ocean. I presumed my own murder was hotly plotted and would follow, but in truth I could not imagine what would happen in my story now as I bumped up against this new state of being alone, of facing what was to come, alone.

At any rate, I took off the dress and the soaked linens. In my bare skin I remember laying the dress on the floor, making the arms neat and all shipshape, the stain of blood on it in the shape of some unknown country. Tadg's blood. It was my very best dress but I knew I could not get the blood out of it, without some tremendous washday washing, with the dress boiled in the pot till it roared for mercy, and then spread out on some beneficent Wicklow bush – a thing that could never be now. The blood was also on my arms and on my shoes. Maybe it was on my face. I peered into the little broken mirror that we had shared there in that poor room. I didn't know who it was, a woman with her face smeared and streaked not only with blood but long black marks of dirt, from what source I could not tell. And my hair all heaped and brittle-looking, like gorse after flowering. I was going to have to make myself again, anew, I saw. I was going to have to restore myself to some semblance of order, if I was ever to venture from that room again.

So I set to, to do that.

When nightfall claimed that little haphazard part of town, I had cleaned myself off as best I could, and put on my next-best clothes, and thrust whatever else seemed useful in one of the cloth bags. The thought of leaving Tadg's bag there troubled me more than you would think it would. But it was like a proof that he would not be coming with me. His few shirts and his spare trousers also to be abandoned. It felt like I was betraying him somehow, leaving his things was an accusation that I had been unable to save him, to keep him in the story of life. I couldn't help it that Hannah would find these remnants of our time together. She would bundle them up, blood and all, and dispose of them I was sure, and scour out the room, as if mere rats had got in after all. And hopefully we would fade in her blameless mind, and become a sort of half-muddled story, among the million wind-blown stories of America, countless as the stars.

PART TWO

Eighth Day without Bill

It's like a sort of TV, these memories. And I don't even own a TV these times, ever since I put the black and white set out under the porch long ago, no longer wanting to see that Vietnam news. Bill very nobly as a little boy pretended never to want a TV, but he used to watch in the houses of his friends.

I can actually *see* some of these old matters. I am here at my table, but I am also combing my hair in the little room I shared with Cassie Blake, away away there in Cleveland. I am using her beloved rat-tail comb. She liked Sweet Georgia Brown hair pomade, and I can smell it as I sit here, sixty years later. And with the smell is conjured lovely Cassie, her backside up in the air as she digs about in her battered trunk for some elusive bit of clothing.

When I was still a young child my father gave me a necklace of my mother's. The first thing a child does with a grown-up necklace is burst the thread. The little cultured pearls poured out on the floor, and made a dash for the gaps between the floorboards. He was able to rescue only a half-dozen, and threaded them back forlornly on the necklace.

The others must still be there, a queer memorial to me and my mother, in the darkness.

A long bit of string and six chastened-looking pearls. Maybe my life is a bit like that.

Cassie's father had been a sharecropper in Virginia who ventured North when everything started to get worse for

95

him, and got employment on the big cargo boats on Lake Erie. He was six foot six, Cassie told me, in his prime. Then he got sick in later life, and shrunk somewhat. He was a famous player on the quill-pipes. I don't think I ever knew what he was saying when he spoke to Cassie, he spoke a queer old lingo then, and so did she, but with me they showed me the mercy of English. He was living in a rooming-house down by the water, and but for that we never would have met, Cassie and me, she never would have rescued me.

She rescued me, and then some years later, she didn't quite see Joe Kinderman coming, as you might say. But she wouldn't have been able, and wasn't able, to rescue me from that, because she was in deep trouble of her own, and . . .

But I am rushing all about. Mr Dillinger would not approve. I am sure he has his own books under better control. This morning my head is like an unbroken pony, plunging about.

This may be the result of the tumult of having Mrs Wolohan and Mr Dillinger in my house at the same time, as happened a half-hour ago. They both drove up, entirely without planning it I am sure, and brought their deluge of conversation in with them, Mrs Wolohan teasing Mr Dillinger as she likes to do, and Mr Dillinger manfully enduring it. They didn't make much reference to me, but I didn't mind that. Mr Dillinger was expressing a concern about the plight of the Shinnecock Indians that live not far from here. Mrs Wolohan, who used to employ a man before Mr Nolan to tend her garden who actually was a Shinnecock, didn't think they had a 'plight', though she listened to Mr Dillinger with great politeness, interspersed with the teasing. She asked Mr Dillinger why he didn't give his garden back to the Shinnecock, since it bordered on their reservation. Mr Dillinger said he recognised that it was her duty to exaggerate in order to weaken his argument. I gathered he would indeed prefer if everyone else went away, Poles, Irish, Old Methodists, millionaires, and all the rest, and Long Island be given back to the Indians. They let this argument go round and round, and laughed a great deal, Mrs Wolohan more or less winning the bout, and then went out and got into their separate cars, and drove off, their friendship absolutely intact. What either meant to say to me I do believe was forgotten in the mêlée.

So then I needed a good few minutes to let the noise clear from my room. And I just sat quietly. And then old matters started to drift again into my head.

Cassie's shapely backside, and so on.

I came up from Chicago in that time of terror on the night train to Cleveland. There hadn't been much choice in the matter because there were only the two trains going immediately, and the other one was New York-bound, and I didn't think I could go back there.

At least I looked quite shipshape by then, with my nice coat and my cloth bag. Thank God I had the few dollars that Tadg had kept in an old tin under the floorboards. I was trying not to scan the evening editions of the newspapers, ranged against me along the station concourse, in case my picture might stare out at me – highly unlikely, since no such thing existed in the world. But I didn't know.

I thought I heard the murderer's step behind me, every step I made. If I stopped, he would stop, I knew, and anyway, I couldn't bear to look around, in case he was actually there. As long as I didn't look back, I could keep him as a phantom.

Ridiculous.

I was fleeing as if I was responsible for the murder, I knew that. But I do not think even now I was unwise so to do. If I had lingered, there would certainly have been a photograph taken, and my face would have been known not only to the indifferent multitudes of Chicago, but the nameless, secret men that had done for Tadg. I could be quiet and unmolested for a long time, and then, just when I felt safe, they would come for me, as they had come for Tadg. This at any rate I could imagine, it was the story of it I had in my head. I do not think it was so unlikely. I doubt if I would exist now if I had not run like crazy. Then there would have been no Ed, and ultimately no Bill. And maybe every life in America depends on tiny dark events like that.

The huge metal snake poured itself through South Bend, through all points east of Lake Michigan, the strange dark city of Toledo, and slowly I substituted one lake for another lake. And all the while, as I clutched my bag, sitting on the dusty train seat, I heard the wheels repeating over and over, *'you'll be safer now, you'll be safer now, you'll be safer now . . .'* If it wasn't the train, it was my own heart whispering up to me.

I arrived alone in a new city, a few sad dollars in my pockets. I was already a prisoner in the open asylum of the world. My solitariness was nearly absolute. I knew as I descended from the train that the citizens of Cleveland already smelled my fear, an odour that drives back human help. I didn't know what capital I possessed beyond the few dollars. My clothes were worn and shiny, and my shoes, once smart and good, chosen with Annie in Grafton Street, and admired by us both for the clacking sound they had made along the Dublin pavements, had an historical air. My best possession was youth, but that of course was invisible to me.

For some half-forgotten days I wandered about. There were hundreds of wandering souls in the streets of Cleveland. My last bit of money was soon expended.

The first night I spent curled up on wasteland, the back-lot of a great steel-mill that spewed forth its smoke the whole night through. The steel dust was in everything, the air, the rivers, the gardens. Those first days, I wouldn't have known if I was among angels or devils. My body became heavy to me, like a spaceman caught out on some planet with too much gravity. It was like dying and being in a queer afterlife. Oh, people were dying in Cleveland, every day. I saw two young policemen gather a body from a park one hazy morning, where an old down-and-out had got to his last breath. They wrapped him carefully in an old tarpaulin, and threw him up on a dustcart.

I was a young down-and-out, right enough. I did not even have the inspiration to beg, though there were beggars all about. I might have been murdered then, and no one notice.

I did have youth as I say. There was a price on that. I could have got a few dollars for my body, but I wasn't at that point yet. There were men, not like the wanderers, well-to-do men that came up to me, importuning me. And there were willing girls and women, speaking every language God had invented, on every sidewalk. I wasn't quite at that point, but it was the next thing, without a doubt.

This memory ends with utter blankness.

I woke in an unknown room, and heard voices talking, and after a little was able to see two forms standing in the square of a window, the bright sunlight burnishing their heads. For a brief second I thought I was back in Dublin Castle, in the care of my sisters and my father.

I had collapsed outside the building where Mr Catus Blake, Cassie's father, boarded, and he had carried me in, against his better instincts; 'I didn't want to bring you,' he said later, in his odd, cold, friendly way. Then he put me on his own bed, 'and you stinking up the place', and decided I was all right there for a while, 'I didn't mind if you died,' he said, and walked all the way over to Shaker Heights to try and borrow his daughter from Mrs Bellow, her employer, 'and I tell you,' said Mr Blake, 'she didn't want Cassie to go. She's not giving Cassie four dollars a week to go out walking with her daddy.'

But Cassie did come home with him immediately on the streetcar and realised I was well-nigh starving, and fed me. Great banging about with the pan on Mr Blake's humble gas-ring apparatus.

Then I was throwing up, and didn't know where I was, and, like Greta Garbo in *Queen Christina*, was clutching at Cassie.

She fed me again, more sparingly.

Then I think I slept for a long, long time.

I heard Catus Blake playing his music on the quill-pipes. 'Old tunes of Virginia,' he said.

'I do not know if I trust the Irish,' said Mrs Bellow. We were standing, Cassie, Mrs Bellow, and myself, in her kitchen.

'Trust is a great part in being a servant. The last girl was selling linen out the back door. All my linen is fine Irish linen. She likely got a good price for it.'

Mrs Bellow wore her dress like armour, expensive cloth with a curious unfashionable thickness to it, like an insulated wall. She was of course Cassie's mistress, and this was Cassie's effort to get me gainful employment.

'I cannot give a job to every stray girl in Cleveland. At least you have the distinction of being Cassie's stray girl. I will not say I do not have a regard for Cassie's opinion of a person. I do. You can find good rich people all over, but good poor people, of the kind you might want in your house, are very rare.'

Throughout this, Cassie was smiling, smiling, her wide face seeming contented and amused. But she didn't say a word. I suppose she knew her river well, and how the fish were in it.

'Well,' said Mrs Bellow. 'I will give you a start. On probation. I dare say you will not find it easy work. You are very small, and you do not look strong.'

With this assessment, she went back into the main part of the house. Cassie gripped me on the shoulders with both hands, her own immensely strong fingers nearly hurting my bones. She turned her head from side to side.

'Thank the good Lord,' she said.

Then she showed me our little niche over the coach-house. One big iron bed, and the walls hung here and there with Cassie's few possessions, a housecoat, a few interesting hats, a washbasin with a big jug and a rough slab of possibly carbolic soap, her oddments and knick-knacks on a little rickety table, her bottomless trunk, and the room in general all spick and span, but I would say never shown a paint-brush since its first going-over with cream-coloured paint a hundred years ago. I could see bits of cloth stuffed into holes in the wall, no doubt the result of efforts in winter to keep out the seeping cold. She had a small gilt-framed mirror, with the gold paint coming off it like a tiny autumn.

She showed me how to boil up the linen pots, and boil the linen, and drag it like bodies into the washing tub, and get the suds going like deep snowfall, and then haul the sheets again into the big coldwater rinsing basin, and slap and punch out the soap, and then her mighty arms manned the mangle like a piece of army weaponry, and she powered the poor sheets through the rollers, the chill water sluiced out. Toilers in the realm of St Veronica, patron saint of laundresses. All the while she told me her story, the way lovers do when they first meet, of her childhood in Norfolk, old Catus a sharecropper there, getting deeper and deeper into debt, and finally breaking north like a child escaping the armlock of a bully.

'A child knows nothing about all that. I just did love Vir-ginia. Chickens coming into the little iron house we had, and birds of every colour and size flocking down, and all the creatures that come and go in the year, that's like a big clock of things, Lilly, and you never saw such a spread of lovely fields, every direction.'

Then she was turning the handle with her fierce and endless strength.

'My mamma was killed by some ruffians going through, they caught her out on a back road, when she was coming back from town with chicken feed. Catus found her lying there in the yellow mess, where they had bust the bag in taking her virtue. But he said nothing about that to me at the time, only that she had gone to her reward in heaven, which didn't seem so bad, though I missed her. I was only five, and I knew nothing. And I don't think Catus ever even *looked* at another woman since.'

I passed muster with Mrs Bellow, and grew into the household duties, my body strengthening from Cassie's astounding cooking. She could make the dimmest-looking vegetables shine anew. Food loved her, and almost stood up and saluted when she came into the kitchen.

There wasn't an inch of her that wasn't beautiful. You don't share a room with someone without seeing all the inches. The depth of safety I felt with her, sleeping at her side, and taking her instructions in the house, caused great gratitude in me. Loving Cassie was where in truth I started to love America. Maybe for me Cassie was America, and if Tadg's old friend the Armenian had seen her, I think he would have been proud to paint her. She was a big, big woman, and it was lucky there wasn't too much of me, or we would never have fitted in that iron bed. Cassie boiled in the covers all night, but I didn't mind. She sweated like those American Falls.

Eventually I dared to tell her my story. From that day on she always scanned the sidewalk first thing at dawn and last thing at night, in case there was a shadowy man standing there.

Mrs Bellow was not beautiful like Cassie. She was a woman who didn't see anything and didn't know anything, but then, she was married to an ignorant man, so I will not blame her. She had her money from a steel-mill down by the lake. We sometimes heard cries in the night, and Cassie would pull the sheet high to her chin, and put her hands over her ears and mutter nonsense, so she wouldn't hear.

Mrs Bellow once told me that her ancestor owned the first house on the banks of the Cuyahoga. She had a map, hundreds of years old, and there it was, a little square house in the blank wilderness. So maybe she also was a sort of picture of America.

I was fifteen years in that house, long enough to learn all Cassie's recipes.

There are all manner of terrors in the world, and bursting with life as she was, Cassie endured her own terror, in the shape of Mr Bellow. He was forever steering her into cupboards or empty rooms in the mansion.

What is a life? What is a citizen? How was it so arranged that a man like Mr Bellow could do what he liked with Cassie, and never a word said against him? It was only gradually I became aware of something amiss. Finally it was Cassie crying in the bed, making her own small cries, that made me beg her tell me what was wrong.

So she told me.

'And I know if I tell Mrs Bellow, that will be the end of us, Lilly, and we will be out on the dusty dry roads of America.'

'What he is doing to you is wrong, Cassie dear. He can't make you do that. Won't we go down to the priest and we'll get him to do something about it?'

Because Cassie's people were Catholic down there in Norfolk, Virginia.

'Ain't no priest going to do something about this,' she said. 'You don't understand, Lilly.'

'Why don't I understand, Cassie?'

'You don't understand, Lilly, is all.'

'He's a low little louse of a man,' I said, perplexed. 'I tell you, he is a tenth-grade devil.'

'Well, maybe so,' said Cassie, laughing despite everything.

Some nights, the great fogs and smokes from the factories far below by the lake would come up the heights and visit us, banishing the fresh air. Big fogs from the lake itself also. In the deep core of winter every blessed thing froze, seven times over, so that the year became so hard you thought it would never thaw out. Then the whole district loosened itself into spring, the poor huddled trees suddenly like a thousand girls, all gold hair and ribbons, and the rows upon rows of blossom-trees in the streets shook out their colours on the air.

At some point that I cannot quite remember, I risked a letter to Annie in Dublin, just to say I was doing okay, and not to worry, and I gave her a P.O. box number to reply to. Well, a letter came back on blue-lined paper, I thought I knew the very shop where she had bought it, in her crabbed writing, like a line of ants held up by an obstruction, and she was loving and kind in her words, but also had to tell me that our father had died. He had died in the county home in Baltinglas, and he had had a peaceful death, she said, though his wits were 'somewhat astray'. She had not been able to be there for the actual moment of his dying. He was buried in the little graveyard of the hospital, she said, under the sycamores, and a poor enough stone put up, she said, because he had only a tiny pension and there was no other money to be put to honour him. I thought it was a sad letter. I thought it was very sad my father had died in such a way. I do remember sitting reading that letter, and feeling as if something vastly important to me had happened, that I had had a great duty to attend to, and had not been able to, because of my wretched exile.

My wretched exile.

Letter-writing. Names, postmarks, locations. Unfriendly eyes.

And I had cause then, not so long after, to wonder if I had been so wise to write after all.

Every day I would be sent to the Main Street to get whatever provisions Mrs Bellow listed. It is almost strange to me that I did that for so many years, season by season.

The mansion was set at the end of its street, and the road ended there. Automobiles often came in unawares and had to turn in the little sweep at the top, where the gates of the Bellow house were. Every house had a coachhouse, and places for tradesmen to park. You didn't see many automobiles on the sidewalk, so this day, coming home with the heavy bags, I did take note of an old jalopy stuck up on the dirt edge, under the old oaks that finished the vista. And leaning against the jalopy in question was a man. I don't know what he had been doing up till then, but I felt that when he spotted me coming in the distance, he rather hurriedly turned the crank on his engine, and sat into his vehicle, slamming the loose, thin door. Then he didn't look at me again the whole way, but kept his face turned towards the scrubby oaks, in an unlikely preoccupation with them. When, in some trembling, I reached the house, and turned down the great latch and started to swing the huge iron gates open just a little to allow me to pass through, he still didn't turn his head.

I saw him make a little movement, and dip right towards

the passenger seat. I don't know why that startled me so, but a fear came into me like a great crowd of rats entering a warm house. Here is the moment, I thought, when he turns and gets out and points the gun, and I am to be killed. I pressed my weight against the gates, and even the tiny gap I had needed to enter seemed to take an age to close. I suddenly sensed how vulnerable I was, how vulnerable any human creature was, bones and flesh, all permeable to a bullet. I was trying to close the gate, I know not why, and he could have leapt out and shot me a dozen times. Why did I not just run like a demon? The human brain is not a logical machine.

It was dark under those oaks. The generous light of June, that ran its fingers through the dry leaves, made the shadows all the deeper. In a strange slow-motion, I closed the gate, and stood there, looking back. I thought, is this the man that took Tadg? Suddenly all I could think of was Tadg. The fact of Tadg, the remnant of him in me, how he lived in my heart, obliterated all my present fear. I was surging with love for Tadg.

My 'messages' as Dublin people say, my packages had fallen from my arms. I had not even noticed. They were lying now at my feet, outside the gate, carrots, sugar, coffee as may be. The man got out of the car and stood in the shadows. His dry-looking hat caused another shadow over his face and eyes. Then I said something that made no sense, and makes no sense even now.

'Is it me?' I said. That's all I said. I waited for the answer with a weird patience. I could not see his face but I could feel him looking at me. I was dressed in my sole summer dress, with the pattern of olives and leaves all over it, well

I remember it. Cassie loved that dress, though it was a cheap thing from the Hungarian market. As he watched me though I began to feel naked, like that dream I used to have when I was a schoolchild, the dream of being in class, and looking down, and realising I had forgotten to put my clothes on. I felt oddly out of place, clumsy. I don't know how to describe that feeling. I felt like I was dying in front of him.

If he had a gun in his hand, and I couldn't see if he did, he didn't fire it. He swung round abruptly and got back into his bashed car. As he drove off, I saw he had a 1923 Tennessee licence plate, I did note that, in the great humiliation of my panic. He must have been driving that Model T drunk through forests to get it in such a state in only seven or eight years. My arms were useless to me, I could barely pick up my packages. My vittles, as Cassie would say.

But I went back into the house and tried to recover myself, get myself shipshape for work. I don't think Mrs Bellow would have noticed if I had come into the kitchen missing my head. She wasn't a woman to notice things maybe. I was even surprised to see her in the kitchen, she was rarely there that time of day, which she usually spent in her bedroom, curtains strictly closed. But she spent the whole afternoon there with Cassie, making three charity cakes for a fête, so I wasn't able to tell Cassie anything till evening. By which time I was like a loosely corked bottle of soda, bubbling away wastefully. It was long enough after the fact now to feel the full whack of it. I couldn't touch a bite of supper, not a bite. I was silent as a Benedictine nun. Which wasn't like me, because whatever had gone on in our lives, Cassie and me liked to talk, we liked to sparkle away a bit at each other, making each other laugh. Well, we were queens of laughter usually.

Now it was well past nightfall and our tasks were finished for that day and we were side by side in the big bed. Her weight created a big dip, so I was always a little sideways, like a lean-to shed against a house in Wicklow. So I told her my little story. Now she was all for telling the police.

'Mrs Bellow won't like that.'

'I don't think she'll want a strange man hanging about, Lilly, I don't.'

Next morning right enough she asked permission from Mrs Bellow to use the telephone in the hallway, and made a call through to the station.

That afternoon a police car came in through the gates and parked under the flowering rhododendrons.

I was not in a good state of mind. I hadn't wanted Cassie to ring and was more and more alarmed she had, thinking about it. I had fled the scene in Chicago. So I would be obliged merely to say a strange man had been acting strangely, which didn't sound very urgent. If he really was an assassin, maybe the game was up anyway. He would surely be back again, and by the savage cut of him in Chicago I didn't suppose any policeman was going to stop him.

All this was going round and round in my brain, and then the trooper walks in, in his policeman's outfit.

I didn't know he was Joe Kinderman just then, of course.

He took the whole thing very seriously, very. I gave an account of the man, on my own in the left-side sitting-room. I hadn't wanted Cassie, I didn't want her chiming in, because out of concern for me she might say too much.

'You didn't know this man,' said the officer. He had a little notebook, and a carpenter's pencil, with thick lead, and when he wrote something, he licked at the lead, quick, quick, snakelike. He had a full mouth with just a line of a moustache above his upper lip, like Cesar Romero. Me and Cassie had seen Cesar Romero at the Saturday picture house. If we had been two ice-creams we would have melted on the seats.

'I couldn't see his face,' I said, suddenly feeling the force of childhood, when a lie was such a fearing sin. I was quite afraid of this man, in his tight-fitting clothes, and his punchy face. The strange man had had a gun, and this man had a gun. It was odd to be sitting in Mrs Bellow's pink and green armchair, Joe Kinderman in a matching chair, trying to tell the truth and yet not to say anything about the past. I wanted to tell him my father was in the same profession, but of course I could not. And Tadg of course, a policeman of sorts. I didn't think this man in front of me was Irish, but still I couldn't chance it. Maybe he knew nothing of Ireland and her politics. I tried to be truthful but sparing. He was tickled pink that I was Irish, when he asked me, I didn't know why, since there were a thousand Irish maids in Cleveland, tens of thousands.

He was heartened when I said I had seen the Tennessee licence plate.

'If you remember the number, honey, we have a good chance to catch this guy.'

'77170,' I said. '1923 I think it might have been.'

'I suppose you don't know the make? Women don't usually look at things like that.'

'Model T,' I said.

He let out a little whistle, or an almost-whistle, accompanied by an unintended comet of spit.

'We had seven women killed these last two years, all over Cuyahoga county,' he said, partly to recover himself I am sure. 'So you look out for yourself.'

I was noticing something about his face then, it was slightly ash-coloured, like I had seen once in the steelworkers' faces when they came up to see Mr Bellow. The furnaces baked dust into their pores. They were human pots being fired all day long, and it left a mark. But Joe Kinderman was no steelworker.

'It's usually quiet up here,' I said. 'Never a soul. That's why he gave me a fright.'

'Sure. And very nice up here it is too. The Heights. Yes, sir. I would sure love to live up here.' And he laughed, like that was about as likely as iron turning to gold. 'Salubrious,' he said, giving the word a breeze of energy.

I found myself liking his fancy word. He might have borrowed it from my father. I liked him, even if I feared him. I smiled at him a little as he sat there, nodding his head, and patting his knees. I thought, *carefree*.

So then he got up and off he went, confident and ashenfaced.

His boot-shoes were so brightly polished I could see Mrs Bellow's windows in them, curtains and all.

Ninth Day without Bill

Well, Joe Kinderman got a name for the car's owner, a Robert Doherty, but it was far far away in Tennessee, two states over. He was thinking now it was just a drifter, on the prowl for what he could get. America was full of uprooted men now, he said, whole families. Cleveland was filling up with them, a city he said that was never going to be an easy answer for anyone. But he had a name and he was going to make sure and certain that Robert Doherty wasn't in Ohio any more.

I knew this because he came back one afternoon, easy as you like, and asked me out to Luna Park. He said I could bring Cassie with me if I liked. He had parked his car and sneaked in round the back to the kitchen, and checked Mrs Bellow wasn't there, all in best policeman style.

We only had one day off a month, and we usually just went haunting the sidewalks round the various stores in Shaker Heights, and looking at the flowers in the parks, which Cassie especially loved. There were places that didn't like Cassie coming in. But we always scrubbed ourselves, and put on whatever we had for finery, and sallied forth gamely.

This was something different, a man bringing us to Luna Park. I had to smile, because I realised properly only then that Cassie had never had a beau of any kind. Cassie was worried that she had been asked too. She didn't want to make things difficult for Joe Kinderman. But he didn't care about that. In his civvies he was all spark and tornado.

Nevertheless when we got on the streetcar all together, and were making to sit down at the front, so we could see everything as we went, the motorman had a word in Joe's ear, and asked him if we wouldn't be happier down the back.

'Don't you worry,' said Joe, showing the man his police badge that he had in his breast pocket. 'I am escorting these ladies. What you're looking at here is out-and-out royalty. This here,' he said, indicating poor Cassie, 'is the Viceregal Consort of the Gold Coast. That's her house,' he said, indicating an anonymous mansion we were passing, 'that's her *palace*, right there.'

'She don't look like no queen to me,' said the motorman, but he was also looking at Joe's badge. 'Just this once, I guess. But this in't the Gold Coast, in general. Folk don't like to see Negroes, all stuck in their faces, in general.'

There was no one else on the streetcar, for all that the motorman had said. Despite the seeming jollity, I knew Cassie so well, I could feel her distress. She was wishing herself twelve hundred miles from that motorman, maybe Cleveland itself. She was wishing maybe she was back in Norfolk, not knowing about the world, getting decked out in her First Holy Communion frock. I knew what that was like. Proud as the first day of creation. And beautiful and shining in the eyes of your father.

Catus Blake had gone living up along 55th Street, he had left the water for good and all. For something of the same reason. Things separating out in Cleveland, like a sauce that hasn't mixed.

These thoughts were still brand new when Joe Kinderman went for that man's neck. He literally went for that man's neck. The sentence the motorman had said had had a much worse effect on him than anyone could foresee. He put his big hands around that scrawny man's neck and he shook the motorman.

'You piece of human excrement,' he said, like reciting a line of poetry.

The motorman was just about to blow his emergency whistle then, and get some help, when Joe let his hands fall away. He smoothed at the man's necktie, nodding his own head, muttering something.

'No, sorry, buddy, but you just mustn't got to say things like that in front of her majesty.' And he smiled his useful Joe Kinderman smile, all nice teeth, and the clipped moustache buckling in an arc.

'You get off this streetcar,' said the man, 'I don't care if you are a police officer.'

So we got down at the next stop and walked our way to the lower part of the city. In the distance we could see the humped-up train tracks of the famous dipper.

Joe Kinderman was even lighter on his shoes now, all that muscle and hardness he had was put floating somewhat on the sea of the world, so at ease that I think not just me fell in love with him then, but every passing soul.

And indeed, a lot of Italians lived down that way, and Joe in his line of work tended to bump into the Italians, he said. The kings of corn sugar, mayhem and such, but also, he said, thousands of ordinary folk, who got into trouble in times past for keeping a still in their yard. Those times were passing, but they knew Joe's face from the fact it had been inserted into a dozen homes there. And it didn't seem unwelcome as he wended down Woodland Avenue. They were on different sides, but they didn't scorn to greet him.

'Hey, detective, now we have a lovely day.'

'How do, Mr Sorello,' says Joe, floating on this air of his own making. 'Good to see you.'

I feel so happy writing this down, because it is about happiness, and here is the day where Cassie was happy.

Joe paid us through the entrance gates of Luna Park as if we were still his little gaggle of royalty. The morning now decided to be in cahoots with us, and the lid of thin mist, which until that moment did not seem able to lift itself away from the city, suddenly did so, and the generous American sky threw all its arms open above us, and above the brightened factories, and the stretching wilderness of the human streets. It was as if the possible paradise of America was revealed, something to replace the unhurt domain that the first white men had found, as Mr Dillinger had explained to me. Something to undo the hurts and terrors that had followed, that first little hut that Mrs Bellow claimed descent from, that first muddled village, then a town flooding its houses slowly across rough fields, and then the great shouting that the city was. Beyond the amusement park the Cuyahoga River, that sometimes had seemed to be like a broken creature slinking away, vast and stinking, abruptly and magically regained her ancient beauty, the filth and darkness of the water turned ever so slightly by the hand of the world, so that its filthiness had only been a humorous coat to hide its gemlike brilliance, its fantastical yellows, its gleaming greens, its browns as lovely as an Irish bogland. My heart lifted like a pheasant from scrub, as if utterly surprised and alarmed by this beauty, its wings utterly opened in fright and exulting.

We passed on in. Joe Kinderman said to me out of Cassie's earshot that there were days when the 'Negroes' were not allowed in to the park, for fear of upsetting the good citizens. And he looked at me with his intense look that I was beginning to recognise. I was beginning to know him. It would have been difficult for me to say why Cassie, streaming along in her best clothes, her face ablaze with the surreal happiness of that day, could have done anything but delight a citizen, much less disturb them. She was the city, the citizen, and the gates of heaven all in one, as John Bunyan wrote in his ancient book. She was like a human person too good for any suitor like in a fairy story. Her tremendous arms, the shine and curve of her lower legs, her bosom that any old mariner would have chosen to grace the prow of his ship, to carry him miraculously through storms, all seemed to me like instances of never-to-be-repeated human grace.

Joe Kinderman's only law that day was that we must ride the amusements, all of them, despiting all fear and reluctance. He bought a handful of tickets like a posy in his fist. He led us magisterially, knowing everything about them, from one to the other. We shied at coconuts like amazons defeating mere men. We collected two teddy bears and carried them with us carefully like the new babies of our strange marriage. All the time, circling about and about, we were deviously approaching the great central attraction, which like a guilty thought hovered in all its twists and turns and complexity above our heads. Whether heaven or hell we did not know.

Then having tasted the mundane delights we were to endure the celestial.

'Anyone ever fall off this thing?' said Joe to the ticketman, just to further infuse me with dread. The ticketman had a long well-combed beard, which he had tied at the end with white string, and God had forgotten to pin his ears to his head properly.

'We don't have no one fall off this thing. You couldn't fall off iffen unless you threw yourself.'

'There, Joe,' I said.

'I heard of plenty people falling off rides just like this, all over America. That right, mister?'

'Not in a regulated place like thissen. This the goddamn best-made fun park in all America.'

'Where you from, mister,' said Joe in his best friendly manner, not wishing to cause offence, 'with your thissen and iffen?'

'Blue Ridge Mountains. Ever been up there?'

'I never been there,' said Cassie, 'but that's Virginia. I come from Norfolk, Virginia.'

But whether the ticketman didn't care for Norfolk, or some other reason, he didn't say anything more. He put Cassie and me into the front of a car when it came clanking up the tracks, and Joe in the row behind us. The seats were made of some grainy metal, and we had an iron bar clanged down across our stomachs to protect us from Joe's stories. Wonderful generous bits of Cassie settled against the bar. The world was made for lesser mortals generally.

'Slipstream,' said Joe enigmatically.

How pleasantly we drew away, some distant engine making mysterious clockwork move, this new beauty of the city uncovered more and more as we rose. The sunlight didn't miss its chance, and as we approached the first high point of the ride, it moved in behind a brassy cloud high above the river, and then suddenly, like a very thunderstorm of light, dropped a cascade of brightness the size of Ireland down on the water, so that the river halved into blackness and brilliance, and you would half-suspect that there was a more mysterious ticketman somewhere, from the mountains of heaven, pulling heavenly switches.

We poised, three beating hearts, three souls with all their stories so far in the course of ordinary lives, three mere pilgrims, brilliantly unknown, brilliantly anonymous, above a Cleveland fun park, with the wonderful catastrophe of the sunlight on the river, the capricious engineering of the tracks, the sudden happiness of knowing Joe, his clever kindness to Cassie, his shoal of looks at me, I could see him, I could see him, glancing at my face, my body, wondering, wondering, his own eyes lit not only by the strange weather of that day, but something as strange within, Joe's gathered stare, like a photograph of some old poetman, that you would see in a magazine, all balanced for a perfect moment, the past somehow mollified, the journey so far somehow justified, Tadg's murder, my own faraway condition, fatherless and sisterless, all poised in the gentle under-singing of the wind, coming up through the filigree of the fun car, raised to heaven, almost to heaven, Joe's face behind me when I looked beaming almost ecstatically, almost frightening, his head back, his eyes closed, his teeth bared, and maybe even laughing, if it wasn't the mechanisms churning, bringing us to the tipping point, bringing us, bringing us, Cassie and me and Joe, here we are, so high, so high, oh paradise of Cleveland, oh suffering America, long story of suffering and glory, and our own little stories, without importance, all offered to heaven, to the sky and the river, to the stories of the houses, the streets, the passing decades, the worrisome future, then, oh, oh, gone beyond, thrown somewhat forward, our weight somehow in conspiracy with this matter of acceleration, our weight as if tearing us downward, as if we were for a moment forgiven by God, and then rejected, in some sort of extravagant humorousness, and cast down, instantly at speed, and then at worse speed and then worse, so that I saw Cassie's cheeks dragged towards her ears, and flappy hollows bubble and boil there, and in the roar of our falling I heard Joe not laughing but calling out, screaming out, words I could not catch, words infected with wildness and happiness, and in me only terror and sickness, and stampeding thoughts, until, until, dropping sheer and sheer, suddenly down to the level we came, bottoming out, and Cassie weeping, weeping, and then holding on to me, her brave arms around me, and me trying to get my arms around her, not succeeding, but holding on, holding, my lovely Cassie, and she was weeping and then laughing, laughing and weeping, as if we had lived all our life in two minutes, two minutes of falling and weeping, and I knew everything that had happened to me was just, because it led to this, and this was my reward, the infinite friendship of my Cassie.

As we came out back towards the huge gates, painted in their white and black squares like a racing flag, a tall man all kitted out in similar finery to Joe, but even sharper, a light linen suit, a sleek brimmed hat as if torn off the back of a seal, and in the colourful company of three laughing women, opened out his arms when he saw Joe and said:

'Joseph, goddamn Joseph Clarke!'

'Sorry, bud, I ain't no Joseph Clarke,' said Joe Kinderman,

laughing. 'You're thinking of some other guy.'

'Oh, I guess. Begging your pardon there,' said the man, bringing up some elaborate lingo in his confusion, and his voice tinged with doubt.

Anyhow, we passed on through the square frame of the gate into the blurred roaring of the city. The efforts of the new light were waning as the day waned, but nevertheless we trod along with contented steps.

That night in the bed Cassie said she was going to rub out the name of Jesus Christ in the New Testament and put in Joe Kinderman's instead. Why, she didn't just think he was Jesus Christ, she reckoned he was God the Father Himself. The Holy Ghost too maybe thrown in for good measure.

I had to stop writing a few minutes ago. In the dark of the evening there was a push on my bell, and I jumped in this skirt, yes I did. I was still at the bottom of that ride, still with Cassie and Joe, and I came back into my little house with a strange jolt. All day there was a series of short drenching showers, and now, being returned by the bell to the present, I could suddenly smell the potato plants in the field between me and the sea, luxuriating I am sure in the rainfall and the new warmth. I folded over this big accounts book, where I am now scribbling, because much to my astonishment I have needed so many fresh pages, thinking at the start I might be done in twenty or thirty. I do not even know why I had the accounts book still, stuck in a drawer, since it dates from the time I ordered for Mrs Wolohan, and is properly hers. So I write my little nonsenses on her paper, properly speaking.

Anyway I rose with a stiffness as infinite as that previous happiness, and wended my way in the darkness of the corridor, where my photographs winked in the odd light, my brother Willie in his uniform that Maud sent me before she died in Dublin, thinking I might cherish it, and Joe Kinderman in his Cleveland police officer's rig-out, looking fairly stupendous, and Ed in his uniform, and Bill in his – not that I could see them as such, but they were vivid and lit as always in my mind's eye.

At the door it was only Mr Eugenides with a covered basket. I turned on the porch light for him, and he stood there silently, the basket in one hand, and raising his nice fedora hat with the other, in his mannerly way.

'I am not disturbing, Mrs Bere? God forbid. My wife says, take this up to Lilly Bere. It is no small thing. It is Mrs Eugenides' best pot roast. She knows you are an expert, but she said, Lilly won't mind me. I said, of course she will not. I hope we don't offend, bringing owls to Athens?'

He seemed immensely pleased and energised when I gratefully accepted his gift.

'Come into the kitchen,' I said, 'I will give the basket back.'

'No, no,' he said. 'Don't worry. I have fifty of them. Some of my Greek produce, hey, comes in such baskets. From the island of Samos, that sleeps in the arms of a Turkish bay. There. Keep it, you will have a little bit of the old country for yourself. Mrs Eugenides says this is of course not traditional Greek cooking, but she learned the pot roast from her best friend, and wishes for you to have it in turn. Her late friend was from Cape May, New Jersey. She has written out the recipe, see.'

'That is so kind.'

'She wishes to hand it on to you,' he said, still in his excess of excitement.

'Well, that is the purpose of cooking. The great purpose. It's all about friendship.'

'*Orea*,' he said, *beautiful*, a bit of Greek I did understand, I had heard him utter it so often in his store. 'Goodnight to you, Mrs Bere. Goodnight.'

'Goodnight, Mr Eugenides.'

It was a lovely pot roast, as I found when I had a little bit of it, with nuts, and cheese, perfection. The face of Mrs Eugenides' entirely unknown friend from Cape May, New Jersey, seemed to hover before me for a moment, as if permanently attached in spirit to her cooking.

Tenth Day without Bill

Being a woman of her word and much more besides, Mrs Wolohan arrived this morning and reminded me she was bringing me to Gerard to get my hair done, which I had of course forgotten. I didn't even know if I *had* known in the first place. She might have said something about it, and anyway, I could think of no excuse not to do it, and gathered up my bag and put on my road shoes and went out with her.

'It is an absolutely lovely day,' she said. 'I was swimming this morning at six. That's a.m.'

'In the pool?' I said.

'In the sea. I went down alone. There was no one there at all. I slipped into the water. It was wonderful. Then I went home,' she said, banging the car door on her side, and taking off with a little whoosh of sand from the roadside, 'and I ate some strawberries and cream. Katherine Mansfield describes a woman in one of her stories as eating cream with a "rapt inward look". That is so good. It is exactly like that.'

Mrs Wolohan is a woman who has endured vast vicissitudes. What has saved her generally in life is not just her courage, which is signal, and her faith, which is solid, but her enjoyment of all the minute pleasures of being alive, something that always gave me pleasure also, in cooking for her. When she was served up, on a dark winter's day, my famous beef Wellington, which in fact was one of Cassie's recipes, though Mrs Wolohan didn't know that, followed by the simple body blow of my autumn pear tart, Mrs Wolohan would exhibit her happiness openly, and create a small speech to remember the occasion. No matter what else was going on all around her, no matter what crushing history was being presented to her. Her whole philosophy was to go on, like a soldier who has lost comrades along the way, and has buried them with due love and remembrance, but who also has assignments ahead that he must go to meet. I think, considering her life, this aspect of her is well-nigh miraculous. It is because of this that I cannot help but to love her.

She is much younger than me, and I was already nearly fifty when I went to work for her mother, and some time after, for her, when she married. Why she has harboured me, why she has protected me, all these years of my retirement I do not know. Why she has allowed this long long tenancy of her little house, which might be put to a hundred other uses, and indeed, in being so near the sea, is very valuable, standing plumb on its little yard, remains to me a mystery.

She is a tallish bony woman, who in a rather unusual way has got more lovely as she has got older. One of her sisters was considered a great beauty. But Mrs Wolohan, like one of those opera singers whose voices only come into full power at forty, is also beautiful, now. Her features are well defined, her eyes are blue, and she dresses plainly in trousers and shirts. She has about ten yards of haute couture outfits hanging in various wardrobes, and these she uses for her charity work, and dinners, and the like. Otherwise she is not too bothered, except I am sure that these seemingly inexpensive clothes cost a great deal and were bought on Fifth Avenue.

Her car is an ordinary mid-range one, nothing fancy, and I love to drive with her in it. When I am close in to Mrs

Wolohan, she will talk away. And there is something in her attitude that makes it so plain that she 'has time for me', as my father would say. That is so flattering that it brings out the best in me, and I never feel old with her, though there must be thirty years between us. I have known her since she was a very young woman, and worked for her or lived near her for over forty years. We have never, ever, had a bad word between us, which I think is very remarkable.

When I was first engaged by her mother, it was actually Mrs Wolohan, now I think back on it, then very young, who interviewed me. It was probably 1950, and it was odd to be questioned by one so young. But all her queries were politely put, and even at that age she showed a maturity beyond her years. She of course loved that I was Irish, being 'Irish' herself, and loving Ireland, where she had been as a child on many visits. People love Ireland because they can never know it, like a partner in a successful marriage. I am a bit the same way myself. Ireland nearly devoured me, but she has my devotion, at least in the foggy present, when the past is less distinct and threatening. When the terrors associated with being Irish have been endured and outlived. As much as I could of my story in America I told her. I cannot remember if I said anything about Tadg. I *seem* to remember doing so, and her being astonished at his fate, but in truth I do not know if I was in fact so brave as to tell her. I *see* in my mind's eye her open, attentive face, her horror that a young man could be murdered in such a manner. I did not give her all the exact details about Joe, how could I? But I think she gathered that I had had my difficulties. More than anything else, it was no barrier against employment that I had a child, who was about four years old at the time. Ed hung about my skirts like a witch's familiar. He was much admired by Mrs Wolohan's mother for being 'well behaved'. If he had not been, I could never have kept my employment there, and I am very grateful to him for that. The casual atrocities that young children commit now and then, however, were well within the bounds of the acceptable. Ed took down most famously a unique piece of Belleek pottery, with the picture of an Irish castle in a wild landscape, and did for it in such an absolute way that it never rose back to its shelf again. This was taken in a good spirit. Mrs Wolohan's mother said she would tie him by the leg like a country dog to the kitchen table if it happened again, but luckily this resolve was never tested.

I am saying all this because I want to record my gratitude. Gratitude has a place, as does commiseration and condolence. *Wirra-wirra* cried the old keeners round the coffins in vanished Wicklow days.

Gerard's salon on Main Street is always busy, because there are a thousand well-tended hairdos around here. This morning he was shouting something at one of his girls when we came in. Mrs Wolohan paused in the doorway, myself just behind her. She turned and gave me a look, as if to say, he is a great artist, and we must overlook his character. As if to say, the cave is full of lions, but we must enter anyway.

One of Gerard's other rather cowed girls took me in hand, and guided me over to the sinks, so she could wash my hair. Alas my hair is thin, and so when you wash it, I do have a sorry bald look to me. So that I would not willingly go to the hairdresser of my own accord. But she was very thoughtful, and whipped a towel around the offending mess, like seaweed on a stone, and brought me over to Gerard.

'Mrs Bere,' he said, as if the name alone spoke volumes, and he need say no more. But what he intended, what he implied, I do not know. With a certain brutal deftness, he peeled off the towel, and dropped it to the floor. He took my poor tresses in his fingers, and drew his fingers through them, again and again, so that he caused a little ache to begin in my scalp. Meanwhile Mrs Wolohan had come up behind him, and was looking not at me but at my reflection in the mirror.

'Mrs Bere would like you to do something uplifting.'

'Of course.'

'Something to cheer her up. Do you think you can do that, Gerard?'

'Yes,' said Gerard, but with an unexpected sadness in his voice. 'Yes.'

'Do you think she should have a bit of colour?' she said.

'Oh, Mrs Wolohan, Mrs Bere does not let me put colour in her hair. I have tried to convince her. But she says, what do you say, Mrs Bere?'

'I am content with the white.'

'You see?' said Gerard.

'Well, I will not try to influence her. She knows her own mind.'

'What I like,' said Gerard, 'is these bones. You have such good bones, Mrs Bere. I could shave your head and you would look just fine.'

'Nevertheless,' said Mrs Wolohan in her best sensible voice, 'don't shave her head.'

'It is very fashionable now in Manhattan.'

'Nevertheless.'

'Of course,' said Gerard.

While he worked, Mrs Wolohan remained at my shoulder. She seemed to get more and more lost in a daydream. Without thinking what she was doing, her hand eventually came up and rested on my right shoulder. She stood there like that for a long time. She was in Gerard's way, but he contrived to work around her. What she was thinking, who could say? I often have thought that she has a lot to think about, if she cares to. If she doesn't just block it out. Her sense of the delicious is maybe part of that effort, not to dwell on terrible things. To continue on. At length she breathed a great sigh, and patted my shoulder, and let her hand drop away again.

Then she drove me home, all coiffeured up, or as much as Gerard could manage. Tested to the limits of his skill. Silent, because Mrs Wolohan was silent. What a long long time I had known her, I thought. I could be the mouse in the wainscot that could tell the whole story of her life, but from a mouse's point of view. The true terror and suffering I cannot really envision. The heart torn out of her again and again. Her true victory over her life though, I have witnessed.

She had brought an old woman out to get her hair done. Old, irredeemably so. Looking just as ridiculous and ancient I am sure, but cheered, as Mrs Wolohan knew I would be. Somewhat.

Telling his beads, o'er and o'er. That's some old poem or ballad, I forget which.

I seem to remember some matters well enough, even in the great mire that is my poor head, but it would give me a great fright to have to put a date on everything. Thank God it does not behove me to do so. For it is just me sitting here, telling my tale to myself, that's what it feels like, mostly, old matters held in the fingers of memory, like those old beads in a family rosary, polished by a lifetime of prayers, and handed down, and slowly slowly no doubt diminishing and thinning as they go from creature to creature. When we were small, my father would occasionally take a great desire to saying the rosary, and we would be down on our spindly knees every teatime for a few weeks. Then this fervour would disappear for a long time, and what it was in his life that brought on these tremendous bouts of piety, in which we were obliged to participate, I of course could not say, then or now. The ordinary stations of a man's life maybe.

Not my father, not my mother, but it's me, Lord, standing in the need of prayer.

But there was a curious circumstance that allows me always to know the year at least of my marriage. You might think a person would be inclined to remember such a signal event anyway, whether or not subsequently they wished to forget. But I am *obliged* to remember it, for it was the year of the great suffering in Oklahoma and other parts. If this country was a marriage between hope and suffering, then one of the partners in the marriage upped and left mysteriously. Or in some great fire, hope was burned off, and suffering was discovered to be indestructible.

Ah, but how easily I slipped over the fate of Cassie Blake. How easily, even unbeknownst to myself. But I will set it down now.

Two years Joe Kinderman 'wooed' me, as he called it. I think he thought it was a necessity, born out of some strange

131

teaching of his mother maybe. Not that he ever spoke of
her, or rather, he did, vaguely, but then another time would
say something about her that sounded like another woman
entirely.

The one big story he gave me was one night walking in
the lovely deep-summer smells of the park close by the Bellow house. The gates had been closed long since, the gate-
man ringing his poignant bell, but Joe though a policeman
did not scorn to climb the railings and hoist me after. And
there we were as private as foxes. Strolling under the low
branches, the air there cooling after the long baking of the
day, every green thing breathing out a sigh of gratitude, the
birds of Ohio skittering about in the hedges and under-
growth, the reckless squadrons of the night flies trying to
keep up with us. And the moon burning in its own bowl of
soft fire.

'You see, Lilly, my great-grandfather was a bandman
down in southern Ohio. I'm talking maybe 1860s, earlier
even. They were building this great tunnel, a whole mile
long, for a canal they were linking up to the Ohio canal. It
was going to bring happiness and prosperity to that whole
district. So, the great day of the opening of the tunnel
came by, and my great-grandfather, Jürgen Neetebom was
his name, was put into the very first state boat was going
through. And they played up this colossal tune, louder and
louder, the trombones and the oboes and the great drums,
and by God it loosened a stone in the ceiling of the tunnel,
and down it crashed, blocking the way. Men leaped down
with hammers and picks and the like, to be breaking up
that boulder. But now, Jürgen he was set to be married that
afternoon in the town ahead, where he was living then. And

132

he was to be wed to my great-grandmother, Hetty was her name. And it was taking a whole heap of time to get that boulder broke up. So finally he cries, "My time's up, fellas," and leaped, uniform and all, into the water, and swam all the way to the other end, and arrived in the church all draggled and soaked, and married his Hetty. And he was some sort of Hollandish man, I do believe, my mother's mother's father.'

The air moved about the trees the whole while, like a crowd of shadowy people, listening, listening.

'The legend of Jürgen Neetebom was that, as a very old man in his nineties, he was standing on one of the canal bridges, where he liked to go and think things out, when the first line of the great Ohio flood hit him. It came pouring down the canal system, bursting all the lock gates as it went, destroying everything, setting Dayton on fire and killing ten thousand souls. Whole cities disappeared. So the water caught up with him in the end. Although some say he was hanged as a much younger man for stealing horses in Texas. Take your pick.'

'So your people always were from Ohio then, if a little more southward?' I said, softly.

'No, I do not believe so.'

The dogwoods, their papery leaves massing in the darkness, whispered *America, America*.

'That's a beautiful story, up to the last bit,' I said.

'You say?' he said.

'I do,' I said. 'Romantic.'

'Romantic,' he said, 'I suppose. I suppose there was terrible work to get that uniform back in order, the drenching it got.'

'I suppose,' I said.

The sort of things people say when almost any words at all give them pleasure, because what the words, any words, seem really to be saying is, *just walking like this and talking nonsense is the best thing I have found to do yet in the world.*

So I could not quite establish what part of the country he came from, but then I was grateful myself for some vagueness around such matters. I did not press him. He did tell me once also that he was Jewish, but I must confess, on having relations with him, he was not a circumcised person, that I could judge.

'Joe,' I said, beholding this, thinking I would broach the subject. But then I didn't, on many counts, not least not wanting to embarrass him. Blindness is a great affliction, except for lovers.

Lovers. When I think of Mr Bellow, with his half-height frame, the head narrowed by the hair being shaven cruelly, pestering Cassie, 'lovers' is not the word that springs to mind.

He considered, without thinking much about it I am sure, that she was available to him in every way. I am sure that is true. I think of all the suffering servants and maids of America, lying down under the onslaught of their masters, which, if it did not always happen hidden from view, would have looked like the map of a great and terrible battle. In the American long ago. At least, I do hope so. Pray so.

Mr Bellow wouldn't ever leave Cassie alone, even though, 'in poultry terms', as she put it, she was no spring chicken.

'He'll get tired of me,' she once said, when I implored her to tell Mrs Bellow. 'You'll see.' But he never did. I nearly said, I don't blame him. But I do blame him, and greatly.

I blame myself. I should have done something, said something, better than I did. What would Cassie's story have been without that? We could be neighbours now maybe, she might have a house there on the Sag Turnpike, we could sit on my porch and chinwag till our chins dropped off.

But, but, in the end of her real story he got her with child, and Cassie couldn't endure that.

I was full of stupid plans. I said she could come away with me and Joe, and we would be a sort of family, and the child could run about our feet, and we'd be happy.

She couldn't bear the thought of carrying that child. She was a mighty woman, and thought she knew what she had to do.

She went down to Lake Erie and started to swim out in the fabulous cold.

The waves glittered all about her and the sun cast worshipful light down on her, as her beautiful back swam out. That's how I imagine it. I read the note she left in our bedroom, and went tearing down on the streetcar to find her, but there was nothing to see, only the endless stitches of light on the water.

Cassie must have scraped about on the bottom of the lake for a week, and then she floated up, it was a miracle she was found at all, but she washed up on the little bathing beach we had often frequented, and me and her father Catus Blake buried her. He didn't have any money, but he found a place for her in the poor man's section of the lakeshore cemetery, where a nice priest was open to his protestations that she was a Catholic woman, which she was, and not a Baptist as might have been assumed. But at the same time the priest was relieved that the casket we found for her would not be open, because he was mighty uncomfortable about putting a black woman in among the others, who were mostly Irish. The grave-markers were only wood, and mostly mouldering. And many of the graves were just bare heaps of clay.

Into the steel-cold earth she was slipped.

Catus Blake stared aghast at the edge of the grave, as his daughter was put into the ground before him. A face of pure grief, like a stricken saint. I knew he had put his pipes in his breast pocket, but he never took them out in the upshot. They made a little bump there, rising and falling with his heartbeat, like a second heart.

Down she went, the gravediggers in their surprisingly dirty clothes, even for gravediggers, slowly lowering her, one of them with a cigarette stuck in the corner of his mouth. Bizarrely enough, I noted it was the Parliament brand.

A goddess among the Irish. So then I did not have my friend, no more. Weeping, weeping. Wept for seven days.

Mr Bellow went around looking abashed. But a silence closed over his great sin. Fate didn't say boo to him. He never paid any price, unless it was the sliver of matchwood he had for a soul, burning, burning to a cinder.

So then Mrs Bellow didn't have either of us. I don't know what it is I could say she did have. I left her to her fate, whatever it was, and was resolved, if I had been ever doubtful, to marry Joe.

We got married in the Irish church in Cleveland, with his police buddy, Mike Scopello, as his best man. The priest said he could marry me to a man who didn't know who he was much quicker than to a man who did, so Joe fitted that bill. Then Joe carried me off down to New York, and we spent a whole week there, getting the hang of our new condition. So, then I was Mrs Kinderman, wife to Joe, who maybe was Jewish but probably not, and might have been Catholic except he wasn't.

When Joe was shaving the first morning in our little hotel, I heard him singing a little hobo's song called 'Canaan'. At least, he said it was a hobo's song, or a down-and-out's, because he heard it sung once, he said, when he himself first came to Cleveland, and was down on his luck. That was the first true-sounding bit of news I ever had about his past.

The whole of America was turning into a mission of sorts, in that time, unless by some miracle of chance you were a toff. Joe was going to hold on to that job of his for sure.

'Sometimes it's the devil's own work, and sometimes it may even be God's, but it's going to keep the meat on the table for us, Lilly.'

There he was, with his surprisingly elegant table manners, eating heartily in a New York chophouse.

Apart from the ashen skin, which he still had, Joe had no problems in the looks department. He was tall as befit a policeman, his limbs were long and smooth, and his teeth were good. I so wanted to write to my father and tell him all, but of course he was poste restante in heaven itself. I was sorely tempted to try and let Annie know. I knew Maud was married so why couldn't I join in the feast of news? But no, I knew it couldn't be, for the moment anyhow. That man in the shadows gave me pause. Then I wondered, was that man always with me? Was he a sort of secret husband, always creeping along near me, or finding out bits of news about me, and coming to find his prey? He might have shot me that day, and not much to be done about it. But he hadn't. I peered out through the great window of plate glass at the flood of people and autos outside. A million lights of every shape and colour like all the souls of the earth since time began, twisting, flooding along the ways. And still that strange dust smell of America I had never become so American as not to notice. That's what kept me a stranger there, a voyager in love with the place of her voyage. And Joe in his youth, making plans for us, eating the food as if it were a stain to be removed from the white plate, cut by cut, methodical. Methodical Joe.

Then we went back to the hotel and took command of the big linen bed. There wasn't too much modesty in either of us. We were glad to meet each other, naked. It was my secret self meeting his secret self. They shook hands. They went at it. He kissed my mouth for an hour. He kissed my legs for another hour. He gave my left ear fifteen minutes. It was like a long train journey, and I was the countryside, with assorted stations. How is it that the human body is designed sometimes to melt into a white lineny bed, in the city of New York, and couples on linen beds in all the cities of the world, trying to climb into each other's skins? That's one queer, wonderful creature.

I am glad and grateful that in my life I knew his love. He didn't need to be from anywhere for me to love him. He didn't need to have a story or a history. He just needed to be Joe, what he was, neither from here or from there. Neither this thing or that thing. And not all the things or from everywhere, either. Secretive Joe. Massively beautiful Joe.

American Joe.

I loved him.

I was grieving for Cassie, but I thought, this man loved Cassie, he saw her, the image of her is in his eyeballs. I can kiss his eyes, because they saw Cassie. I was thinking a lot of daft thoughts at that time. In love as I was.

Another of those precious days we went to see *In Old Chicago*. Don Ameche as an Irishman. With great happiness and contentment we watched Chicago burning in 1871.

That night we lay again in the hotel room. We made love, and this time Joe used a sheath, which puzzled me just a little.

In the morning when we woke, there was a strange reddish light in the room, and outside the window the light was redder, and yellower, and stranger. There was a big wind howling along the avenues of the city. The whole room, the bed, and our limbs, were covered in dust. Joe's face beside me was a queer brown colour, as if the dust had baked itself onto his skin, using the sweat of the night as a mixer. He looked like one of those voodoo dancers, but the other way round. He was almost blackened. Years later Mr Nolan, who hailed from the mountains of Tennessee, and knew bits of Irish that he didn't even know were Irish, used the phrase *cailleachaí dóite*. Which means, old women burned by sitting in by the turf fire all the time. Mr Nolan said, and wise it was, that we had better be happy in this life, and get what we could from it, because soon enough we would all be *cailleachaí dóite*. Actually *cailleach* means hag, so I suppose I qualify now. But then, in my heyday, full of love, waking beside a strangely altered Joe, I was no *cailleach*, but a youngish woman almost bursting open with life. New York had to be careful with me, or I would swallow her up. In the full flush of my love, I wasn't really fearful for that time.

There is a defiance that comes after fear, but really is a sort of sister to it. That really is the fear itself, with a new aspect. The sight of Joe, and myself also when I gazed in the mirror, I do believe returned me to what it properly was. The fear that arises from the simple sorrow of the world. And therefore can't be got away from.

The storm blew its sorrowful dust about all day, covering everything and everybody. It must be still there, anciently, in the cement mixes of that time following, lying in the little lines of the sidewalks, deep in the very heart's core of the citizens. In Mr Dillinger's newfangled DNA. The dust of that day, the day that the gigantic wind brought all that dust from Oklahoma, bringing it six hundred miles and more, all the way to New York. All the way I will be bound to Chicago and Cleveland. The dust of dreams, of farms, of Okie talk, of lullabies and lovers' promises, the dust of America's blood and spit. The wind brought that. *And the Lord was not in the wind.*

The time of my marriage. Just after.

So then we set ourselves up in a small house in the Irish part of town, a fact which obliged me always to keep back from my neighbours. It put the wind up me to be surrounded by all the Irish names, but most of those families were second- and third-generation in America. They didn't know much about my Ireland. Not that I did myself, or do now. I cannot imagine it. It is like a huge graveyard, with my father and my sisters buried in it. A blankness has grown up in my head over the years. Someone has been painting out those old scenes. White paint over everything. Willie is in Picardy of course.

Joe liked being married. One morning he told me to be sure to be standing out on the sidewalk at six o'clock when he was due home. I stood there faithfully in my best dress, thinking it was an occasion of some sort. It was a blowy day, and I felt strange standing out there, with the secret world of our house behind. The little brown kitchen that had only a small window looking out on the neighbour's yard, our sitting-room the size of a cat litter-box, and up the tight stairs, our bedroom, or 'the ring' as Joe dubbed it, where we 'wrestled for Cuyahoga county'.

Anyway in the blowing dust of the evening, and it may have been summer then so, up came a big new automobile, with huge white wheels, that you don't see nowadays. Mrs Wolohan's chariot is a very small affair beside it. How they got those tyres off I don't know. It had enormous lamps, shining with chrome, and it was great excitement to me to see Joe sitting up in that behind the wheel. He must have brought his civvies in to work with him, because he was in his mass-going suit, and his white hat with the thick black ribbon. His 'gangster's' hat, he called it, and indeed it had been given to him by an Italian gentleman he knew.

'Some machine, eh, Lilly? Get in, Lilly, let's go for a spin.'

We drove out along the lakeshore, and back into the city, and sped along Woodland Avenue, acknowledging as we passed the strange castles of Luna Park, then away out to Shaker Heights, the big engine surging and trembling, passing the turn to Mrs Bellow's house that I knew so well. But we had done with all that, we were turning our faces to the future.

'The past is a crying child, that's for sure,' said Joe, 'but it will all be made up to him in the coming times. Yes, sir.'

Joe liked to make enigmatic statements like that. It cheered him up.

Eleventh Day without Bill

Well I remember when Joe's partner Mike Scopello came to see me. We had been married about three years. A man had come into the Cleveland police department and started to clean everything up. There had been too much money sloshing around Cleveland, and Joe said there was a lot of officers and detectives on the take from the Italians. Mike was an Italian, and a Sicilian at that, but from the north-east part of the island. The first night he had supper with us, and I astonished him by serving 'the best plate of fish' he ever ate, he showed me a tattered but treasured photograph, not only of his grandmother and grandfather, who he had never really known, but also the old farmhouse where his family had farmed for hundreds of years.

'I don't know, Lilly,' he said. 'Maybe it's a ruin now. I heard it was all right.'

Mike didn't like Mussolini much, but otherwise the Italians worshipped him. We could drive through Little Italy and see banners with the great man's face on them. There was even a hope that Mussolini would come to America. He was going to make Italy like it was in the time of the Romans, people said. Anyway they took pride in their distant leader.

'Old house still probably going to be a ruin, with or without Signor Mussolini,' Mike said. No, he didn't like him. 'I don't like all that show,' he said. But he certainly liked that fish.

He was also mighty fond of Joe. Two times they were in gunfights together, with the racketeers. Joe said they were always looking for clever new ways to break the law. All the old still-men, all the families that had lived off the sugar-corn trade, all the kids that had gone to school with the dollars of that trade keeping them in shoes, they were young men now, and eager to make their fortunes.

'Like trying to get bats out of your roof,' said Joe, sitting that first night in the afterglow of the summer evening. Our little house had a view of the lake, just. You had to crane your neck, and all you saw were factories and jetties, but it was there, the water. The lake had its own aroma, from a hundred ingredients, mixed by the god of that lake. There was great soothing in that smell. I didn't like to have to go away from it; sometimes we drove northward along the lake shore, there were places up there to visit, restaurants and the like, and that was fine, but I didn't like it when Joe cut inland in the big motor. He loved cities, and wanted to see Toledo and maybe even Chicago, but I was loath to go, back along those shining train tracks.

I had told Joe as much as I dared about myself. In the end I did tell him about Tadg, but I didn't say I was there, and I prayed to the good God that he wouldn't look into it. I thought I owed him that much of the truth. Not that I seemed to get much truth back for my trouble, but maybe I wasn't with Joe for truth exactly.

'Your story,' he said, lying up in the bed, his legs too long for the end of it, and his upper body naked, only the bottoms of a set of striped pyjamas to cover himself. His big right hand was holding a cigarette, which he was gratefully smok-ing. He loved his tobacco. 'Your story there, about your Irish friend, reminds me of something. Mike would tell you the story better, but Mike isn't here . . . There was this little Italian woman, from southern Sicily, very young and very pretty, the way those Italians can be, long jet-black hair, anyway, she was found killed out on Lakeshore Drive, riddled with bullets and shotgun pellets. This was maybe five or six years ago. Turned out, her brothers had killed her. They had all fired at the same time, so all would take equal share in the killing. Five boys seemingly. I never saw them. They were back on a ship to Italy before anyone like me caught up with what they were doing. But this informant guy, this little snitch guy,' and he took a long draw from the cigarette, making it fizz with heat, and then blew the smoke slowly through his teeth, 'yeah, this guy, I catch up with him, and he tells me the story behind it. She grew up in Sicily and wanted to make something of herself. Her brothers chose her a husband, but she wouldn't take him. So she sneaks off on the boat and finally fetches up in Cleveland. The worst damn place ever in America she could fetch up in. All these Italians. In no time, her family found out where she was. The brothers are sent over. They kill her. Their own sister.'

Then Joe said nothing for a long while, not until he had burned the cigarette to the last ring of paper.

'Mike's not like that. He's a good guy.'

He lay there, tapping his left foot on the brass bedstead.

'Your story kind of reminds me of that.'

'It's something the same,' I said, but nervously. I didn't want to be talking about it any more. I didn't want Joe to have married a shadow, even if he was a shadow. But it made me so fearful, stories like that, my story, and that poor girl's story.

Anyway, Mike was not like that, he was just in mourning for that old house, and denigrating Mussolini. I was glad at any rate I had cooked him the fish, even though of course I hadn't known his village was by the sea. He carried the photograph of the house about with him like a holy picture. There were long black rocks at the end of the land, reaching out into the water. I thought I could almost hear it, and wondered how that water smelled. What the god of that water had mixed for a smell.

So it was a couple of years after that, when I knew Mike quite well, that he came to see me, but there was no Joe with him, and it was the middle of the afternoon. I was just back in from the store, and was just blanching some potatoes, which I was going to fry then for Joe's meal, with a length of the softest steak that a policeman's pay-packet could finance. Mike Scopello usually took an interest in anything cooking, but not this day. He divested himself of bits and pieces, he even took off his gun-belt and gun and laid them on my kitchen table, because he had quite a stomach, Mike, and it was awkward for him sitting with a firearm digging into his stomach-folds.

'We're looking into something,' he said. 'It's just routine stuff. I wanted to ask you a few questions.'

'What about?' I said. I didn't think I knew anything about anything, living quietly there, but I was willing to assist him.

'You know Joe's machine, that fine automobile . . .'

'I won't answer any questions about Joe,' I said, after a moment, holding up a hand, which happened also to hold a spatula dripping with fat. The oil splattered against the back of my hand, burning me ever so slightly. Mike jumped up and grabbed a cloth and put it under the cold tap.

'You all right?' he said. 'You burn yourself, Lilly?'

'No, I'm all right.'

'Okay,' he said, and sat back down, wary now I could see, a little different, maybe trying to figure out an acceptable way to ask his questions.

'I love Joe,' I said, after a short silence.

'Of course you do,' he said. 'I love him too. I just need to ask some questions. It's routine. We got all these new procedures now. Everything has to be followed up. We got rid of forty-three officers in the last three years. Forty-three. We're a clean outfit now. I just need to ask some questions.'

'But I won't answer any question about Joe.'

'I'm not saying he done wrong, I'm just clearing something up.'

'I don't mind answering when Joe gets back.'

'Wouldn't be any use asking you if Joe was here. I actually don't want to upset Joe. He's my partner. He's pulled me out of things, plenty of things. This is a bad city sometimes. People want to kill people all the time. Joe has my back, the whole time. He's the safest partner in the department, everyone says so. Even when some of the boys were taking money, big money, Joe never was. This isn't about money.'

'All right,' I said. 'What is it about?'

'That car of his, does he go out driving in it late at night sometimes? I mean, men do that. Blow off steam. I see them all the time, just cruising round. I don't even mean going down through the markets, nothing like that. Maybe he does that? Some nights?'

Well, I knew Joe did do that sometimes, not often, just now and then. 'Deviation,' he called it. He had looked up the word 'deviate' in the dictionary, and was intrigued to see

it meant to wander from the route, among its other mean-
ings.

'You better ask Joe,' I said. 'It must be nearly six o'clock
now. He'll be home soon.'

'We'll talk about it again,' said Mike, getting up, and
starting to put himself together again, throwing the gun-
strap from long practice around his shoulder, and inserting
the blunt-looking weapon into its nest.

'I don't think so,' I said.

'I'll see you soon, Lilly. I would appreciate it if you didn't
mention this visit to Joe. I would. It ain't nothing, and I
don't want him to make anything of it.'

'You need to talk to him straight, man to man, eye to eye.'

'That's not how it works. I'll see you now.'

And out he went, his thick legs rubbing at the thigh.

So then I was watching Joe, a little, I couldn't help it. It
put a disturbance under the wall of things, dislodging a
few stones of the foundations. 'There's trouble making a
start,' Mr Nolan used to say, staring up at a gutter slightly
fallen as may be, and soon he would be back with his ladder and his box of tricks. But we had no handyman to
be seeing to us. The Celestial Handyman tends to let the
house fall.

So I was watching him the next morning, as he per-
formed his ablutions in the little bathroom, ferocious
splashing of the face and neck, vigorous warblings, and him
singing *Little birdie, little birdie* . . . Shaving always gave
him some pain, because his skin was tender, and inclined to
red spots and little weals, hardly noticed, so he might sing
a line of the song, *Little birdie, little birdie*, and give a yelp,

and then go on with *why do you fly so high?*, scraping away all the while, valiantly. There is a certain courage needed in a man like that in the matter of shaving, every morning. Then he was applying his unguents, whose nature I didn't know, but it was called Silver Birch Balsam on the little tin, I do remember. And he was mixing up in a pestle and mortar some stuff he bought in little packets from the drugstore, and what they were I couldn't know, and he didn't say. But when he knocked a bit of water into it, there was a slightly unpleasant worrying acid smell, and as he applied it to his poor raw face, I was fearing for him, that he might burn the cheeks off of himself. Then a huge wash again, copiously applying the lovely cool water of America, and shaking of his head, and all the while the little song kept going, in broken snatches and silences, and groans. *It's because I am* – silence – *a true little bird* – silence – *and do not fear to die* . . . Then he was throwing the uniform dutifully and excellently ironed by myself onto the bed, which was my viewing station just then, before I would launch myself into the day and fry up his eggs and bread. Grab the whole thing on the hanger and with a small violence cast it onto the bed. Dear Joe. And he was climbing into the trouser legs then, tottering in his vest and pants. A man dressing in the morning, in his youth. My husband. My beloved. And truly I loved that man.

I could have asked him what he made of Mike Scopello coming to talk to me, but something stopped me.

It wasn't anything particular. It wasn't the unguents or the strange abrasive ingredients or the tottering, or his general beauty as a man. It wasn't anything in particular.

He was the man who had defended Cassie Blake. He was

the man she thought better than anyone she knew, barring her father, Catus.

He was that man.

We lived unmolested by any further thing Mike Scopello had to say, right up to the beginning of the war in Europe. The new war brought the thought of Willie vividly back to me, and I was thinking of all the young men rising up from their peaceful beds, thousands and thousands, the weather of whatever place they happened to be outside their childhood windows. It's only ever one soldier you might think goes to a war, the one single soldier that leaves a household to sally forth from the place where he is loved. He goes to the war carrying his heavy pack but also the burden of that love. Little by little it grows heavier, he cannot shed the thought of home, no matter how much he might like to, or need to, just to be able to fire his gun and survive. That's what Bill told me. The pull of home, he said, is what crucified him and his buddies in the desert. They tried desperately to break that cord. With beer, with music, with wild talk. Deep deep friendships grew around their suffering like scar tissue, in the great stillness of waiting for battles that never seemed to come.

Homesickness, he said, was like the energy surging into the electric chair. A soldier was a sitting duck for it.

In the night-times now Joe would go out and work as a fire-warden, as if they expected those German planes and rockets to reach Cleveland shortly. He would knock on doors all night and tell people not to show their lights in the blackout. He said people were just plain stupid, and broke laws like Christians broke bread. He was mighty flustered sometimes, arriving in home, stumping up the narrow stairs in the small hours, wearied by the great law-breaking stupidity of Clevelanders, as he saw it. But it was really just that the war seemed far away, up to the time families were obliged to send their sons to it.

The Italians went out to it, Mike Scopello one of the first, even though their country was on the other side. The Irish went out to it, even though England was on their side. The Poles, the Germans went out to it, the Japanese wanted to go, the Jugoslavs, the Quakers, the Protestants, the Indians, the Dutch – everyone was American then, completely and vividly, and everyone went. There were bands to send them off, and the boulder of God fell out of the ceiling of the heavens. It was an earthquake, tearing at the sons of America, trying to swallow them up. Beautiful, beautiful, beautiful sons, that women had reared, had kissed and screamed at, and that fathers had stared at intently in their cots, to see themselves in the wondrous mirrors of their babies.

If I had known Mr Dillinger then, he might have spoken to me of Thucydides and Herodotus, as he did when Bill was set to go, years later. How ancient it all was, he might have said.

'The beginning of everything human,' Mr Dillinger might have said, 'and the end.'

Mike Scopello survived the war and came home, but he couldn't get back his job as a proper police detective, and took up work in a private capacity, working mainly for poor haunted ex-soldiers, who wanted the movements of their wives watched, gloomy work like that. We all went out a few times, me and Joe and Mike and his girlfriend, but I always thought there was something bothering Mike, he certainly didn't act with his old full-hearted nature. Joe thought it was because the war had hurt him, deep in him somewhere. Joe felt bad himself because he hadn't had to go. Although he was as healthy as a goat on the mountain, the medical board had found him wanting in some way, Joe didn't specify. He thought Mike was an absolutely A1 hero to have gone, to have put his life on the line for the safety of the world. And at the same time, the thought of it also hurt Joe. If you can be jealous and loving at the same time, that was Joe with Mike, more or less.

Myself, I was pregnant.

I was jubilant. I have to confess Joe was not as jubilant as I had hoped, coming home from old Dr Schwarz with the news. I was forty-three and just as I had begun to believe it would never happen, it had happened. I was not the sort of woman to believe that if my husband was not happy about something like that, he didn't love me. I knew Joe was not playing to the normal rule-book of life. Someone had scribbled out for him a very particular scrawl of rules, only proper to him. I knew that. But I was hoping for joy, to give him joy. He *said* he was happy. He used the right words. But I knew he was not delighted, because now in the morning he seemed to redouble his efforts with his unguents and scarifiers. I thought he was going to rub his poor face away.

It was beginning to be odd, confusing times. Not the great drama of a world war, but a little tiny war fought in the corner of a small Cleveland house. Wherever I stood those times, I was in confusion.

Then Mike Scopella dropped in alone a second time, maybe carefully choosing an hour when he knew Joe was out at work. He had lost a lot of weight in the fighting of his war, there wasn't a pick on him. He would have had to take in his old police uniform if he had got to wear it again. He was hard and lean now. He had always given me a great impression of honesty. Now he also exuded a sort of right-eousness, maybe not all that attractive now I think of it. But he was one of those men who, in despair of the world, have decided that there is indeed a devil in things, evil abound-ing, and begin to think less about angels. Joe told me that Mike was a regular mass-goer now. He liked to chip in at church festivals, he had helped carry the Virgin Mary float during the last procession though Little Italy.

'It's always good to see you here, Mike,' I said, hoping of course it was an ordinary visit, though he never did just drop in, aside from the previous occasion. I had never men-tioned that to Joe, and between one thing and another, my pregnancy, not to mention an entire world war, it had fallen away helpfully into the past. But there was something tug-ging, tugging at me now, some intimation, like a drop of lemon in a jug of milk, to sour it for the soda bread.

'You'll be thinking me a bloody tenacious son of a bitch,' he said, rolling the four words together in a less objectiona-ble blur. 'Always things nagging at me, worrying me. I don't sleep at night sometimes. Becky tells me to go sleep on the sofa. The sofa is not comfortable, Lilly. Tossing and turn-ing.'

Again my best refuge was silence, polite silence. I smiled at him as beatifically as I could, to lance the boil of his com-ing words.

'You'll remember I came before. The reason I came was because Joe's nice automobile, that he had in those days . . .'

'He's still driving it,' I said. 'The shine's gone off it a bit, but it still goes well.'

'Well, in that time we had this series of murders. They were attacks, followed by murders. Women, you see. We kept getting these descriptions of the man, but sometimes the guy would be a Negro, you know, sometimes a . . .' – and he seemed to fish a moment for a word – 'white guy. And. Then two times, two times this automobile was seen parked near a particular murder scene. One of the detectives noted the occurrence. He was writing down all the plates, you know, to try and get a picture. Because we didn't know who was doing these things, we didn't have a clue. So Detective Brady gets these two numbers, for the same car, parked at completely different sides of the city, a mile and more between them down by the water. So he goes looking for the name, and it comes up Joe Kinderman, which was really really strange, since Joe was working on these homicides himself. So what was going on? Joe never brought his machine into work. He was afraid of getting it scratched in the compound. No, he hopped the streetcar. So at that time I came to you, and saw how upset you were, I reckon I did hope for the best. And I did sort of let the whole thing drop, and Brady never said nothing further, and then the war came, you know.'

He sat there at the little kitchen table. The mug of coffee I had given him sat untouched on the smooth, scrubbed wood. Now he was nodding at the mug, as if agreeing with something the mug had said.

'So just this month I'm looking into something for this guy got himself in a whole heap of trouble, and I get this sergeant I know to, you know, slip me out some sheets, and

I'm going over these sheets for this something, and I see these new homicide cases mentioned, that happened during the war, I mean, while the blessed war was on. I hadn't seen a newspaper all that time, maybe you read about them. And whoever had written them up thought they looked like the same guy that likely did the murders years before. There was a way of going about them that I won't go into detail about, but it was nasty, decisive, and, boy, I don't know, my ears pricked up. All these new murders happened at night. And Joe, you know, what did he do for the duration? He was a fire-warden. In the goddamn blackout. I was thinking about that.'

'Mike, you're frightening me.'

'Yeah, I know. I'm sorry, Lilly. And you expecting and all. I know. I don't feel good bringing this to you. I just need to ask you, you ever see blood on Joe, you ever see him flustered or worried about something, he ever come home really late, and you not knowing why, he ever act strange to you, maybe even, you know, rough you up a bit, I don't know?'

'No, never.'

'All right.'

'Mike, you look tired. You need a rest maybe. Mike, Joe loves you. I mean, you're the only man he would give a one hundred per cent grade to, as a human being. He thinks the sun rises out of Mike Scopello.'

Then Mike was shaking his head instead of nodding it.

'I know,' he said. Then unexpectedly, he started to cry. So he wept then for a good minute, a little waterfall down his weary-looking cheeks. Then he dried his face with a handkerchief and blew his nose. It was slightly comical, loud.

'Sorry, I do that. It's not Joe. It's the war.'

'I know, Mike,' I said. 'You were very brave. You got that medal in Italy. What were you doing there, Mike, that you got a medal?'

'Tanks. Wounds received. Nothing,' he said. That was it, Mike's account of his valorous action in the war, that he got a Purple Heart for.

'I do remember saying to you before, talk to Joe, man to man. He's got this on its way now,' I said, patting my belly, 'Joe's as straight as a preacher, he'll tell you what you need to know, set your mind at rest.'

'You could be right. I shouldn't be bothering you. I'll talk to him. You're right. And look, Lilly, I don't see him killing nine women. I don't see him killing anyone or anything. It's just when these bits of evidence are put before me, I can't stop thinking about it. I can't stop thinking about it.'

Then Mike went off. I noticed his thighs didn't rub together any more. I don't even know if he got talking to Joe, he probably did, but I never knew for sure.

I only heard it, then quite swiftly smelled it.

Next day the paper had the story of it, but in the moment that it happened, it sounded like Babylon falling as promised in Revelation. Or the Japanese had decided to send a last squadron of bombers and sadly drop them onto Cleveland, though the world and its uncle knew Japan was on its knees and her emperor dead. But the thought flew through my mind. Or that Hitler had risen from the dead and was flying a host of ghost airplanes. A sense of vengeance was in it, great harm, evil intent. But it turned out it was only an accident.

A bit of gas started to leak out of a new storage tank, that they had proudly built to help the war effort, up at the East Ohio Gas Company. It must have just put its white swirling face out, sniffed the Ohio air, liked the sense of freedom, and decided to sally forth. But it had not been born to know freedom, and as soon as it mingled with that air, it blew up. The whole storage tank blew up, in one vast end-of-the-world whoosh of fire, the fire grew into armies, and with a devilish hunger devoured whole streets of houses. You could imagine the wives of that morning maybe on their knees polishing their kitchen floors, the postman whistling between the open gardens, the birds sewing with their beaks through the cottony air, all the normal to-do of the day, seen and unseen. Old folk lying up in their beds, tapping the floors for attention with their sticks. Someone weeping. Then those ferocious flames cancelling them. Babies in their cots.

You would pray to God that time that God did exist, to welcome their souls into the halls of heaven.

Then a second tank went up. A whole square mile up beyond 66th blown flat, a miniature Hiroshima. And queerly, whole streets spared in among the charred ruins, the inhabitants staggering out, choking on the mean-hearted fumes. Then in a violent aftermath, such gas as had not burned off pouring along the gullies of the streets, down into the sewerage and the city drains, now and then erupting into explosions, like the fits of a thousand lunatics, manhole covers thrown a thousand feet into the burning sky, the very tunnels and crawlways and arrangements of the underground distorted and cast asunder.

One hundred and thirty souls called early, many 'vaporised' as the paper said, and I thought of Willie in the war, when poor soldiers would be blown to atoms by the falling ordnance. In the moment of death all human persons are innocent. God takes everyone, I would hazard, and I rest my faith in that.

Though I didn't know what I heard and smelled, I heard it and smelled it. I rushed out into the street. A low-sweeping wind brushed against my lower legs, it seemed to be confined to a foot off the ground. It was like water, that wind, a sort of flood. Immediately I thought of Joe, out there somewhere in this unknown catastrophe. A colossal plume of black smoke cut through with white burgeoned and rose in the distance. Other women from other houses and lives stood on their steps, their hands over their mouths, gasping with wonder and terror.

'Mrs Kinderman, Mrs Kinderman,' my neighbour called to me, a little slight thing with a veritable swimming cap of black hair, all firmed down, 'do you think the war has come back?'

'I don't know,' I said, 'I don't know.'

All day I waited, trying to reach Joe all the while. His station-house was in a ferment, because the survivors had to be marshalled into a local schoolhouse, and some enterprising madmen were said to be looting out the abandoned homes, which was hard to credit. The whole area was toxic with that violent smell of gas that seems to run a spike into your tongue. When the cause of the disaster was opined, grief took up the places in the brain where terror had nested. Great grief spreading out through the city like a gas itself.

Joe didn't come home at tea, or at suppertime, or even at midnight. I sat in my chair in the little hallway, with the door open, waiting for his patrol car to drop him off, waiting for his footfall along the dew-dampened concrete sidewalk.

I heard my heart in my ribs the whole time, ticking away.

That's when you know you love your husband, all things considered and taken into account. In balance. Love, which puts its two hands around your throat and starts to squeeze. Which bangs at your heart with an angry hammer, never ceasing, till the poor muscle flips and flaps in despair like a landed fish. Love so pressured it wants to unpack your body like a kit, just like Bill in the army had to learn to strip his gun, and reassemble it.

Joe disappeared.

He just vanished.

Vaporised, I thought. Joe, vaporised, made into a million million water drops of one kind and another, and then gone into the blue ether.

I sat in my chair then with my two arms neatly on my legs, all symmetrical and parallel. I was trying to hold on to my baby, for fear my fear would drive it out. I knew enormous shock could unmoor your baby. The little skiff of your baby slip its rope that tied it to your womb. Sitting there, holding on, holding on to Ed, probably an inch long. Inchelina.

Twelfth Day without Bill

Joe's last partner was an Irishman called Deacy and he arranged a ceremony to remember Joe. There were all the other funerals for the bodies they had found, and parts of bodies, and then a few ceremonies for the disappeared. Detective Deacy was a real Irishman, from Ireland, and I was still fearful of such a person, even in my fog of grief. I took some comfort that he was from Mayo, on the far side of the island from Wicklow. He had also been in the war, but all in all he seemed to me a cheerful soul, sociable and bright, although all such qualities dimmed by the passing of Joe. I don't suppose he had had all that much time to get to know his partner. And it was his first time joining the cops. But nevertheless he was inclined to give the little ceremony full dignity. He was one of those persons who loved life, but was willing to give Death his due. He was a big hulking sort of a man, with a sort of stoop to his shoulders, that reminded me of Annie. He looked like he had carried a boulder across some great distance, and it had left him slightly crushed down at the top.

Anyway he spoke very finely about Joe and Joe's many qualities as a person and a detective. It was poignant to hear someone I knew so well described by another, so that in fact he sounded like someone different. I didn't really recognise Detective Deacy's Joe. He told a story about him being taken captive by a bunch of corn-sugar merchants years before that I knew nothing about, and how Joe had convinced them not to kill him, and then when he escaped, made sure they were arrested and did their time for the corn-sugar, which would only have been a few years, tops. And how at Christmas time the men sent him a card, thanking him for convincing them not to kill him, which would have given them the electric chair. His fellow officers there were smiling wryly, chuckling a little. Stories of Joe unknown to his wife anyhow.

There was a bit of a desperate difficulty then because there was going to be a long process working out Joe's bit of money, if any, due to me, because they had no body, and no death certificate, and I was going to have to wait before the courts could declare him legally dead.

'It's kind of strange,' said Detective Deacy, in my kitchen, in just the same chair where his predecessor Mike Scopello had liked to sit. 'It's not just the death cert. We can't even find a birth cert for Joe. We can't find any sort of cert for him except his marriage licence. Any information he gave when he started his training doesn't quite tally with any actual document. There's not one piece of paper can tell you anything about him. But he died in the line of duty more than likely, so we're not making much of that. But you might think, aside from the fact that you married him, and we did clap eyes on him every day, that he never existed.'

'How would that come about?' I said. 'Do records get lost a lot?'

'No, it ain't that so much. No. People change their names. And then they cross state lines like invisible men.'

'Oh,' I said.

I didn't want to talk much more about that.

'Aliases. I arrested a man last month had thirty-nine different names. He kept a list, in case he forgot them. But I'd have never known that, except he was a nut, and was confessing to petty crimes across eighteen states. Eighteen. Wanted them all taken down and noted, and given to the press. The press couldn't care less. He was very disheartened. He's doing five to ten in the Cleveland correctional.'

'And do good people change their names in America?'

'I don't know,' he said. 'Good question. Maybe not.'

Then he gave me a bag of dollars he and his buddies had got together in a whip-around. He had asked his wife what would be a good move for me and she had said go talk to Sister de Montfort over at the women's hospital.

'All right?' he said, rising like a bear. 'Can't tell you, Lilly, how sorry I am, how sorry we all are.'

'Thanks, Detective,' I said. 'I know.'

So I eked out the dollars, and my baby grew inside me. How is it that we do not feel less lonely for the presence of our children? I think I thought that the little life gathering force and purpose inside me would assuage all my troubles. But it was fearsome lonely in the old bed, when there was no Joe with his long limbs stretched out, the feet hanging over the end of the bed, the cigarette in his mouth, gassing away about everything and nothing. And it was quiet, so quiet, all that summer, in the house, the cheap clock on the mantel timidly ticking and chiming, almost embarrassed to be breaking the convent-like silence. Every morning without mercy I threw up into the toilet-bowl, I retched so hard I thought my baby would pop out my mouth.

I risked a letter to Annie, though I hated the thought I might stir the dark man again. But I had to think, it was so many years later now, decades later, surely those old orders must be falling away. Surely even assassins grew older, indifferent to vanished causes. I prayed so. I wrote to Annie at the last address I had for her, telling her my story, more or less, and a couple of weeks later picked up her reply from the post office, still not daring to supply an actual street address. She told me that things were not going well for her, she had had to throw in her lot with our cousin Sarah Cullen in the townland of Kelsha, little farm, bed, and all. She also for good measure filled me in further on my father, telling me his pension after independence had gone mysteriously awry, and he had been obliged to throw himself on the mercy of the new state. Now she described his grave for what it was, a pauper's one. Maybe her own increasing poverty, and single state, had worn her down, and she had reached the hard nubs of certain truths. Maud, she said, much to my alarm, though married to her painter and with two sons, had lost a little girl to scarlet fever, and having buried her in the angel's acre in Glasnevin, where all the little ones of Dublin were put, had taken to her bed, and had not risen out of it for some years. Annie did not believe there was much wrong with her, except her head was not strong enough to endure her loss. This was all terrifying enough, and yet I pored over the letter even so with a strange gratitude, eager for details, no matter of what nature. I longed, longed to be home, out of this American chaos, and back in an Irish chaos I understood better, and would not be so alone in. And yet I sensed in my sisters a huge loneliness, each in her own way. I could imagine from all she said that Annie had no money at all, and yet she included in her letter a folded red ten-bob note. The bank on the corner gave me four dollars for it. I was so grateful to her for it, and wrote to thank her. That letter received no answer that I knew of.

I was about five months along now and thought I was doing quite well. I could just manage the rent on the house, and to feed myself. I went to the big Italian market once a week, and the wonderful ladies there filled my bag with spuds and carrots and the like. There was a butcher down there, Mr Donelli, who was a great expert on the cheap cuts of meat, because his customers didn't buy much else. I had all of Cassie's teaching to make me adept at cheering up these items with a bit of clever cooking. I was cooking for my child, I thought. I was setting out my meals, and had the magical sense that there, right in the heart of me, my little one was joining me in the repast. I used to chuckle to myself, thinking about it, I hardly know why. I was one of those daft women who talk to their bellies. When the baby moved the first time, as I was lying half-asleep on the bed, my eyes opened wide, and I could feel a sort of bright light as decent as the sun burning softly through me, through my breasts and my loins, a sort of wild happiness in the guise of light. I don't know how else to describe it. It was as if some person inside me was signalling to me. *I am here.* Maybe in truth I didn't feel any the less lonely, but I certainly felt *fiercer*. If any demon, devil or evil person had come near us, I might have torn out their throats.

So I was classing this as doing quite well.

Then I got a letter. The postman brought it, right to the door. It was in a scrawly black writing I knew. Out of the blue, the untrustworthy blue.

I had to fish into my box of things just now to find it:

Dear Lilly,

 I am writing this to you without return address. I want you to know the rumors that Mike Scopello told you about and threatened to tell the cops are not right. I know for a sure cert if I stood before a judge and jury they would find me innocent. Anyway Lilly the reason why I went is not the rumors. I cannot even write it down here. Now I am writing this and my next thought is how much that I love you. Nothing is bigger than that. The thought that comes next is of what is in you. Our baby. I will send you money every month as long as I know where you are and can send it without seeming to send it from anywhere. I pray God who understands everything will forgive me.

 Joe.

Then he wrote in Xs and Os like a child and then he crossed them out.

I got in touch with Mike Scopello. He hadn't come near me in my present predicament. He too had thought Joe was dead, killed in the explosions. Now it looked like Joe had only used that as a cover. Mike said, yes, he had threatened Joe that he would bring his suspicions to the police. They already had the licence plates business on record, the mysterious presence of Joe's auto at two of the murder sites. He said Joe was very worried, very black and angry about it. He swore blind he had had nothing to do with the murders. It was all coincidence, he said, about the damn automobile. He seemed really shocked, said Mike, which had thrown Mike a bit.

The thing was, Joe was telling the truth.

Just about the same time as the letter came, just a few

days later in fact, it so happened the actual murderer was discovered, and he confessed all. It was some mad Swede from Illinois. It was in all the papers. Joe was sure to read about it, I thought.

Mike Scopello came back over as soon as he heard and said he was sorry he had suspected Joe. He said, anything he could do, he would. I didn't know what to say. I asked if there was any way we could get a message to Joe. He said no one would find Joe Kinderman. I begged him to try.

'I will try,' he said. 'And if there's ever anything you need, anything at all, you just ring that number. I don't feel good about this at all. Not one bit. And you expecting makes it all the worse.'

Even so, he said he would have to let the station know that there had been a letter, and that therefore Joe was still alive somewhere. I knew that meant there never would be a pension. But I thought, it doesn't matter, Joe will come back now.

Then after a good many days, beginning to despair, I read his letter again. It was right there. He had already told me, it wasn't the rumours had made him go. *I cannot even write it down here.* Write what down?

It was something else was keeping him away it seemed. That he couldn't say.

It was nearly twenty years before I found out what that was, and I don't know if I understood it even then, or understand it now.

And whether he could not risk the sending, or thought better of it, or his letters went astray, I never did find a letter from Joe with money in it, so I suppose that first and only letter, which I have kept – and have been copying out here, and marvelling at his atrocious spelling, and correcting it – was not all honest. Why had he left me, why had he left *us*? I thought about that, full with child. I thought about that. An anger flooded through me such as I had never known, even when Tadg was murdered, or anything else that had happened to me in my life. I had never been brought so low that I had cursed at someone, even, God forgive me, cursed at God. But I cursed at God and Joe that time.

Whatever society the human creature finds itself in, it tries to live in it. We desire so greatly to be respected. Otherwise even wide gardens and palaces are a sort of prison. I didn't think there was going to be a lot of respect for a single woman with a child. It wouldn't look right, plain and simple.

But Mike Scopello seemingly couldn't shake off the feeling he was somehow responsible. Even though I said a half-dozen times he was not, he made it his business to try and help me. When I went into the maternity hospital, he told them he was my brother, and when Ed was born, contrived to delight in the birth of his nephew. He brought me flowers and cards and all the news of the city, and many nights he sat in by my bed, talking quietly. The other women were charmed by him, never questioning how an Irish woman and an Italian man could be sister and brother.

His new plan was to drive me up to Washington, where his real sister lived.

'Why would your sister be happy to see a stranger with a newborn baby?'

'She's a saint,' he said. 'I've been suffering from her saintliness all my life.'

When Ed was strong enough, he was to fetch me from the hospital in his automobile, just as family might.

The appointed day came, and I wrapped Ed in his blanket, and fetched on what finery I could muster of my own. I kissed some of the other women and said goodbye and even thanked the nuns. I stepped out into the winter air and the cold of the night gave me a fright. It was a heavy, damp cold, that had come up from the lake. There was a powdery snow blowing about and everything was eerie and strange. It was a shock to hear again the huge surging movement of the city. I could see automobiles pouring in great black snakes on the distant roads along the lake. I went on down the granite steps, afraid of the frost and the approaching darkness, one arm clutching Ed. The cold had already laid a tiny rheum of ice on his face, deep though it was in the blanket.

I stood out on the sidewalk on weakened legs and waited for Mike. Good as his word, it wasn't too long before he pulled into the kerb. I thought I recognised the automobile.

'Get in, Lilly,' he said, leaning over and pushing the passenger door open, 'for the love of God. It's warm in here.'

'Thank you, Mike, thank you. Is this Joe's car?' I said, settling in, gratefully. I felt Ed's tiny self stirring in the blanket. At least I hadn't killed him.

'It is. I bought it off the pound for a couple of dollars. He left it parked down by the railway station. I thought, I'll buy it, and give it back to him if he turns up.'

'You weren't able to trace him so?'

'Not a sign of him. All I can say, he is somewhere in America. I guess he changed his name again. Who knows?'

Then Ed woke up properly and started to cry for milk. I put his tiny mouth to my breast.

'Okay,' said Mike, embarrassed as hell, but putting up with it. 'Okay, okay. Washington, DC. Here we come.'

Mr Dillinger did come after all. I hadn't been expecting anyone. I had seen no one for a couple of days, and thought that was right and proper. Sympathy has its term. They had done their duty, and a thousand times more. But he had been in New York, he said, attending to his new book. He said he was very excited about it, and also full of dread. He laughed heartily at his own two-headed self.

It was already dark when he arrived. There was a bird, most likely a marsh owl, calling out on the potato fields somewhere. I answered the door to him and we stood in the salty night air and listened to it. Mr Dillinger has travelled everywhere on the earth by all accounts. There is hardly a valley he has not peeked into, hardly a desert he has not endured. But tonight on the porch he declared this spot of God's earth – whether he meant my house or the Hamptons in general, I could not tell – balanced in that moment in a state of earthly perfection. I asked him did he think it was 'unobjectionable'. He laughed at the odd word, and said yes, that expressed it perfectly.

Then he moved into the strange gear of condolence. His body hunched, and he took one of my hands in his big hands. His long face, like a challenging sheer rock, pitted and lined, seemed to narrow further, and he leaned in.

'I would be honoured if you would allow me to dedicate

my new book to the memory of Bill. Do you think that would be possible? I know it is a big thing to ask. I would just put *In memoriam W.B.*'

'Put William Dunne Kinderman Bere,' I said, 'put his full name.'

'Will I? Then I will. I will do so. I will do so.'

I was tearful as I brought him inside, but the hall was dark and I could conceal my tears. I sat him down as always, and made tea, as always, though it was getting so late. My brain was rushing with gratitude, and though Mr Dillinger could not know it, a doubt came into my mind for the first time.

I had acquired great strength, I suspected, from my resolve not to live on. Mr Dillinger had shown me an example of the enormous effect of courtesy brought to the act of remembrance. Suddenly I was wavering. Now, sitting here, writing this out, I am not so sure. But for those moments he had brought me back to the pact we make with life. That we will see it through and live it according to the length of time bestowed on us. The gift of life, oftentimes so difficult to accept, the horse whose teeth we are so often inclined to inspect.

Then, his great action done, he relaxed. His very bones seemed to soften and he lay back in the chair. There was an old song that used to be sung by my brother Willie, called 'The Spanish Lady'. In it there's a line sung by the man in the song, who has told us about the great beauty of the Spanish lady, a harlot in Dublin, years before. And now, he says, 'age has laid her hand upon me'. Age has not laid her hand on Mr Dillinger.

Willie sang that very song at a singing competition organised by the Capuchin Friars down by the river Liffey.

Luckily the song is so mysteriously worded that an innocent listener would never know the poor Spanish lady was
a harlot. He had a heart-rending voice, and even when he
was only seven and did not know what the words of a song
meant one way or another, could make people cry with his
singing. *Who should I see but the Spanish lady, washing her feet
by candlelight?*

But Mr Dillinger was telling me a story about his days in
China as a young man. It was his first voyage out of America, and he had acquired a great wish to see Peking and the
Great Wall. He received permission to do so only after an
enormous effort. In Peking he met a young man who came
from northern China. Mr Dillinger struck up a friendship
and was asked if he might not like to journey home with the
young man. It was a part of China apparently that had not
seen a Western person in two generations. They boarded a
rackety old train dating from colonial times, belching great
plumes of steam. On the way he was obliged to eat from
the stalls on station platforms, cooked insects, scorpions
and the like, which Mr Dillinger found delicious, if a little
numbing on the tongue afterwards. With great difficulty
the young man explained to him that he was not meant to
eat the tail. Mr Dillinger became ill, and retreated to the
primitive lavatory on the train, with that hopeless sickness that descends when the body has been poisoned. As
he strained and despaired, cursing his wish to see China,
he became dimly aware of a small screeching. His bowels
loosened, exploded, but relief was his. When he opened the
door, there was a tiny woman, screaming at him, tinily. He
had been defecating while they stood at a station, a terrible
sin. He felt the deepest shame.

When they reached the home of the young man, he was heartily welcomed. The young man's family stood around him, and touched Mr Dillinger's face, and climbed up nearer him on boxes, trying to match his great height. He was given the best bed in the house, and he was feeling fine again. How extraordinary to be in such a place, he thought. In a wooden house, in a wooded valley of almost violent green, heaped up to the very heavens. It was beautiful, austere, and silent. Then his door opened and a woman came in, the grandmother of the young man. It was dark in the room and he could barely see her. She was talking in Chinese, and gave him a little box, and was gesturing to him to eat, but Mr Dillinger didn't dare do so, because of his recent illness. The old lady went away very disgruntled. In the morning he went out into the daylight with the little box, and looked in. It was a white moth with its wings removed, still alive, a great delicacy, the young man said, and a great honour to be offered it. He really should have taken the risk of eating it, the young man said. Again, great shame.

Here Mr Dillinger stopped. He smiled a rather private smile in the gloom of the kitchen, perhaps a gloom equal to that vanished Chinese gloom.

'Sometimes,' he said, as if this were the moral of his story, 'it is dangerous to be honoured.'

PART THREE

Thirteenth Day without Bill

It's nearly two weeks since Bill was buried, according to Mr Eugenides' calendar. Every Easter he hands them out. *Vangelis Eugenides, prop.* With pictures in it of the islands, Paros, Naxos, Sifnos – you can sail among the islands all year, in Mr Eugenides' calendar. His own home town, not very beautiful to the stranger's eye, and on the mainland, always gets April, when, he says, he misses his homeland most. Then he is thinking of the wild flowers lining the stony ways.

I had a good thought this morning about Mr Nolan, I must guard against that. It is something to do with the two weeks. I have been making an effort not to think about him, to banish him. I have refused to mourn him in any way. I have not wanted anyone to mention him to me, especially Mrs Wolohan, who probably thinks I am doubly bereft, why would she not? But I was suddenly sorry he was gone. A simple emotion, like a dog might have. There was a huge wall built against feeling that, but I felt it. I was thinking of the first time I met him, in the house where he died, a man in his late fifties, smoking a short slim cheroot, with his hair still brown, more or less, but shaved tight, like a military man. I thought he might have been somewhere, Korea maybe. He looked like he had come in a long way, from a war or a wilderness anyhow. With his boxes and books and gun-cases, all more or less as he had put them the day he had moved in, and never moved or improved as far as I ever saw.

Sitting in his canvas chair, properly a beach chair of some sort, looking very serious. Mr Wolohan had sent me over to him, I had to search for the house among the spread of small dwellings along the Sag Turnpike, where many of the gardeners and other men offering labouring services lived. It was to tell him he would be starting Monday. A vanished Monday in the lost history of Mr Nolan in his prime.

He was very startled to see me, I thought. I had knocked on his porch door, but hearing no answer, ventured in. The old cream paint was peeling off the wooden-panelled walls. There wasn't a picture hanging in the place, nothing.

'Oh, thank you,' he said, when I told him why I had come. I believe he had offered himself for work a few weeks before, but that place was already taken by Mr Cuffee, the Shinnecock man. But Mr Cuffee had gone off, taking a violent dislike to the large new mowing machine, which he deemed 'no damn good'. So now the Wolohans did need a man after all, to follow the mower around their acres of grass, and a thousand other tasks. 'I was just wondering, did I need to be thinking of moving on.'

In those days it was said work was more plentiful, but work always needs to be gone looked for, no matter what they say.

'I'm really glad,' he said. 'I guess you work there in the house?'

'I cook for the Wolohans,' I said.

'And I bet you're a fine cook.'

'Not so bad,' I said.

'You an Irish woman?' he said. 'Just going by the accent?'

'Oh, yes,' I said, 'long ago. Long, long ago.'

'I know,' he said. 'Tennessee myself, but – you know.

178

Nolan. Inishmore, my grandpa was from there. I couldn't say I'm just certain where that is. Ireland somewhere.'

'You can come Monday, anyhow. Grass is coming up round our ears.'

'You tell Mr Wolohan I'll be there, bright early. Really good to meet you, ma'am.'

'That's all right,' I said.

So I was remembering that. Nothing really, chit-chat, although vital to Mr Nolan's well-being, or so I imagined at the time. It is a nice task to go over to someone and tell them they have a job. Work is the oil of the soul.

We ride to our doom, like the cowboys, we surely do. But not that time.

'This is my sister Maria, the saint,' said Mike, when we got to her little apartment in Washington.

'Now, that's what he says, Lilly,' said Maria. She was wearing a lace-trimmed skirt and a lacy blouse. Her hair was in a motionless perm. 'Me, I'm no saint. I never met a saint. I suppose some saints did good things. Our mama, she loved St Agatha of Sicily, whose breasts were cut off by the Romans. You can see her, Lilly, in her paintings, with her little breasts on a plate in front of her. They look like two baked buns. And that's why she is patron saint of bakers, which was our father's trade. Sensible work.'

'Now I hear about myself, how *stupido* I am to be in this line of work,' said Mike. 'But it's good work.'

'Cheating couples. That's not good work.'

'Aiye . . .'

They were already rowing, brother and sister fashion, and I was hardly in the door of her apartment. Even as she spoke, turning her head to me, appealing to me as a woman for sense, like a little volcano of energy she had taken my baby, and was changing him on her kitchen table. She had already been primed up to get napkins for Ed, who right enough was wearing one so heavy with pee it was as big as the rest of him. Tiny and soft, as gentle-looking as the first thing in God's creation to be called gentle, he made a miniature murmur under her ministrations.

'And you can have your bath, Lilly, I have so much hot water in the cistern I could set out to sea with it like in a steamship. My God, I wait and wait. How long it take to drive down from Cleveland?'

'A long, long, long, long time,' said Mike, and I knew, exhausted as I was, that he was also in the deeps of exhaustion, the endless great river of headlamps on the highway having poured so much light into his brain he must have felt like he was permanently in the heart of an explosion. Ed had slept and fed, slept and fed, and I had followed suit, inescapably, but when I woke, every time, I said a prayer to God to thank him for sending me Mike Scopello, who seemed to me a winged man that time.

And I think the Sicilians could pray to St Maria of Washington if they wished. I bet she would get their prayers answered, double-quick time.

I must have been with Maria three years, and when I was fit and well, after a month, worked with her in the great fruit market outside the city, where the enterprising women there kept a crèche for the babies. There were lots of babies, Italian babies, and one Irish, or whatever Ed might be.

I was all the world for Ed, and hardly knew it. There was a carousel he loved set up in a wide street of lofty trees that had the breeze living in their leaves like birds. The low roofs of the city made me think it was a pristine Dublin. All the great buildings ranged about, and me and Ed among them, in the half-noticed paradise of his child-hood. Half-noticed by me, because my mind was often on other things, and half-noticed by him, because he seemed to have forgotten so much of it when he was grown. 'Ed, do you remember when you loved to roll down the sloping gardens?' 'No, Ma, I don't remember that.' 'We did it every Sunday, Ed, without fail. You were mad keen for it.' 'Maybe I remember it, a little, Ma.' That hand in mine, that wound-able hand, the woundable hand of every child, us moving through the gentle public gardens of Washington. My hand stained permanently yellow from packing the pears and the apples in the market. A woman approaching fifty, and a lit-tle neat boy with close-cut hair. Our smiles mostly for each other, and every stranger a possible demon or bear, till they proved otherwise. Then reaching the fabled carousel, and waiting till his favourite horse came free, he would ride no other, then round and round to the tinny music, swelling up into the dry trees, and when the carousel man held out the token, all the children would fiercely try to spear it with the rings provided, Ed's face the most fiery and determined of all. The great days when he bagged a free ride, the triumph in his face, and the darkening street rescued by the lamps coming on, one by one, with their electric *ping*. I see that carousel in my dreams, it goes round and round, and Ed rides there eternally.

Then I got work with Mrs Wolohan's mother. I don't know where I had earned the luck for that. Maria was so pleased for me. It was she who saw the notice in the paper, Situations Vacant, and that an Irish woman was preferred. There was going to be fancy cooking involved, said Maria, I could bet my hat, and she had borrowed some books from the library, so I could brush up. The biggest one was called *The White House Cook Book*, which was all the recipes that the wives of the White House had put together over the decades of American history. What they had been cooking while the story of America progressed.

'This family,' said Maria, 'big high-up people, and they will be used to cooking like that. You get this job, you can spit on my head, from on high.'

'Somehow I don't think I will want to spit on your head.'

'No, but you could, if you get this job. From on high.'

It wasn't anything to Mrs Wolohan's mother that I had a child. In fact it was almost a good thing. Mrs Wolohan's mother believed in good deeds, without the colossal molasses of nonsense that usually goes with them. She believed in Fairness, with a capital F, and people making their way, and the principle of the Helping Hand.

I gave my name as Bere, not Kinderman. She liked that my name was Lilly, because she was a very Catholic woman, and grew Madonna Lilies *religiously*. She had an old painting in her house of the angel Gabriel presenting a lily to the Blessed Virgin. It's a strange name, because some years later Mr Eugenides said he liked it because in Greek weddings the bride wears a crown of lilies. Mr Dillinger liked it because in the old Greek story Zeus slept with Alcmene, a mortal person, and put the resulting baby at the breast of his wife Hera while she slept, so that the child would be more divine. She woke up and cast the baby from her, and the spray of milk from her breast became the Milky Way, and the drops that fell to earth became the lilies. Mr Eugenides never mentioned that story though, even though he gave a book of Homer to Bill.

'When my son was killed in the war,' Mrs Wolohan's mother said once, 'I thought of the Blessed Virgin at the cross.' I have thought of that often. She sitting in her smart suit, at her elegant table, saying a thing like that, to pull the heart out of your chest.

I cooked for that woman like I would cook for God, if He were ever so human as to be hungry. She was mistress of a vast American mansion, with marble pillars and pink walls and cushions with scenes of men hunting deer in France. Porcelain ladies danced on her high mantelpieces. Presidents and emperors and kings and dukes had dined at her table, including Michael Collins and De Valera, years before.

'But not on the same night, Lilly,' she said, rightly laughing at her own wit.

She professed to like my cooking but it didn't stop her bringing in a French chef, two of them, three of them, when she thought she needed them. Her grown-up sons and daughters glimmered in the house on family gatherings. One of her sons was a senator just up the hill in the Senate house.

It's a fact that once upon a time one of the richest women in America was also one of the nicest.

When my Mrs Wolohan, her daughter, married, I followed her up to the Hamptons. That must have been the mid-1950s. I was sad to leave her mother, but life was lived at such a speed in her house I was also a bit relieved to reach the quietness of Bridgehampton.

It was *nearly* the wide open spaces that Ed seemed to dream of, even as a little boy. He loved books that showed the lost places of Texas, the Rockies, the deserts of the western coast. At least the great beach was there to entrance him. There were no red escarpments like west Texas, but there were mighty heaped-up yellow dunes for his nine-year-old legs to conquer.

There was the little school locally for his lessons. In his white shirt and blue shorts.

There was a lot of happiness, and then there was a lot of sadness.

When I see photographs of the fifties, everything is always so clean. The sidewalks are clean, the tar on the highways is clean, the shirts of the men are starched, the women's skirts haven't a pleat out of place. I don't know if it was like that. I hardly remember. Maybe. Everyone wanted to do well, live better, after the war, which had eaten up so many sons, including one of the sons of Mrs Wolohan's mother. The world had come to an end like in the Bible, and now it was to be created anew.

But as they used to say in Ireland, *the devil only comes into good things.*

But it was good for a long time. It was also the mid-fifties, I suppose, when Mr Nolan showed up in the locale. As soon as he was working in the same house, or in the same grounds at any rate, he would drive Ed back and forth to school. We strolled down, the three of us, to the picture show, a thousand times. We stuffed Ed with Mr Eugenides' soda and pie.

Mr Nolan threaded himself into our lives. I suppose it befits a handyman to be constitutionally helpful. It was curious how deeply he entered into my life, and yet how lightly. It was a sort of fact of life. Mr Nolan, a presence, like the sparrows in an Irish town. It was Mrs Wolohan of course paying him for his work, but for me everything was done gratis, so lightly and almost invisibly that I never thought twice about it. I *liked* him, but did I *see* him? Was he not almost not there, a lot of the time, even when he was there? He applied himself to Ed. No task seemed too much for him. He had a beat-up old auto, that he loved more than he did himself. Himself he tried to poison, many times over, with mammoth drinking bouts. He fought his own soul and spirit, gloves off, with alcohol. Mr Nolan.

He used to read to Ed at night. He possessed an old volume of *Winnie-the-Pooh*, and they liked to read that together. I would hear them, in the American evenings, so unlike Irish ones.

One night, when Ed was about eleven, going in to give him his kiss goodnight, I found Mr Nolan sitting on Ed's bed. The both of them were weeping. Or rather, Mr Nolan was shedding a dark tear, and Ed looking blank and stunned. They had just got to the end of the book. Christopher Robin, Ed told me, was going off to boarding school, and Pooh wanted to know if he would still exist when Christopher Robin was gone.

'It's about the end of childhood,' said Mr Nolan, inconsolably.

He was a good man for things like that. He was also, now I think of it, a connoisseur of birthdays. I had forgotten that. He liked to give you store-bought flowers that day, and chocolates he used to get from the chocolate-maker in Sag Harbor. One particular birthday, he went to Mrs Wolohan and begged a free day, and drove me all the way down to Cape May, starting at first light, on our own, without Ed, 'to see the lighthouse'. There was an old concrete gun emplacement in the sand there, still waiting for Hitler. Mr Nolan put himself in the water for a swim. It was so deathly cold he was only under for a second.

'Well,' he cried, 'that is the end of the Nolan dynasty!'

We climbed to the top of the lighthouse, up a cramped stone stairway, and at the top we were speechless with exhaustion. Mr Nolan admired the stonework, admired the scorched vista of the sea, and kept smiling and smiling.

We came in home in the small hours, with that weariness in the corpse than only a long auto journey can give. Mrs Wolohan to my astonishment had with her own hands made sandwiches for us, beef sandwiches indeed, waiting for us on the kitchen table with a note, on one of her blue windmill plates.

And Ed, who knew Mrs Wolohan nearly all his life, loved her. He was never the least bit shy of her, in her own shyness, and I must confess she put manners on him. I suppose he could have dined at his ease with kings by the time she was finished with him.

This was all in the context of little meals sometimes, rarely enough I suppose, with her, when the table was put out under the colonnades in the summertime, with the lake brought a little closer therefore to Mrs Wolohan's blue-slippered feet. When she was eating, she was at her wittiest, and she teased Ed into a magnitude of good manners, as if she were preparing him for the diplomatic corps.

But in his deepest heart Ed loved those big spaces. That's where he was trying to get to, all his life. He loved all the cowboy films we saw with Mr Nolan, and that the old film house owner loved too, and delighted to show to the good people of Bridgehampton, even though we were a little short of endless expanses of American landscape, with cattle and cowboys in them. He was a small dark man called Mart Pelowski, who had swapped his potato farm for the cinema, off a man called Billy Waldron. Mr Pelowski had trouble getting prints of the new films in those years, but he got them. He would go down to the New Jersey distributors, and beg the prints off them. His little premises only had a hundred seats, and therefore in the good weather, and for a popular film, he would move everything outdoors, and people would bring their chairs in the back of their pick-ups and station-wagons, and he would show *The Man of the West* and *Last Train from Gun Hill* on the gable wall of the building. The whole town, workers and nobs and in between, and especially every man jack child among them, would exult in our island of perfected peace, watching the wondrous mayhem on Mr Pelowski's wall. Next morning everyone would have red bites on their ankles, from the mosquitoes, and the wide plains of Texas in their hearts.

All the summers he was down on the beach, growing brown as a chestnut. The dunes were his Himalayas, the sands his Sahara. Mr Nolan would be there on a Sunday decked out in his ancient chequered shorts, and myself in my sensible bathing-suit, with a touch of gay colour, but that would nearly stop the blood in your veins with its wires and bones and gusset.

Mr Nolan's body hard-looking as dried logs. Myself getting older, that strange map of blue veins on my upper legs, a map to nowhere.

As Ed got older I sat further away from him on the dunes, so he could revel in a new aloneness, the fake aloneness of childhood, rich and intoxicating. His joys could be tiny. Nothing more wondrous to him, more desirable, than to hop, skip and jump over the burning sand to the ice-box man, a nice Shinnecock called Charlie Heat, and bring back the treasure of a Coca-Cola, so cold it was a form of heat, that he could hardly hold in his paw, and sitting on the merciless sand, and defeating the half-death of the summer by downing the icy liquid. Then in his mind he was a desperate traveller across Death Valley, who had found a sudden oasis in the realm of doom.

That was Ed's vision of America, all in all, and when he finished high school, he wanted to go there working. And when that season was eventually approaching, I found an agricultural college in New York that would take him. We were all set. My hope for him was boundless.

But that was the decade of assassinations, and Ed was young in it. Like a good youngster, he took it all to heart, he took it all personally. No one was shot without Ed feeling the bullet go through his own self. Medgar Evers was the first one, and then all that rosary of death after, with every bead a soul.

It was one of those deep dark summer nights. In Ireland in the high summer the light stays good till eleven. On rare hot days, people would linger down at the Shelly Banks till the last moment of daylight, strolling along the butter-yellow stones of the Great South Wall, the children flinging themselves into the shallow oily sea. But even in summer the Bridgehampton night seems to come early.

Mrs Wolohan's brother the senator had driven up for dinner, and with him had come the famous preacher Dr King. Mr Dillinger was also there, and the four of them talked quietly under the gathering darkness, the flowers of the wisteria slowly fading above their heads as the night blotted everything out. I had cooked scallops for them, and I had been asked by Mrs Wolohan to make pecan pie. I was worried, because I had never made it before. It wasn't even mentioned in my *White House Cook Book*. Making something for the first time can have evil consequences. But I made something that at least looked like the illustration on the recipe Mr Nolan dug out for me.

In the kitchen, with the windows open on the lawn side, I could hear them talking and laughing.

Ed was going in and out with dishes. He was already nearly a young man. He hadn't grown his hair like some of his school-friends. He liked Bob Dylan, and sang his songs quite tunelessly around the house. He seemed to worry a lot about things. The atom bomb especially haunted his very dreams, like it did so many in those days. At school they had showed him how to get under his desk should the world happen to blow up. When he came home that evening, he had made me practise too, under the kitchen table. The two of us looking out, and all the good earth gone to ashes.

But in truth it was hard going out into the world, when the same world might be removed in a sudden great flash.

After the pudding course, he stayed out a long time. I thought I could hear Dr King's pleasing voice talking to him, and Ed's own smaller voice responding. It made me happy somehow. I washed the dishes and the platters with enjoyment, which a person wouldn't ordinarily. Ed came back in.

'Dr King wants to say thank you, Ma.'

'I'm in my dirty apron, Ed, I can't go out there just now.'

'I don't think he minds things like that.'

'No?'

'No, I don't think so.'

So I went out. Mrs Wolohan was telling a story. She only really spoke at length when she was at ease. Sometimes she was content just to listen. But she was telling a story, and the men were laughing as she went along the stations of it. I don't remember what it was. I just remember the ease, and the happiness at the table.

'Oh, Lilly,' said Mrs Wolohan. 'Dr King wants to compliment you on your pecan pie.'

'I never made it before. I was frightened making it.'

'It was the best pecan pie I ever ate,' said Dr King.

'That's so kind of you,' I said.

'You have a fine boy there. What do you think he will do after high school? I questioned him to the best of my abilities, but he wouldn't tell me.'

'He wants to do something with farming, you know.'

'A fine boy,' he said again, as if somehow he were clearing up a mystery. Which in a way he was. A fine boy. Yes, Ed was. Ed was a fine boy. A magnificent boy.

'I'm very proud of him,' I said, and added, though why exactly I could not say, 'I love him very much.'

'He could do anything he wants,' said Dr King, opening his arms wide in the dark air to illustrate this 'anything', and smiling.

'Thank you, sir.'

That was more or less what we said. How is it that often-times the most important things that happen are at the end of the day composed of chit-chat?

When God is happy I am sure he chats with the Son, and the Holy Ghost.

I went back into the kitchen in a strange state of excitement. I was shaking as I rubbed down the surfaces with an old cloth.

I had hoped to save a bit of that pecan pie for Mr Nolan, since he was a Southern man too, but when the plate came back empty, I didn't mind.

It's an easy phrase to say, and harder to say what it means, like faith itself, but it was true, I saw it, I heard him say the words, Ed 'loved his country', just like Bill did later. I loved Ireland, in spite of all, and I was so grateful to America, for finally offering me sanctuary. But Ed, flesh of my flesh, was of America. America made him and America unstitched the gansey of him.

I am remembering the morning he came to me, with his draft letter in his hand. He is standing there in my narrow wooden bedroom, and he wants me to read the document. It is official-looking, urgent, full of intent. Of course it is not a death warrant, but it is a warrant of sorts, that's how it reads to me. I look up and his face is deeply serious, like a philosopher's. His father's face shines through his features, the man he never knew, and that I knew but barely understood.

'That's the letter they send, you know, Ma,' he said, unnecessarily.

I was gazing at him. I was seeing I thought something for the first time. His features were regular, square, like a portrait. He stood before me, and I gazed at his face. I think I saw how doubt wavered there, and courage, and of course the blessed ignorance of what was truly to come. I thought I knew what a war was and I certainly did not wish him to go. If I had been asked I would have said so. But no one had asked me and now I said nothing. His face, a portrait of someone lovely to me, looked suddenly unfinished. The thought made me dizzy, panicky. Those finishing touches, that it is the work of a good mother to supply, were missing. I was thinking that and felt the terrible treachery in the thought. I didn't even know where the thought came from, and hardly what it meant. I had failed in something, I had failed. I had not managed to *complete* him. And now I would have no more time to try and do so.

He was called up and of course he went. He might have squirrelled out of it somehow, with his college place, but he didn't.

Some weeks later, there we were, in Bridgehampton, the army bus pulling in. Ed wasn't the only one waiting to board. I recognised the boy who had worked all year in The Candy Kitchen. One of the Yastrzemski sons also, Joe, who was going to take over his father's farm some day. All the mothers and fathers standing back, smiling and waving, I am sure under strict instructions.

I held my unfinished son for as long as he would let me, until he pulled away gently.

'I was going to leave my old Buick with Joe Yastrzemski, but I guess that won't work,' he said.

'You won't be gone too long, honey,' I said.

'You ask Mr Nolan to turn the engine over now and then, okay, Ma?' he said.

'All right, I will, Ed,' I said.

'Okay, Ma, you look after yourself.'

'I will, Ed. You be sure and do the same thing, you be sure.'

When Ed had been in Vietnam for two years or so, and my little black and white TV was telling me every evening things I did not want to hear and showing me things I did not want to see, but had to hear and see, because that was the fearsome hell where my Ed was, something happened. It happened out of the blue, pure coincidence. I was down in New York city on some errand for Mrs Wolohan, I do not even remember what it was, that part of the memory has fallen away. I may have just looked in on her city apartment or fetched something there, but I had crossed back over towards Central Park, and was heading down Third Avenue – going where as I say I do not know.

I wasn't paying too much attention to anything I am sure, but somehow or other I became aware of a little group of people coming towards me on the sidewalk. I was soon staring at the man in this group, because, although twenty years had passed, I thought I knew him – I thought it was Joe Kinderman, to the life. He was bobbing about in that springy walk of his, and talking, and waving his hands, all very normal for him, and characteristic. So vivid to me that the years fell away. If it wasn't Joe Kinderman, I thought, it's his double. I don't know if I wanted it to be him. I don't know what I thought about it. I might have dived away into a cross street, I might have turned on my heel and hurried

193

back towards Central Park. Instead I stopped and watched him coming towards me. He seemed to be caught in that little crowd of people, maybe theatre-goers returning from a matinée show, I thought, there was a woman, a black woman, and three younger people, maybe her daughters, and they were just strolling, strolling along.

All the many details of Joe and his story flooded into my head. I saw Mike Scopello in detective mode as of old, with his conscientious face, and the rats of fear from those days poked their noses back into view. I watched him coming. So far he was quite unaware of me, in fact he was laughing now, as if he knew the people around him.

Now we were only a few feet apart. He caught my watching eye.

'Joe,' I said. 'Joe.'

As if it was the most natural thing in the world, and he was some old friend. I wondered bizarrely is this how it always is when people meet who have had strange history together, jailer and prisoner, or the like, hello Sam, hello there Sol? And the dream the prisoner had of killing his jailer when he got the chance melts away in the powerful pull of politeness?

Joe, for it was certainly him, though that bit older, with his curly hair greyer as you would expect, and his face somehow longer, narrower, and the skin itself greyer, stopped, and touched the shoulders of the two girls nearest him, as if he might protect them.

'Is that you, Lilly?' he said.

'It is me,' I said.

'Who is this?' said the woman with him, very politely, smiling, a fine, strong face.

194

But Joe didn't seem to know how to answer her, so he just stayed there, dumb for the moment, the cabs on Third Avenue as raucous as rooks, the half-hearted blue of the sky looking down at us. I do not suppose God loved me much then, because my heart stirred with a murderous desire, the humiliation of what he had done sluiced through me, the memory of his abandonment flooded me as if I was some sort of storm drain. I dared not move a muscle, in case I sprang forward and tried to do him some harm, tore at his throat with my teeth, hit at him with my bare hands, which would not have been wise in that indifferent New York street, but was an almost irresistible impulse.

'Ella,' he said to the woman, 'would you go back to the hotel with the girls? Would you? I just have to talk to this lady. I won't be long. I will be down to you directly.'

'Of course, Joe,' she said, trustingly, I thought, I noticed. Trustingly. 'Is everything all right?'

'It is,' said Joe. 'Surely is.'

The three girls and the woman – yes, a fine, curvy woman, I thought, I noticed, in one of those sheath dresses, and all smooth and nice, and her skin so dark it shone with a private, secret light – turned back along the sidewalk and left us there.

'Well,' said Joe. 'Lilly. I knew we would meet again some day.'

'Did you, Joe?' I said. Oh, I felt wretched there. There had been some dark trick of time. He looked like a man in his very prime, but I felt shrunken and old. I had had Ed so late. Maybe I had had no business bearing a child so late. Maybe that was it.

'Do you want to step in?' he said, indicating the door of the

Italian deli that was just there. 'We can talk in there, Lilly.'

'All right,' I said. I followed him in. Unwanted thoughts kept hitting at my brain, unwanted. The allure of Joe, his oddness, the fact that you couldn't ever get a handle on him, decide definitely who he was. The pleasure it used to be, to be with him. This was not the way to be thinking. I should have held on to the fury, I knew. Then there was the choosing of the table, the waiter shepherding us, Joe asking for coffee for himself and tea for me, it was hopeless, it was like years ago . . . For all I knew this man was a murderer, maybe that mad Swede had been falsely accused, he certainly had a cruel heart, cruel enough to abandon his pregnant wife.

He seemed content with the silence that sat between us then, for a long time. The little scabby-faced waiter came with cups and pots and we were given what Joe had ordered.

'This is stupid,' I said, 'sitting here. I should go.'

I wasn't talking to him really, but to myself. What could I say to him? He had left his pregnant wife without a word why and never a word since.

'I'm so sorry, Lilly,' he said. 'You can't be thinking too well of me. Sure was unforgivable, what happened. I should have maybe written it all out in that letter for you, at the time, but I didn't, I know. I didn't. Just a short stupid letter I sent. Lots of things I didn't do. I look back from this vantage, and I wonder at myself. Why did I do that? How did I do that? I suppose I can look back and tell you why I think I did it, why I think now, I mean.'

'I was pregnant, Joe. You just left me. You just disappeared. One day, Joe was there, and then the next, no Joe. Who was that woman, Joe, who were those people?'

'That's my family, Lilly.'

'What do you mean?'

'My wife, my daughters.'

'You got married again, Joe?'

'Lilly, yes I did. I went back to where I come from, where I am known, where people know me for who I am, and I married a girl that was local.'

He shook his head, like he was hearing someone else's despicable story, and then at least had the good grace to repeat: 'I'm so sorry.'

It was my turn to say nothing, and I knew well enough that he would wait till I did speak, and not break the silence. But I had to wait for the strange sludge of grief to die away in my throat. A whole minute probably passed. Then I managed something, but it didn't sound like talk, more like a little engine starting to chew up its own spinning parts.

'You have a son, Joe. He's in Vietnam. He never knew his father.'

'I always did want a son. Tell me, Lilly, forgive me asking, but is he white, my son?'

I was completely surprised.

'Is he white?' I said.

'Yeah.'

'Why, Joe?'

'Well . . .'

'Your other family there, they're black.'

'Yep.'

'But you're not black, Joe. You're as white as me.'

'Not as white as *that*,' he said, and gave a little laugh. 'Lilly by name, and Lilly by nature. You see, Lilly, years ago, I had this great fear, this great fear that . . . I'm not saying I know if it's right or wrong, but being with Ella and the girls

197

is right for me, because . . . My great-grandfather, the one who swam the tunnel to get to his wedding, you remember? He was white all right, but his bride was black, and all his children. And Jurgen Neetebom, he was the only white man ever in my family. And when I was born, his great-grandchild, by God if I wasn't so black at all, which I know now can happen, it's, you know, skipping generations, and I was very confused in those days, Lilly, and I was afraid when I got out into the world, and was able to live as a white person, that people would find out about me, or that my skin would turn back, so I used to use all those lotions, you remember, and the bread soda and God knows, and when you got pregnant, I feared, I feared so bad the child would be black, and I knew you would leave me, I knew I would lose everything, so . . . I couldn't face the thought of standing there, peering down into the cot, and I would see my true face, my true face in the face of my child.'

'But Joe, your true face, that's a good face. I wouldn't have minded one bit.'

'I wouldn't feel that now. All that fear. Times are different now. Changing, anyhow. I feel such pride in my race, Lilly, I do. I love my girls.'

'Of course you do, Joe.'

'But back then . . . I can't tell you properly what that was like. It was being burned in a fire. The thought of losing everything.'

'Losing everything, Joe? You did lose everything.'

'Yeah, that's right. I left before it was an established fact. So, I chose to stay there in my home place. And that's what I did.'

'And all the trouble with the police, Joe?'

'Well, that all was all right, Lilly, that man was caught.'

It seemed to me suddenly that Joe was a very unusual man, he was a very unusual man sitting across from me. I remembered him as being a tower of a person, a beacon. And he still was. It seemed to me sitting there, angry and resentful as I may have felt also, that he still was. He was Joe, Joe in America, with his own particular and unusual story.

'Joe, it wouldn't have mattered to me one tiny bit what colour you were, or Ed was, for that matter. Not one tiny bit.'

'Oh, but, it mattered to me. That was the fear. You live in a big box of fear. You start that sort of subterfuge, Lilly, and then it's fear all the way. And I am mightily sorry for you being mixed up with me like that. You're a good person, Lilly, of course you wouldn't have minded. But I didn't know that. I was thinking, thinking, thinking. All fear, crazy thoughts, strange thoughts, things that madmen are thinking. You were better off without me.'

'That's what you say. But I loved you, Joe. That would always have been enough for me. I know what fear is too, Joe. I didn't feel afraid with you.'

'You were so lovely, Lilly, and it was a privilege to be with you, yes sir.'

'I don't know whether to thank you for that, or throw this scalding tea over you.'

'I wouldn't blame you, one bit. Are you all right for money, Lilly? I have a cab business down home, it's my own car, I could send you something?'

'I'm fine, Joe, God knows. I've been lucky. People helped me. Mike Scopello helped me. Lots of people.'

'I'm glad Mike helped you. He was always a king of a man, a king.'

Then Joe pushed back his chair.

'I better go, Lilly. I am mighty proud to think my son is in Vietnam. I think he is so brave. I will think about that. And if you want to tell him I am thinking about it, do tell him.'

Then Joe got up. He breathed out a long heavy breath, and nodded his head. It was so like him of old. But this wasn't of old. This was the dry fields of the future.

'Do you have a picture of him?' he said. 'Of my son?'

'No,' I said, lying. There was always a picture of Ed in my purse.

'I thought about that baby a million times. I didn't even know if it was a boy or a girl.'

'It would have been the easiest thing in the world to find out,' I said.

'Maybe,' he said, and nodded again. 'You often talked about America, Lilly, I remember, you said a lot of things about America that was wise, how strange she is, and deep, and wide. I often think of that. I often think of you. I am not a heartless man. But I am not a good man.'

Then he turned towards the light of the street. Somehow in the contrasting glare I could see him better now. His face was not just ashen as it used to be, but deeply lined. There was something in those lines more eloquent than anything he had said. I felt it was almost reprehensible even as I felt it, but I felt sorry for him suddenly. There had always been a weight on Joe that no one could see, not with human eyes.

'You could cause a lot of trouble for me with Ella,' he said. 'And that would be right and just.'

'I'm not going to do that, Joe. I probably don't even know your real name.'

'My name is Joe,' he said, and smiled. Then I knew he

was going to go. 'If you want to tell the boy about me, you . . .'

'You already said that, Joe.'

'Right. So long, Lilly. I'm sorry, like I said. I'm real sorry.'

Then he went off towards the door in that strange slow canter of his. There was something in his apology that touched me again. Maybe in some ways a useless man, maybe even a coward. A bigamous man for sure. Who had caused me immense grief and confusion. All the ways confounded. Everything that is once builded shall be torn down. So that again I thought, I could with justice kill this man now. Maybe when I stood up then, I stood up to do so. There is a part of me wishes it was so. Joe Kinderman, or not Joe Kinderman, just Joe, some Joe.

He paused at the till, just to pay the cheque. Joe the gentleman. Then he was nearly out the door. Nearly gone. Nearly too late. I hurried after him, and *arrested* him, as one might say, I stopped him in mid gigantic step, the heavy metal door was propped against his right foot. I stared up at his face, and then my head went down, scrabbling about in my bag. I found the damn thing then. I handed it to him, the picture of Ed when he was off to his debs night with a vanished girlfriend called Janet. Joe took it, held it in his slender fingers, those ridiculously beautiful hands of his. He looked at the photograph. He looked at it. Big tears started in his eyes. He looked at me again with a last look, and almost fell out into the street, clutching the photograph. Then he plunged away, to what he thought was his proper life, into the river of people, the confused torrent of people, into Canaan itself.

Fourteenth Day without Bill

About this time, Dr King was shot.

Ed came home on leave, and he was an absolutely unsmiling young man that time. The man on the TV said the tragedy was all the greater because Dr King had been killed in America, 'on Canaan's side itself'.

All the cities I had lived in were burning, and all the cities I had not lived in also.

Ed had never grown very tall, not nearly as tall as his father, but he was a serious person now, an army man, and it gave him a strange gravity, so he *seemed* taller than he was. He gave me a sort of vertigo looking at him, a panic. He was a very handsome-looking child, like his father also. He was so precious to me that my blood wanted to stop flowing through my veins until I could discover a way to help him. I was his mother. I had nothing to give him, nothing. *All the king's horses and all the king's men.*

His first night back I made him his favourite dinner. He ate it all right, but he didn't seem to notice it particularly, and he didn't say anything about it.

This wasn't long after I bumped into Joe in New York, but I never said a word about that. I thought I would, sometime, but there was another emergency in my boy just then. It was the emergency in a child when he is full of new intent, whose nature I probably would not have understood even if he had taken the trouble to explain it to me.

Ed went back to the war. Then yet another great soul was pulled suddenly from the song of life.

I was watching TV in my quarters. It was my day off as it happened. We were still living in a few rooms in one of the wings of Mrs Wolohan's house. I always tried to keep up with the war news. It was a way of getting Ed through it, a sort of magical procedure. If I watched the war unflinchingly, he would come through it. But a news flash came up. I stood up, gasping. Disbelief, horror, misery, all crushed into my heart. It wasn't news of Ed, it was Mrs Wolohan's brother. He had been gunned down in his own America. Murdered in his own America. The story of his life ripped right through by Death.

I went down the wooden corridor. The little knick-knacks and things she liked, often worthless in themselves, were ranged as always on their calm tables. Photographs, the father she adored, her mother, her clan. There was a grey winter storm blowing outside, but it barely ruffled the peace of the house. I knocked on the door of her sitting-room, as I always would, and, hearing no answer, went in.

She was standing at one of the windows. Her right hand rested on the window-bar, the other arm straight at her side. She was wearing a blue cardigan and white trousers. She was just looking out the window, at the silenced storm. The light of the storm played on her features, the blue eyes stirring with the light.

I never, even in my own life, saw anything so sad.

1968, the year you could *feel* something ending. I didn't have a name for that something. Ed said it was the death of hope, and many people said that too, everywhere you went.

Mr Eugenides said it was the death of hope. Mr Pelowski at the cinema said it too.

For Mrs Wolohan it was another great mountain of sorrow to climb, to plant her flag of courage on the top.

As for Ed, his face grew all the graver.

After all, he had met some of those poor killed people, at Mrs Wolohan's table. He had talked to them, they had talked to him. He was just the cook's child maybe, but in America a cook's child might do anything, and Ed was bright as June sunrise.

I don't think he thought he should shoot his way out of his anguish in Vietnam. In fact, I know he didn't. He was in the engineering corps, and had lately taken to specialising in landmines. He used a water diviner's stick to find them, ashwood, like they were wells. It was a talent he had. Lots of his buddies were blown up doing that work. But Ed had some knack. He aimed to exercise that knack, to put something tiny in the scales of history, tiny, but the only thing he had. He stayed on in that country I had only strange glimpses of, on the murky black and white TV. He saw it all in full colour I suppose.

Ed never spoke too much now. He had become a closed book as a young man. I myself had to divine things.

I don't know what broke in him. Plenty of things maybe. Wires burned up in him, and then he couldn't get a signal on whatever sort of radio he was. Or send one out. My Ed.

I wondered if it was my fault, whether the nature of my life had affected him, innocent as he was. As soon as I had that thought, it shook my hand, and moved in with me. There is a price for everything, even in a story. How much truer that is in real life. I thought I had caused, if not the demise, at least the demolition of my son's inner spirit, his secret self. I had contaminated him, like Typhoid Mary had unwittingly killed those who found themselves near her. The poison, the extract of deadly nightshade in me, was history.

I had needed help, sanctuary, deep sanctuary. I had found it with Mrs Wolohan. Her suffering was sometimes so great in that decade, she would heal you where you stood of your own troubles. She was never anything but constant to me. She offered me safety, she gave it, and she has never taken it away, in forty years, when oftentimes she had no safety for herself. When that strange angel of death chose, and chose again, among the members of her family, with his pointing finger. If the gunman following me had found me in the sixties, and shot me in cold blood on some street corner, no one would have taken much notice. Because that was a decade burned black by grief. There were a half-dozen men with guns waiting in dark spaces in those years to fire their weapons. Fixing their hats on their heads and laughing at the evil they were about to do. To kill America, and if she didn't lie down, fire into her soul again. Point blank. Love and murder both just need intimacy. Many great souls were killed in the sixties, and my small soul would not have registered, that's for sure.

It's so strange that I can write this, and feel that my years have no width or length, have no dimension at all, just the downturn of a bird's wing. So quick, so quick.

I am trying to catch things in this web of words, things that were important to me. But just like the stronger houseflies, sometimes they get free, in spite of all. There's a big spider this year on the lavatory window, so I don't clean just there. She tries her best to catch the big summer flies for me. Suddenly I'll hear that mighty focused buzzing, which is the requiem of the fly. But now and then, one in a hundred, a fly does manage to gain its freedom.

I am trying to gather my thoughts, finally. Some of the thoughts are strong enough to elude me, I know. They want to be wandering about generally, along the ditches, counting the wildflowers, then maybe float down to the flowers in the dunes. Casual, and free, and strong.

I am thinking the thought, again and again, that I undid my own son.

Ed must still be out there somewhere. In this big wide country. I would so love to see him before I go, but I don't think that will ever be. Last time I saw him, I think I saw a man that could never come home, because the compass, that most people have, had been ripped out of his memory, out of his very heart. Ed died clearing landmines in Vietnam, I mean, he did not die, of course not, but in the long toil of defusing bombs, out in the wild jungle with a buddy to hold a torch on the work, or his own sweat making his hands dangerous to himself, Specialist First Class Ed Bere as good as died, or at least did not come home, or ever could find his way. This was the child I loved, fed in an automobile from Cleveland to Washington, and put food and words into for twenty years.

Of course Ed came physically back from Vietnam. I knew the time of his plane's arrival at the base in Pennsylvania, I had received the letters of notification, I had prepared his room for his coming, and slew the fatted calf in the form of Cassie Blake's beef Wellington, his favourite food on earth. But he just never arrived.

I had to throw out the beef Wellington, uneaten. No news came of Ed. Like his father, he was out in America, somewhere. I wrote to every agency I knew of, and Mrs Wolohan, despite her own Himalaya of grief, helped me. Of course agencies try to be confidential. Even if they lock your child up, they don't really want to tell you about it. But he seemed to have drifted out beyond the ken of agencies. He didn't seem to be using a bank account, or drawing money, or if he was, he was doing so under an alias, another family tradition, because I couldn't find a trace of him. Furthermore, I was trying to be careful, because I had an idea that he had more or less gone AWOL, in contrast to his previous devotion and strange meticulousness towards the army.

At night in bed, trying to sleep, I kept doing the worst thing I could, playing in my mind the old reels of our times together. Simple films, of no interest to anyone else. Everyone's private cinema. His first walking, that I nearly missed, and only caught because Maria Scopello, who was looking after him, screamed down the Washington street for me. His first word, which was 'Dada', of all things. His first day at junior high, in those blue shorts. Nonsense things, the deepest, most important poetry of my life.

I was nearly going to write to Mike Scopello, who I hadn't seen now for years, but who always sent me a card at Christmas, and I him. But like me, Mike was getting old, I knew. Also he had rheumatoid arthritis, his sister had told me in a letter, and I didn't think he wanted to go slipping about the country, howling with arthritic pain.

But unknown to me, Mr Nolan had begun his own enquiries. How he did it I do not know, but he got information on Ed. He took a Saturday and Sunday off – indeed, Mr Nolan never retired, until he got ill – and went off mysteriously. He said he was going to Tennessee, which was usually his way of saying he was on a two-day drinking batter. He liked to drink hard with some of the other gardeners round where he lived. He liked to 'close the curtains' as he called it. I suppose even then I knew he had his own demons, Mr Nolan.

But he mustn't have gone drinking that time.

'Well, Lilly,' he said, 'he's up in the Smoky Mountains, way way off in the backwoods, with some other vets and hippies. A crowd of *pocaidí dubha* and other such characters I guess.'

'Where's that?' I said.

'North Carolina,' he said. 'He's in there somewhere, I'm told, back of the Cherokee res. Long long way in, in the old-growth trees.'

'How did you find that out?'

'You just have to keep asking round. You can trace a skeeter in America, if you know how to keep asking.'

'And could anyone find them in there?'

'Reckon I could. You'd need some class of a mountainy man anyhow. You want me to try, Lilly? He mightn't want to see me. He might want to be left alone. Not be found.'

I thought about that for a day or two, but then I had to ask him. I kept seeing the boy in his faded blue shorts. I knew he had seen the merciless mayhem of that war, I knew he was a grown man, but I kept seeing the boy.

'I would like you to try,' I said.

Mr Nolan now owned an old black Town Car, that Mr Wolohan had bought for a few dollars a few properties over, when some ancient millionaire died. He gave it to Mr Nolan, because he knew he needed something to fetch the plants in. Mr Nolan had the back seats taken out, and a wooden plate put in, which all worked as good as a pick-up. And Mr Nolan was more proud of that huge scratched car than he could ever have been of a truck.

Anyway he begged a few days from Mrs Wolohan, but didn't trouble her or himself to say why. He was most ever close by and often came over to do things outside his times, so she was graceful about letting him go. Indeed she wasn't so much critical of his drinking as interested in it. She liked to hear of his adventures, and how things were over in the shebeens along the pike. As a Tennessee Irishman, it was expected he would like a drink, I suppose. So maybe she thought that's what he had in mind.

The next morning early he loaded his car up for a couple of days' driving. I hovered about, waiting to say goodbye. He knew how to load his own automobile. He had an old knapsack which he threw in the back. It made a heavy noise when it landed.

'That's my old gun. Guess I shouldn't be throwing old guns around. I sometimes put a Lilo in there and sleep,' he said. 'If I find myself over by Montauk, you know, late, done in maybe. This is the world's best automobile.'

Then he climbed into the front seat and slammed the

door, and wound down the window, hardly missing a beat.

'I'll hook up with Highway 81, and that will bring me nearly all the way where I'm going, New Jersey, Tennessee, North Carolina, and then I'll just sling a left somewhere and get across to Cherokee.'

'I am so grateful, Mr Nolan. It is so kind of you.'

'You ever been in Tennessee, Lilly?'

'No.'

'All the tobacco fields you'll ever need to see. I'd like to bring you down there sometime.'

Then he was singing some old song he knew, 'Little Birdie'. He wasn't in a rush to go, I noted. He was relishing something about the moment.

'I knew another man knew that song,' I said.

'That so?' he said.

'He used to sing it when he was shaving.'

'It's a good shaving song,' he said. 'Wouldn't want to get carried away on that high note though, and slit your own throat.'

Then he switched on the big engine, and gunned the pedal.

'I know another good song, "Oh Death", but I'm not singing that.'

'You can sing it if you like, I don't mind.'

'No, I better not sing it.'

'Just sing a little bit of it,' I said.

'*Oh Death,*' he sang, '*Oh Death, won't you spare me over for another year.*'

Except he didn't say *year* like I did, he said *yare*.

'When you sing that song you sound more Tennessee.'

'You can't sing it any other way,' he said.

211

Fact is, I wanted to kiss him, I felt so grateful. But he didn't need a seventy-year-old woman kissing him.

Then he drove off into the early morning glitter.

I suppose he had often driven down those roads, going home. Or did he ever go home? I knew his people were dead now, so he said. Well, he could be pretty mysterious, Mr Nolan, but it wasn't as if he was the first mysterious man I had ever met. You can be expert in things you'd rather not be expert in. Or that weren't so good for you, like Ed's gift for bomb disposal.

At this time I had just retired, and Mrs Wolohan had arranged this house for me. She had spoken a little speech for about ten minutes in the hallway of her own house, by the old mirror and the knick-knacks I had polished a thousand times, itemising my years with her.

Mr Dillinger was in Africa, and there had arrived, with a dozen stamps and postmarks, looking weary but triumphant, a card with a picture of an elephant: '*Here's to many happy years, Mrs B. Cordially, S.*'

So I was new enough into the house, and was still busy arranging the few things to my name to my satisfaction. Knowing that Mr Nolan was on his quest, on my behalf, felt like a fortune in the bank. I was rich with expectation anyhow.

Three days later, towards suppertime, I was in the backyard, and heard the chain of the lavatory going in the house behind me, and I turned to go back in. I didn't fear intruders, not in those times. I hadn't turned on any lights, and my kitchen was dark.

I almost didn't see the child, because the child also was

dark. He was about two years old, and was draped, swaddled nearly, in a shirt of Mr Nolan's. I hadn't heard the old Town Car drive up, but I could see its black shape outside, where Mr Nolan must have parked it on the road. The first call on his time had been his bladder.

The child just stood there, in the centre of the floor, looking at me. A thin little boy with a heap of black hair.

Mr Nolan issued forth from the lavatory.

'Oh, sorry, Lilly,' he said. 'I didn't think you were in. Nature called.'

'That's all right, Mr Nolan. Who is this?'

'I guess that's your grandson, Bill.'

I stood there, and slowly slowly I put my hands on my head. Rested my two open palms on my head.

After a moment, thinking I might be scaring him, I hunkered down to him. I was nearly afraid to embrace him. But he moved first. He came into my arms like a known child.

That night Mr Nolan told me his story. The beautiful, unexpected child was exhausted, and had gone straight to sleep in Ed's old room. He lay in the sheets for one long moment with his eyes fixed on mine, burning softly in the soft light, and then the lids closed.

Mr Nolan sat out on the porch with me. The fireflies burned themselves on the bulb above us.

I knew he was tired from his journey, but he also needed to tell what had happened, and I needed to hear it.

He had got down to Cherokee in about fourteen hours, he said. There was a friend of Ed's waiting, a Cherokee called Nimrod Smith, who also had been in Vietnam, the man who a few weeks before had told him where Ed was, when Mr Nolan first looked into it. Now Nimrod Smith wanted $50 and Mr Nolan promised to send it when he got home. Mr Nolan waited all day while Nimrod Smith went into the forest on his motorbike. He wouldn't just bring a person in unannounced. So Mr Nolan was left to twiddle his thumbs in the motel. But it turned out to be a good idea, all in all. Nimrod Smith came back in the darkness. Ed was anxious to see Mr Nolan, he had something he needed to tell him. He had said he would meet them about halfway along the trail. Next morning Nimrod Smith brought Mr Nolan into the mountains on the motorcycle. Ed was waiting in a small glade, and he had a child with him. Mr Nolan was overwhelmed to see Ed, he suddenly realised how much he had been worried about him, like he might his own son, if he had had one. Ed had let his nice hair grow, and he had a rough mountain man's beard. He embraced Mr Nolan. He said the child's mother, a girl called Jacinta Riley, had died in hospital in Knoxville, and the mountains just weren't any place for a child. He said he was desperate for his son's welfare. He asked could Mr Nolan take the child out, maybe take him back with him to me? He said his ma would know what to do.

That I would know what to do! I hadn't the slightest notion, except I was so grateful Ed was alive, and that he had had the sense not to try and keep his son in such a primitive place. Maybe I wished he had come home with his son, and sorted himself out, for his son's sake. But Mr Nolan said there was something very sad about Ed. Mr Nolan was deeply affected by seeing him, I could tell. He wept when he told me how altered he was, 'the boy', as he called him, just as he always used to call him, when indeed he was a boy, in the days before he went to Vietnam.

'Like an empty house with a ghost in it,' said Mr Nolan. 'God help him, Lilly.'

'You did a good thing, Mr Nolan, you surely did.'

'Bringing you a little lad two years old? What are you going to do, Lilly, rear him up? What the heck are you going to do?'

'I'm going to live a long time,' I said, not having any other plan.

'You're going to keep him?'

'I'm going to keep him, till Ed recovers. Some day he will recover. That's my prayer, Mr Nolan. Until then,' I said, 'I'm going to be looking after Bill.'

'Well,' said Mr Nolan. 'You are certifiable mad. But I'll help you. God knows I will.'

'Thank you, Mr Nolan.'

Fifteenth Day without Bill

I woke this morning so tired, so bone weary, I dragged myself more than walked to the lavatory. I am beginning to think this writing things down is as much hard labour as an Irish country washday.

But I also got a little gift of happiness out of the morning too. The constipation that had been bothering me all week finally surrendered to my prayers and imprecations and what followed was a feeling that I do not think would disgrace the citizens of heaven, in their famous contentment.

To remember sometimes is a great sorrow, but when the remembering has been done, there comes afterwards a very curious peacefulness. Because you have planted your flag on the summit of the sorrow. You have climbed it.

And I notice again in the writing of this confession that there is nothing called long-ago after all. When things are summoned up, it is all present time, pure and simple. So that, much to my surprise, people I have loved are allowed to live again. What it is that allows them I don't know. I have been happy now and then in the last two weeks, the special happiness that is offered from the hand of sorrow.

I had to disclose our new arrival to Mrs Wolohan. I was obliged to, though a corner of my mind feared she might object. I couldn't have been more wrong. Another child she could get ready to dine with kings. She took the matter into hand, and wrote on my behalf to the hospital in North Carolina, and was sent the death certificate of Bill's mother, and his birth certificate was located also, and sent on. His full name, presumably entered by his father, was William Dunne Kinderman Bere. It was poignant to read this name, containing all and more of my own history as a human creature, and look down on the small bearer of it. He had more names to himself than years. He was in fact two years, three months, and five days old. He had had his mother till he was two. She had died of sepsis following on from peritonitis.

I brought Bill to Dr Earnshaw, at that time not long in practice, as I remember. He seemed to take a dim view of the whole matter, or so I thought at the time. But in fact of course it was just Dr Earnshaw's manner, which I grew to understand better over the years. He gave Bill a thorough going-over. Much to my surprise again, there wasn't much wrong with the child. He had been fed wisely, and Dr Earnshaw pointed out to me the little tiny shellfish marks of his inoculations.

'I will do these all again, of course,' said Dr Earnshaw, 'but this is not a neglected child.'

I had no photo of Bill's mother Jacinta, but something of her, even by these minute traces, seemed to come through to me, and I wondered about her story. I wrote to her parents in Knoxville, an address that Mrs Wolohan had from the hospital, but was much distressed to get a strange, hurt letter from a Mr Riley, her father. He went to the trouble of pointing out that since Ed was a white person, the boy could not be his, and for their part, said Mr Riley, they had no further interest in the matter, and were still grieving for the loss of their daughter, who had gone off the rails in her last years. He said that if I intended to have the child adopted or put into care, he would fully support me in my endeavour. However he enclosed three photographs of Jacinta, one as a baby, one as a high school student, and one on the day she married Ed. This I peered and peered at, marvelling at it. They had been married for whatever reason in Harris County, in Houston, Texas, a 'furtive five-minute job, among what looked to us like Texican shotgun wedding-parties, not a word of English spoken, and all the brides expecting' as Mr Riley described it, obviously not approving, or, more likely, deeply offended by it. But even in that present chaos, I was proud of Ed in his best jeans, and hair in a long Indian plait, which he wore down his left breast. And his wife Jacinta as glad as a rose, beside him, with the sign for the courthouse behind them. They looked like any other young couple, all their years ahead of them, blessed with youth. I prayed it had given Ed a few days of happiness, whatever ailed him generally.

I prayed also that in time his wounded self would recuperate, atom by atom, at whatever pace it took, and that some day I might see him again, and that he might see his son, the one restored to the other. I prayed for that.

Some weeks later, Mr Nolan dropped down to me, as he was doing regularly, to see how I was getting on in this realm of great changes. I think he also liked just to clap eyes on Bill.

'Did you get a chance to send that $50 down to Mr Smith?' I said.

'Didn't know whether to tell you or not, but. I was glancing through Mrs Wolohan's *Times* week before last. Just two lines about it. Cherokee man called Nimrod Smith found dead in Knoxville.'

In the Second World War, one of the tortures in the prisoner-of-war camps was to keep waking the captured soldiers all night. Not let them sleep, disorient them, drive their spirits into their boots. But a two-year-old child will do just the same thing. For a whole year Bill woke every hour. He wasn't looking for anything in particular. I think he was just checking I was there. One time I slept through his calling. He slept in the little bedroom near mine, just separated by the bathroom. He must have been nearly three. I opened my eyes, and I saw him there, in the dark room.

'Hello, grandma,' he said.

And then, having got a taste for talking, he got talking as good as the next child. Somewhere in the dark gap between his bed and mine, he must have reached a decision.

I do not want to dwell too much on the beauty of that child. I think my heart will break if I do so. But just to record the fact, Bill had beauty.

My aunts in Wicklow used to say to us, when we were children, snagging up in their skirts, 'You're lovely, when you're asleep.' And I know what they meant. A child is hard labour. There is nothing so onerous and exhausting as a small child, nothing. I have sympathy for men digging on the road when I pass them by, in the height of summer as may be, and I always say hello, because digging a ditch is nearly the hardest work on earth.

The hardest is rearing a child. Even when you're young.

Bill liked the little push-car I got for him, but boy, he

really liked to be carried. He loved it. I would have to carry him till I was well-nigh about to die.

Then all the pleasures of having a child also seem to carry a searing pain with them. A kind of after-pain. That day you ready them up for their first day at school, their shorts and shirt all shipshape, their lunch in its new box, and going along to the gate of the school, handing him over to Miss Myers, his young teacher. And her reassuring smile, and Bill, happily going forward with her, into the schoolhouse. The little crowd of mothers, heroic beings really. It was a curiosity of the district that in the time of Ed's childhood, most of the kids in his class were white, and yet in the time of Bill's, most of them were black. Mr Dillinger said Sag Harbor had been an important station on the freedom train long ago, which was one of the reasons some of the Shinnecock were black. So in that way, our district had a history of bright goodness, along no doubt with darker matters. Which was lucky for Bill.

Wonderful, but then, going home along the sea lane with my heart scalded. The days of having him about the house over. The days of innocence so deep in him, it was like wisdom, like he knew something important that he was always on the cusp of telling me. The days of me and Bill knocking about. Bringing him to see what he called 'the river', but that was really just Sag Pond. The first time he swam in Mrs Wolohan's pool, with his bizarre armbands, some strange creature off the TV. I never had a TV since Ed, so he would go down the road a bit, to a friend's house. Every child in his class was his friend, and suddenly I had twenty new friends myself, the mothers of those children. Toing and froing, exhaustion, hard labour. Head down, no let-up.

Every moment of your day filled, appointed, anointed.
Paradise.

Mr Nolan liked to bring Bill fishing. They'd go off together to some bit of water. Mr Nolan had a favourite spot 'near the Shinnecock hills' and the two of them would head away in the aged Town Car. He started to teach Bill the songs he knew, from his own childhood. One day he put Bill up on the kitchen table, and had him sing a new song. Well, it was an old song, called 'Kevin Barry'. A rebel song, as it happened, and I don't think Tadg Bere would have liked to hear it sung, all things considered. But the strange fact was, Kevin Barry had been born in Rathvilly, as my father was, so that was a rebel song I didn't mind, for old times' sake. I didn't tell Mr Nolan any of that. I didn't tell him either that Kevin Barry had been exactly the same age as me.

> *Another martyr for old Ireland,*
> *Another murder for the crown,*
> *Whose brutal laws to crush the Irish,*
> *Could not keep their spirit down.*

Bill sang it forth. He sang like a linnet. Mr Nolan beaming. The voice filled the kitchen, this very kitchen. Bill stood up on this very table, in his blue leather shoes, raised up his two arms as Mr Nolan had taught him, and gave the song everything he had. Which was considerable.

'This boy has a sweet voice,' said Mr Nolan. 'I never heard a voice like that.'

But I had. His own great-uncle had just such a voice, Willie himself, whose name he carried, who had asked my father once if he could go and try and make a go of it in the music-halls. My father horrified. 'No, Willie,' he had said. 'That would never do. What would your poor mother in heaven think, if I let you do that?' And the truth was, our mother, according to Annie, had loved Willie's voice. She would have been proud if he had made a go of it in the halls. Willie and his *Ave Maria*, and his 'Roses of Picardy'. I can hear him now. And as I hear him, I also hear Bill, chiming in. The two singing together in my old head, that never even knew each other in life, killed seventy years apart, in two different wars.

I pointed out Willie's picture to him in the hallway. From then on, Bill always said hello to Willie as he passed, or gave him a quick greeting with his hand, a sort of salute, because of Willie's uniform. He was his great-uncle really, but Bill always called him just Uncle Willie.

But he called me grandma. When he was seven, he began to ask me about his father and mother; he worked out somehow that he must have had such things once. All his friends' mothers were still in their early thirties mostly, in their twenties. Why was he met at the school gate by an old crone? Not that he said that. He was never afraid to be seen kissing me, or holding his grandma's hand. I was so old I could have been his great-grandma.

I told him the simple stupid things I thought I should say. I told him his mother was safe in heaven, and his father was on a long journey, and I didn't know when he would be back.

'So is he going to heaven to see her?' he said.

'See who?' I said.

'My mother.'

'I don't think you can go to heaven until, you know, you . . .' And because I was a grown fool, I didn't think I could say the word 'die'.

'Die,' said Bill.

'Yes, until you die,' I said.

'So where's he going?' he said, his voice clear and easy, just looking for information.

'I don't know. He never told me that, Bill. But I know he's gone, and it's a long way.'

'As far as Montauk Point?'

'Further than that.'

I could tell he was impressed.

'As far as the moon?'

'Not as far as that.'

When Mrs Wolohan heard Bill singing, she didn't think of a kitchen table for a stage, her mind went straight to the Metropolitan Opera. She got Mr Dillinger to phone his good friend Signor Devito, the famous teacher, who had one of the new mansions right down in the dunes. And then I was obliged by all these efforts to bring Bill to see Signor Devito, and have him sing for him. I sat in the big sunny room in one corner, while Bill and the Signor sat at the huge black piano. Bill was eight, but I was a mass of ageless suffering, on his behalf. Signor Devito was exceptionally kind, but asked Bill to sing some scales, which Bill didn't know how to do. He had no training whatsoever, aside from Mr Nolan's efforts. And Mr Nolan was just a mountainy Irishman from Tennessee.

'So you sing me a song you like,' said Signor Devito, his long brown fingers bedecked by rings, whose gemstones were so considerable I could see them quite plainly across the room, glinting in the shuttered light. He had his Italian name, suitable for opera, but Mr Dillinger had confided in me that Signor Devito was in fact Greek, from Alexandria. He might have been any age, with one of those smooth lineless countenances, with no trace of a beard. Mr Dillinger said he had helped Marian Anderson prepare for her debut at the Met, when she was already fifty-eight, but this meant nothing to me, beyond thinking that it sounded impressive, whatever it meant.

So Bill began to sing 'Roses of Picardy', that he had got Mr Nolan to teach him, after I told him it was one of his great-uncle Willie's favourite songs. As I say he was only eight, and his youthful voice, singing a soldier's song, made me cry, secretly, where I sat. Indeed I wished Willie could have been there to hear it; perhaps he was, his shade creeping near, from Flanders to Bridgehampton. To cock an ear to such sweet singing, with all his own suffering and the suffering of his companions contained in the song. As if, a ghost for some seventy years, he was hearing his own young self, magically renewed by the mercies of history. Through Mr Dillinger's DNA.

Afterwards, he sent Bill out into his vast hallway, so he could have a word with me.

'Like others of his race, he has a good voice. I don't know, Mrs Bere, if it is exceptional. I want you to bring him down to New York to hear some proper singing. I will organise the tickets. In the world of opera, you live in a storm of wind the whole time. Like the sailors who do the passage round Cape Horn. You have to have it in you to make such voyages.'

225

Some weeks later, Bill and I sat in the magnificence of the New York Met, listening to a singer called Mr Shirley. The opera was called *Turandot*. Bill seemed to me very small, young, and slight in the seat beside me. As the opera progressed, I thought he became smaller, younger, and slighter. Before the end, the two of us slipped away, bought pizza, and ate it waiting for our bus home.

When I first put Bill into the single bed in the box-sized bedroom, he was about the length of a pillow. By the time he was eleven his feet reached halfway down the mattress. That's how I measured the passing of time. Life may be brief, and childhood briefer, but there is a sumptuous brevity to a grandson's childhood.

The downturn of a bird's wing.

One time in the late fall I was just tucking him into bed when I heard, or thought I heard, someone stirring along the porch. For three days we had been buffeted by the very edge of a hurricane, which had blown itself out away somewhere on the sea, giving us only hints of its anger, enough to rattle my shingles and put my heart into my mouth. Huge rolling stumbling gusts had come in from the beach, pulled viciously at the earth of the withered potato plants, and given the impression that it might, with just a small effort more, tear our house from its foundations and deposit us elsewhere. Now in the glowering aftermath the moon was being snatched at by the last storm clouds, hurrying along like city crowds in the rain. The planks of the porch were firm enough, but they were ancient and twisted, and you could not walk across them without making a small screeching music.

I lifted my head from kissing Bill goodnight and thought I saw the outline of a person unknown in the dim window.

I hurried to the front door to check the bolt was on, as fast as my arthritis would let me. I was my own watchdog in the world, so it behoved me to be fearless. I switched on the porch light by the inside switch. Now the narrow space gained a poor light, a few feet of it at any rate, and there was a person there, but he did not seem to care much about his sudden revelation. I knew immediately it was Ed. No creature ever unchained a door so fast. I nearly threw myself out on the porch, my dress catching in the hook a moment, ripping ever so slightly. When I tugged at it, freed it, and looked up, I half-expected Ed to be gone, gone like a ghost. But he was not. He was there.

He stood immobile on the old planks, watching me, nodding his head, his face turned away from what light there was. He was crying like a child, trying to conceal his tears. But the moon betrayed them, catching into them, making moonstones of them. He didn't wipe away the tears. The wind was interested in the open door, it wanted to go into the house and frolic about there, so I clicked the door shut.

It may have been 1982 or so, so Ed was about thirty-six. His hair was cut very short, and there was a V of skin at each temple, where his hair had given up. He was dressed in a loose linen suit. I couldn't see any sign of a suitcase or a knapsack. The brown weather scumbled about behind him, the strange dark yellow light of the fringe of a storm at night framed him, so that he might have been a creature issued by the storm, pushed forward by it. He didn't say a word for a long time. I didn't mind. The animal I was, all that I was, was exulting in his mere presence. I could think of nothing, no recrimination or argument, to meet him with, except that natural joy.

'You're looking awful well, Ma,' he said.

'Not bad for eighty,' I said, or thereabouts.

I was afraid to say anything except in answer to him. I was afraid I would scare him away, like a bird in the garden.

'Bill's looking awful well too,' he said. 'I'm glad you were able to keep him.'

'He's the best child ever was,' I said. 'And plenty of devilment in him too, thank God.'

Ed laughed there, in the stormy darkness.

'He has a good person to watch over him,' he said, and followed the statement with utter silence, the silence that comes after a person has spoken their inmost mind, perhaps not meaning to.

I wanted to say, it's cold enough out here, won't you step into the house? I wanted to say, why don't you tell me what troubles you so? Why don't you step in and see your son? I couldn't say any of those things. I was afraid that by trying to get him into the house, I would lose him from the porch. I was content to shiver there. The wind was not so bad. It was something else was making me shiver. All the bits of the history of my life.

'I want you to know, Ma, it's not lack of love keeps me away. I often have thought maybe you thought that. When I try to write to you, my hand freezes. I often thought when I came down to the town, I might ring you. But I never have done any of those things.'

'Sure I never doubted that,' I said, noticing myself falling back into an Irish way of saying something. 'Never.'

'I often think of my father, which you might think would

be a blank thought enough. But it's not. I think of him, out here in America somewhere. Father and son. And all the time I am thinking of Bill. Do you know, Ma, his mother was a very dear person to me, but she died.'

'I know,' I said, still fearful to add anything, in case he would think I had been hunting him down.

'I want you to tell Bill that his father loves him dearly, will you do that?'

'Of course I will.'

I was thinking, it's hard for a child to understand a love like that. He would rather go fishing with his father than hear such a declaration. But I knew Ed existed in a parsimonious place. He had only the farthings and pence of love to give.

'The war did something to me, Ma,' he said.

'I know, son,' I said.

'I can't find the end of the string. I can't remember the tune.'

I nodded. I knew the least attempt to turn this conversation would make him disappear. I knew that. I knew he would disappear anyway, I knew it, but I didn't want it to be me who had scared him away.

All the same I went over closer to him. I could see he did not flinch away. I could sense Bill inside on his bed, maybe dreaming already, while his father, a dream figure, stood near him out in the dark. Ed was not a tall man, but he was taller than me, and I got so close I could see the dark grey stitching in his jacket. I put out my two arms, and held him gently at the elbows. He seemed to hang his head a moment, and then lifted it again.

'I'm sorry, Ma,' he said.

229

'That's all right, Ed,' I said.

He pulled away from me. 'Wretched' was the word that occurred to me. The saddest man on earth.

Then he was gone.

Sixteenth Day without Bill

Bill liked to sit out on the porch alone, playing the guitar, aged sixteen. It was the remnant of his musical ambitions, maybe. I didn't pay much heed to it, till he sang one day a song about the Cuyahoga River catching fire, from all the gas and oil and trash in the water. I sat up then and listened. I can almost hear it still, if I sit quiet enough. *Burn on, big river . . .*

Bill, sprawled across the chair, one boot thrown up on the rail, head back, eyes closed . . . All he was missing was the cigarette in the corner of his mouth, to be the image of his grandfather Joe Kinderman.

Unobjectionable.

If he began in wordlessness, he ended in it too, but only the general wordless condition of the teenager. Age ten, he was full of a beautiful intimacy. Age fourteen, he began a long retreating walk into silence. As a child, he was like the library of Alexandria, full of stories and rare items. Then life seemed to burn most of that away, page by page. I never knew, and still don't, if there was anything I could have done about it. Maybe it was just growing up. Travelling light as a man. But I felt something was being traded, word by word, till there were no words, only a handful anyhow.

He tensed up. His muscles hardened and pulled on his bones. He lived in his private mind, but I didn't know what he kept there, because the door was bolted. I didn't get noisy, I didn't bang on it, clamouring to be let in. I thought, I knew it was what they call a phase. He was going to grow through it, and eventually reopen that door, and step out into the light, bathe in it. I was absolutely sure of that. The reason was, he was a person so deserving of love. His beauty even as a child had turned into another sort of beauty. Mr Dillinger, who liked to take photographs, took one of Bill, that I have inside beside my bed. It was the day he was going to catch the army bus in Bridgehampton, to go down for training in Georgia, like his father before him. There were about a dozen boys on that bus, from the district, just as before, but a new generation. Mr Dillinger came by with his fancy-looking camera. He didn't even pose Bill, he just took a snap, as Bill stood in his uniform, drinking coffee by the draining board. The light of Bridgehampton sits on his face, the salty strange potato-field light of Bridgehampton. Bill's home, his native place. An American in America. A child in my heart. He is just lifting the old blue cup to his face, it's got halfway there, eternally. He's going to drink from it, without thinking. Just a cup of coffee. He knows nothing about the desert where he is going, to fight for his country. He has used that exact phrase, just seconds before, putting me back to my father's old sitting-room in Dublin Castle, and Willie making the same fateful declaration. That's how it begins, and it is there in that photo. There is no photo for how it ends.

When he finished high school, Mrs Wolohan came over to me and said she would be happy to help with college fees. She said it would be her privilege. This is her way of doing a great favour without attaching any burden to it. Bill did have half a thought that he might like to join the Forest Service. He had read somewhere that away off in the national parks they had stations where men and women watched for fires, and studied the life of the forests. Mr Dillinger had spent many hours with him out on the porch when Bill was a child, telling him about the Native Americans, and all the things that interested Mr Dillinger. So all this must have been in Bill's head. So in an odd way, his imagination was filled with scenes of the wilderness not unlike his father's had been, but from another source.

You had to have a qualification in forestry to do that work, and the college in upstate New York was expensive, far beyond my means.

So that thought was in there, in his private mind maybe even, but there was other stuff too. He liked to drink beer with some friends of his over on Sag Turnpike, children mostly of the people there. Mr Nolan told me he had begun to see Bill over there, because that was the stomping ground for Mr Nolan's binges.

One night Bill brought a girlfriend back. He asked me was it all right if he slept on the couch, and she could take his bed. She was a slim, small girl, called Stacy. The first night, I heard them laughing in the small hours. I didn't think he was spending much time on the couch, but I didn't say anything. I must confess I was bothered by Stacy, because she would never speak to me. Maybe I seemed so old to her, I wasn't worth the trouble. I just didn't know. She came in and out of the house, and though she ate my cooking, I remained invisible to her. Mr Nolan knew her father, a gardener, 'best gardener round here bar myself', said Mr Nolan. Then I got to know her father, for a few moments, because we stood together in the courthouse, while Bill married Stacy. He just did it, suddenly. There wasn't one scrap of preparation. They went away to Las Vegas for a week, honeymooning. I had been happy to pull a few dollars together for him.

It was a time of some confusion. He bought a cheap bed for his room, and it just about filled the entire space. Stacy moved in there with him, and the house vibrated with their conversations, and their silences too. He got a job at the gas station, and all talk of college and forests ceased. Most confusing of all, most desolating, was I had no means to talk to him. He was like a shadow of the child I had known. I couldn't read his face, and just to confess it privately here, I was hurt, immensely, immensely. I was raw with hurt, day after day. It felt like I was dying. It felt like a sickness. I wanted him so much to go out upon the world, as the man he was. To flourish, in America. I thought he had a good chance to have a life without fear. I thought he had a good chance to enjoy some sort of victory over fear. Because the heart of him was good, I was sure. I never stopped thinking that. I never stopped loving him.

One evening about two years ago he came home on his own. His overalls were painted as always with oil, his hands were blackened by it, where he had wrestled with equipment maybe, I didn't know. He came into the kitchen where I was baking, and stood there. Usually he would go on to the WC, where he had a bottle of stuff that washed his hands clean. But he didn't go on there, he just stood, becalmed. In the corner of the kitchen was his guitar, propped up. He hadn't played that for a long time. He hadn't sung for a long time, the songs had died away into the general silence. Sometimes it had felt like everything had died away, everything I thought had significance, including my own strange history. Maybe, I had begun to think, I am near death. My story is dying in my mouth. I was eighty-seven years old, after all. I knew I was very old, because I hadn't bought new clothes for about ten years. I don't know why I thought that was a sign of great age, but I did. So that was a young, young man, spare of frame, with maybe a few beers in him, standing in the twilight near an old, old dame. The two of us, in some sort of present moment I didn't understand, just as I had not understood any moment really for a long time.

'So I guess I'm getting divorced,' he said.

'Bill,' I said. 'That's awful sad news.'

'Well,' he said. 'I guess there's nothing to be done about it. She don't love me no more.'

'Why don't you wash your hands, Bill, and sit down, and we'll talk this whole thing through?'

'I guess,' he said. He didn't go into the WC, he washed his hands at the sink, with the carbolic soap I kept there, for scouring things. I suppose he was scouring his hands, scouring generally speaking. I knew suddenly something about him, at last, even if it was such a sad thing. The thing I knew was that he had loved Stacy. He didn't even weep for her, he was well beyond mere tears, but I could sense his suffering in the very curve of his back, the very slowness of the gesture of washing his hands.

Then he sat down as I had bid him, and I made him a cup of tea, with due ceremony. He talked about things, for the first time in years. He said he was very sorry he never had a father, though he knew his father had had his own troubles. He said he just didn't know what to do with his life,

235

he didn't know where to put his feet, as he phrased it. The boy I had known, I gradually saw, was quite intact inside this man. The true beauty of him was, he was no hero to himself. He had no opinion of himself, and therefore he was entirely without bitterness. I don't know how I had interpreted his silence those previous years. I think I had committed the sin sometimes of thinking the worst of him. I think I had. It was a very great and serious sin.

Like other young men who don't know where to put their feet, I suppose, he decided to enlist in the army. I tried to keep calm when he told me. I tried to believe it was a good idea. But my mind was shouting out Ed's name. If I had thought it would do any good to get down on my knees and beg him not to go, I would have. But, if I didn't know much about the world, I knew Bill. By the end of the year the war had come to the desert, and so Bill went there.

He went off with Mr Eugenides' book in his pocket.

What he found, by the few small things he told me, was not Homeric. Whether it was heroic, I don't know. I am sure it was, in part. I would like to say it was, for Bill's sake. Like Willie before him, I know Bill loved his platoon. He loved his captain. But it sounded like a very curious war, to me, back home, in Bill's few letters. Vietnam, which had hollowed out my son, was protracted and seemingly endless, and when it did end, ended in what they called defeat. If Willie had survived the First World War, he would not have been thanked at home for his efforts. Even though Ireland was a victor in the war, Willie and his like were banished from thought, in the upshot. He was part of his father's world, of loyalty and empire, and all that passed away. So it is possible to come home unthanked, even in victory. How much worse for the boys of Vietnam, who came through ceaseless slaughter and defeat, only to be spurned and scorned at home. That was what put Ed into the mountains, partly. I am sure of that.

Bill's desert war was short, victorious. But he came home stunned, like a calf in the slaughterhouse. In the slaughterhouse, they drive a bolt into the brain of the animal. There is a moment when the calf balances between life and death. I mean, it is neither alive nor dead. Perhaps its short time in the meadow streams before its eyes. All the particulars of a life, human or otherwise. The unnoticed, myriad, unimportant parade of images, not prized in particular by anyone else, but surely beloved of God.

He did not speak about it, not a word. He did say some things to Mr Nolan, whom he regarded as a man he could trust, in some ways as a father figure, or the best approximation of one. Mr Nolan in turn told me in great confidence what Bill had confided. He said Bill had seen the oil-wells burning, he had seen the desert set on fire. He had seen the enemy soldiers fleeing in a great convoy, defeated, trying to get home across the ruined landscape. Thousands upon thousands in cars and trucks. The sight had so terrified him, Mr Nolan said, he no longer understood the meaning of the word 'victory'. The defeat of the enemy seemed to Bill like his own defeat.

'I wish I could say I didn't understand what he meant,' said Mr Nolan. 'But I did.'

He spoke with his own private sadness. Mr Nolan had been unwell for some time. Dr Earnshaw had sent him down to the hospital in Brooklyn, where he knew a special-

237

ist he could recommend. It hadn't been good news, I knew, because Mr Nolan was famishing week by week, thinning and thinning.

It was early morning, the birds of Bridgehampton were singing to beat the band, as always seeming indifferent to us, to our suffering. And there was a great deal of suffering in that little room where Mr Nolan lay. Up to this point I may safely say I revered him, I loved him, in that simpler way of friendship, where everything more or less is known, accepted, and for the great part rejoiced in. A person who has attributes that excite in you a continuous desire to see them, who, on coming in through your front door, seems to create in you a strange satisfaction, may be deemed a friend, and the devil take the reason. My friend then, Mr Nolan, lay within in his room, as was usual now, with his laboured breathing, my own footsteps already like the beginning of a conversation. *Where everything more or less is known.*

On his little battered radio, with the perished tape and the grubbied-up knobs, could be heard indistinctly the news, a dry report on the burning of the Kuwaiti oilfields . . . They had not ceased to burn just because my Bill was gone out of them.

I must have made some slight clatter coming in, because Mr Nolan woke, his throat in the first instance full of a dreadful spittle, which he had to clear with a horrible effort.

He looked like death, like Mr Death himself. In the usual gloom of his bedroom the boxes and whatnots of his life were ranged about him as always. Here was a man who had never entirely moved in, anywhere in his little series of abodes, the little series we all have a version of, in this restless country, where it is so easy to move, and oftentimes so troublesome to stay still. Cardboard boxes he had hauled about with him, and had thrown in here over thirty years ago when first he came to Bridgehampton, bringing his grey-looking skin, his ruined straw hats in all weathers, and his much-valued friendship into my life. The boxes that maybe held clues to this mysterious man, who had alighted on Bridgehampton like a storm bird so blown about by the storm that it no longer knew its own history, the name of its own species.

'Oh,' he said, a sigh reeking of silence, of being alone, and thinking, as if I had been in the room all along, or was not in the room even now, 'and so we come to the moment I have been dreading all these years, and knowing it would come, and sometimes wishing an automobile might run me down before I would have to tell you. I would almost ask you to hold my hand, Lilly, so I can adjudge the precise moment you draw back from me. What I am going to tell you will not please you.'

He stopped for about two minutes, just stared into space, his mind maybe gathering his story, I don't know. Even the birds had gone quiet outside, because the sun had crept up willy-nilly, crossing the flooded bays, touching the rich houses, and this little house, inexpensive and bleached under its few trees, the sunlight slowly slowly trying to rub it out, but rather hopelessly, like a schoolchild with a dirtied page. Everything here was holding on, against the efforts of the childish sun. Nothing more so than he. How old was Mr Nolan now? Probably in his late eighties, and yet up to a few weeks ago he had been working as always, clearing the gutters for Mrs Wolohan, shimmying up roofs to fix shingles as if he was a very sprite of shingles.

'The first day I ever came here, looking for you . . .'

'Looking for me?' I said. 'How so, looking for me?'

Old fears rushed back. Even after all these decades the very thought of anyone 'looking' for me put terror back in my heart, if the terror had ever left it, and wasn't just there like a pile of kindling waiting for a spark.

'I was looking for you, Lilly, if no longer under instructions indeed to find you, and the moment of finding you, which so happened to be for the third time, coincided with the moment I wished to be done with everything that had brought me that far, and, and of course I should have told you then, but.'

Then nothing for a few moments.

'In America,' he said, 'everything is possible. Everything is both true and untrue in the same breath.'

It is possible that no one can tell you anything that you don't already know. The brain, some part of the brain has picked up the information already, but not the 'top' brain, not the bit that thinks it knows things.

'The old gun-case there,' he said, 'you see? The old black one. Yes. Lift out the gun, it's not loaded, and do you see the little door in the velvet there? Yes, yes, put your hand in there, you'll find them, photos and clippings and letters and documents and such things. Yes, yes. Fetch them here. Lay them out on the bed.'

I did so, with strange obedience. I didn't even have the papers on his coverlet when I recognised one of the photos. It was an old photo of Tadg in the long ago, in his Tan uniform, maybe that very morning he had joined up. Why did Mr Nolan have that? How did he have it? I did not even have it myself. There were newspaper clippings about

240

Tadg's murder in Chicago, an awful photograph of him lying up against the museum wall in a great welter of blood, and there was a letter with the letterhead of one of those American 'Irish' societies, with shamrocks and banners and harps and all. The letter was typed and it was addressed to someone called Robert Doherty. I glanced through and it was obvious even to me that it was a letter of instruction, telling this Robert Doherty to go and kill the traitor Tadg Bere, and telling him where Tadg might be in America, and they had intelligence from sympathetic places, port workers in New Haven, policemen here and there, and the letter also included details about myself, and that I was to be killed also, and the letter writer expected to have photographs of both of us when the post allowed.

I looked up at Mr Nolan. I was in great perplexity and indeed he didn't look any better. His face, already wracked by pain, had a further icing of pain on it.

'Do you see what it is?' he said.

'What is all this stuff?' I said.

His face looked like it was ticking, like a clock. The clock had lost its hands long since, but somewhere in the old face there was a ticking, or a whirring, like the works gathering for its chime. Perhaps I was so sensitised now, so alert, I could actually hear the blood pulsing through his neck. The old heart wearying itself with a last weariness, a final effort. Truth is everything. We do not know it, we do not know how to get it, we do not have it in our possession, God will slap it on us like a police warrant as we arrive breathless at the gates, it is entirely beyond us, truth, bloody truth, but it is everything.

He did speak, but with all the charm and horror of a death rattle.

'I am Robert Doherty,' he said.

'The man who killed my husband?'

'I am that man. Lilly, they knew you were in America even before you got here on the ship. Our organisation had a cable through, and me primed to do the work before ever you set foot on land. And then Chicago, though it did take a while to track you down. Your real names were on the ship's manifest, but I couldn't find out where you had gone after that, and I thought you were going to get away with it. But then I thought you might try to link up with relatives here, so I worked that angle, and your cousin Cullen, wasn't that his name, quite a well-known man in the lumber trade, I found him easy enough in Miami, and pretended to be a friend, and sure enough he'd had a letter from the old policeman your father that had reached him late, because it had gone to an old address in New York, and in his innocence he told me you had a second address to try in Chicago, and he was very distraught that he hadn't been able to help you, and I said, ah sure, no bother, I'll do what I can for them. And then, and then, the business in the gallery. Then I went up to Cleveland after to kill you, Lilly, when I found out you were there, and that wasn't easy, because no one on earth knew where you were, until your own father wrote to the police in Chicago, and asked if they knew the whereabouts of his daughter Lilly Dunne alias Grainne Cullen, and he was very concerned about you, naturally, with Tadg Bere dead. And I had a good contact there among the detectives, and he was in touch with me, and said you might be in Cleveland, your name had turned up there, but I lost heart for the job when I saw you again. In Chicago I had had a clear chance to shoot you, as I had been bid, but had not taken it. And I was even less able that second time. You in your nice dress and as pretty as Bette Davis.'

My brain was whirring, my compassion for him curdling in my breast, like lemon dropped into milk, and I was about to go and leave this wretched man, but I knew one thing in my confusion.

'You should have killed me,' I said. 'You had no right to my friendship all these years. You took away my life when you took him anyhow. I should kill you now. If I had strength in my hands I would do it.'

'I'll be dead in a day anyhow. The doc just told me. He wanted to bring me into hospital, but I told him, never you mind. I have the little morphine pump going, do you hear it? He fastened it to my breast somehow. Oh yes. The nurse will come shortly to watch with me. Kill me if you want. I am so sorry, Lilly. So sorry. Please, please forgive me. We thought we were doing good for Ireland. When I saw you I could not harm you. I changed my name and my history. I never forgot you. And I went and had a life of sorts automobile-building in Detroit, and married and then when my wife died I didn't know what else to do with myself, I came up here and found you, and decided to – what? – nest near you. Make a stop in the long trek. I always felt so bad about what I did. I was trying to make it up to you. I know that's ridiculous, all things considered, ridiculous, ridiculous, in a ridiculous world. The young know nothing, or worse, less than nothing. But I didn't know what to do, and I always meant to tell you. And then bit by bit, I loved you. And then I could not tell you. Forgive me.'

'No,' I said, 'I cannot do that. I curse you.'

And then I did turn about, and then I did go out, and leave him.

My instinct was to stay with him, to assist at his going. It shocked me that such an instinct was so deep, so independent of a righteous anger, even of hatred. My heart, in some strange fashion, bled for him, as his own body bled. I knew his whole lower regions were destroyed, I knew he suffered monumentally, and that the borders between his intestine and upper body had so broken down that he had endured little bouts of faecal vomiting, a very terrifying and monstrous betrayal of the body, when the very shit itself comes out through the mouth. I knew what he was suffering, I knew what he was in essence, but now I knew more, and I could not stay. I did not think I would have to apologise to God for it. I would expect God to understand. Yes, I would.

The nurse, a beautifully turned-out Jamaican woman I knew from the market, was just driving up in her battered sedan. She was round, shining, and wrapped in all the colours of the West Indies. I mustered the shadow of a smile. She gave me an infinitely cheery greeting. Happy in her work. Ushering out the souls.

Did I really understand what he had told me? It is days and days after now, long after, and I am not sure I understand him even now. He had been young, we were young, Tadg and myself. I do not to this day know what Tadg did in his police work. There may well have been terrible crimes against his own soul. Of course. A killer perhaps, a young killer, in his own country in his own time. Not without guilt, dark guilt. Maybe the stories about the Tans are all true, I fear they might be. Dark lads. One story I read in a book, that gave me pause, thinking of Tadg, long after he was dead, a Crossley Tender on the move near Gort, a woman at a doorway with her baby, shot for the sake of cruel cruel devilment as the lorry passed, the bullet passing through the child into the breast of the mother, so that her family rushing from the cottage interior found them both slain on the threshold. The threshold of a new country. My own country that is foreign to me. Mr Nolan required, instructed in a letter, to fetch about America and her neatly drawn states, for my husband, for the life of my husband, his little handful of years, and all the years of his future. Mr Nolan had just told me what he had done, he didn't need to tell me the story of it, because I knew it, I had been there, I had half-seen Mr Nolan approaching across the great entrance hall of the institute, for it had been he, half-seen half-sensed the approaching horror, I had plucked at Tadg's sleeve as he stared and stared at the picture 'of himself' as he had put it, the face of another man long ago, the fierce, folded, suffering face of Van Gogh, I had tried, tried to alert him to his danger, *no, no, just a moment, Lilly, just a moment*, and that dark figure approaching, unknown, blank, in a dark coat, in a dark hat, drawing something from the dark interior of the coat, something blacker than black, lustreless, blunt, a gun of course, and me not able to turn the tide of the story, *Tadg, Tadg, come away, come away, we are in danger, there is something, something terrible approaching, what is it?, come away.* And then that figure so close, so close in, intimate, like he meant to embrace Tadg, oh, just an inch from him, and the arm stuck into his side, and the enormous blast, the enormous blast of a gun in such a huge marble space, oh my Jesus, and Tadg falling immediately, like a cow in a slaughter yard, the bolt into the brain, the bullet into his side, catching him somehow, maybe whirling around in his body, skidding off bones, because the bullet did exit, I saw it smash into the wall, just missing the painting, bizarre, terrible, and that bleak dark figure, that young man with his letter of shamrocks and harps telling him, instructing him, go and find and kill Tadg Bere, folded somewhere into his pocket, and now the old photograph loose on Mr Nolan's bed, that young man . . . My deep dear friend of these last many years. Lying here destroyed by the devilry of his own pancreas. A story of misery and terror.

I am an old foolish woman. I had loved Mr Nolan just as well as I loved Tadg Bere, and even, to give him his due, poor Joe Kinderman. Murder everywhere, and blood, and the very shit of his own body coming up out of his mouth.

I stood on the sidewalk. Mrs Sanford's fields were all to my right, her potato plants showing themselves shining and green in the sunlight, a queer forest, a thousand bonsai trees.

If I had been cursing him, now I was cursing myself. Stupid, ancient, shrunken Irish cook that couldn't even abide by her just anger.

I would have to put revenge aside, lay it aside for the few hours it would require. When he died, when he perished, I would curse him then, I thought, in a great steam on the meagre little sidewalk outside his house, I would strike at his coffin, and wail, and wish him in hell, as was my duty as a loving and plundered wife.

But I knew I had to go back in, and assist the resplendent and shining nurse, who doubtless needed no assistance, and be there at his bloody side while he, my former friend, the murderer of my husband, died.

And he died that evening.

Seventeenth Day without Bill

It is a beautiful morning. Of this there is no doubt. I don't think God is mocking me.

I come full circle. I feel it in my bones. Just after waking, as I brewed up the tea, and wondered did I have the true desire to drink it, I stopped what I was doing, and put my two hands to my face.

When I received the phone call, asking me to come to the school, I had no idea what it was for. It was some years since Bill had attended, and it was a Sunday. Furthermore it was only nine a.m. But I went, dutifully enough. I wondered had they confused me with someone else, or had dialled the wrong number, and would be surprised to see me instead of the person they had in mind. I called a cab, and nice Mr Jensen drove me. He was giving out about all the new people in Bridgehampton, even though I suppose it gave him more work. He didn't like what had happened to the price of land. He said his own children would not be able to afford to build houses there. He thought the government should do something about it, but he didn't think they would. America was all for the rich now, he said.

It was the usual cab talk, soothing in its way. Change happens everywhere, and we could never be immune to that here. I was grateful for my niche. It was a beautiful morning, and I was inclined to optimism. I was sure in my heart that Bill would recover from his difficulties. I knew he was drinking far more than he used to. Stacy had rung me just the day before, saying he had come to her house, and had stood outside and shouted up at the windows. She had asked me if I could ask him not to do that. I thought I might ask Mrs Wolohan to revive the college plans, and see how Bill responded to that. With all that had happened, even so, I thought, well, he's young, and the heart recovers. All it needs is time, and people to be thinking about you. Somehow I could imagine him, manning a forest station, watching out for fires. The sunrise itself out there in the wilderness a sort of fire, the sunset a conflagration.

Nonsense like that. Comforting stuff. Delusional, I suppose.

They brought me down to the boys' lavatory. I am not sure if I was ever in a male urinal before. They had already cut him down off the cubicle door. The hook was absurdly low, as if placed for a young child, high school though it was. I marvelled in a strange way that he had managed to hang himself on that. His army tie had been cut from his neck, and he was lying on a stretcher. I asked had there been efforts to revive him, and the ambulance man said he didn't know. He said they had waited for me to come, but he had to get back as soon as possible, as there was a fire on the highway out past Southampton. There was a nice cop there I recognised from the town, and a nurse. The doctor had been and gone, apparently. All this I saw and registered nowhere except on the very top of my brain. Nothing sank in further than that.

He lay on the floor, slightly turned, his legs bent at the knees. He looked awfully young. Not as young as when he came, but young. I wondered had he been brought out of the mountains to anything good. I just did not know. I knew that I had loved him and would have gladly given my life for his, a thousand times over.

I suppose his face was altered by the way he had died, but I don't remember it like that. In my memory, his face is beautiful and soft, his hands with their long fingers lie open like the flower Honesty. There is no breath in his body but the eyes seem to be still looking at the world, as if by looking on even after death he might penetrate to its mystery.

There should always be rain for a funeral, or if the weather is to be dry, frost, and snow deepening spoonful by spoonful, although this would make the work of the gravedigger harder. Nowadays they have a little digger for that work. They made a cut into the earth about three by seven feet, very expertly. I imagine the men finished off the work with the spade, it was so neat and clean. Like lads up on a high bog in the Dublin Mountains, slicing the sods of turf with a precision that only the water-hen and snipe can see.

But that day – and long ago it seems, but really only the length of this strange 'confession' – the sun moved through the trees like water. The trees were solemn, full-leaved, and stately, and the sunlight poured through them. It might have been a liquid or a thing you could touch. Something you could take a portion of, weighing it out or cutting it, and add into a cake mixture. The sunlight moved through the trees like a gold wind. It was full of things, human things, whispers, old bits of talk, past matters, and the cancelled future.

There was a thin, inching wind. They were lowering his body down in its veneered casket with the oak lines painted onto the pine, the idea of a better wood onto the true and honest wood. He was going down into the earth. The sunlight poured through the trees like a liquid. His companions in the army had come out, and one of the young boys blew a bugle, and his sergeant unfolded the lovely flag and spread it over the mock oak, and down he was lowered by his sundered friends, and soon enough he was there, at the bottom of the hole, and they, after their appointed ceremony, slowly went away, to do whatever young soldiers do after a burial like that. I cannot say, I would not say. The sunlight moved through the trees, approaching the rim of the grave with its own simple gravity, as if God Himself had taken the form of sunlight and was timidly looking in, afraid of his own creation, to view the matter bare and unadorned, afraid of what He had done, or what He had let happen. The old trees shrugged in their absolute magnificence and luxury, and the boy who meant more to me than my own sere life was packed away like a store of potatoes into a potato pit, for which the cottager will never return.

Afternoon

I will go out now into the village and fetch my few and mortal messages. I have the house neat and tidy of course and it will be no trouble to Mrs Wolohan, and I am sure she will forgive me the slight untidiness of this body, lying completed and still.

It is only one last bit of a life that I undo. Lord, it is nothing, absolutely nothing. A year, or two.

I don't leave much. I have put such things as I value into a box, but who will want them I couldn't say. No one. I wonder if there might be anyone in Ireland who would want them, if I had an address. The photos of Ed and Bill and Joe, which might only seem unimportant to someone else, even a relative. The letter from my father about Maud, and the three letters from Annie, sent in the 30s, the 40s and then the 1960s, the later one asking me to come and visit, but in characteristic fashion, supplying no address. And I thought it was better left, busy as I was, and settled with Mrs Wolohan, and believing, oh believing in the ancient adage to let those sleeping dogs lie. But Maud and Annie and Willie and my father never left me anyhow. There is never a day goes by that we don't drink a strange cup of tea together, in some peculiar parlour-room at the back of my mind. Then there are Ed's army papers and suchlike, and Bill's letters, and both their drawings from school, Bill's drawing of the hanged man that so upset his teacher Miss Myers.

I suppose all will be bagged up and set in the trash. At last Mrs Wolohan will have her little house back. God bless her for her beautiful and infinite patience.

I am thankful for my life, infinitely. I am thankful for my father, my sisters, Tadg, Cassie, Joe, Ed, and Bill. To take your own life used to be a mortal sin, so mortal that the priest would not let your body lie within the boundaries of the graveyard. It very likely still is. But that is all the guesswork of mortal men. No one should say they know God's mind, you cannot speak for God. I confess it is a little while since I made my once customary journey to Our Lady of Poland church in Southampton, to make my confession to the nice Polish priest there. It is a long long while, in fact.

But now I have made my confession here. Let God weigh it up, and see what must be done with me. I am taking the risk of going before I am called. I wish to present myself early at St Peter's gate.

I fancy just up the track inside the gates will be a figure waiting, and that by the agency of God's mercy I will be let through. I wish, I wish to walk forward hurriedly to that figure, to embrace him again, just as, standing that first day in my house, he once to my astonishment embraced me.

Night

Mr Eugenides, who bears the cleanest face in Christendom, was deeply solicitous, as only a man can be when he has married his public to his private face, which as always was discreet, and in the same moment sincere.

'You will be sorry and weary,' he said, in his eccentric phrasing, 'for a long time. Believe me, Mrs Bere, I do know. My own father was lost in the fighting in the Peloponnese, ah, ah, many years, many years ago. Sorrow, sorrow! The sorrow of countries, and our own private souls. Never grows lighter.' And indeed as he spoke I caught a full measure of his sorrow. It mingled and danced with my own.

'Thank you, Mr Eugenides,' I said.

And with an elaborate eloquence of gesture he smoothed at his smooth counter, with both hands, as if he might soothe the lost tree itself it was made of, and nodding his head presidentially as he did so.

And I told him I was not sleeping well, and ought I go to Dr Earnshaw for a proper prescription? But Mr Eugenides would hear nothing of it, and he found on his computer evidence of a recent script for me, and he proposed to add to this, or 'stiffen' it, as he said, whatever he meant by that, he hardly intended it to mean like putting additional spirits in a drink. But at any rate then he would take no money, would have nothing to do with the bills I fetched from my handbag, as I thought I must, since I had not the intention to pursue the pills on my insurance – but no, no, he would have nothing of it, he pressed on me a half-dozen cards of sleeping pills – 'Samples anyhow, Mrs Bere,' he called them, which I don't think they were, judging by their pristine appearance. I left the shop with his consoling voice behind me and the little set of pills in my bag, splayed out loosely among the old lipsticks and compacts, like a strange hand at cards.

My road home seemed all the more vivid to me as I wended along it. The trees with their leaves crackling in the breeze, the little parsimonious vistas of yards and shining cars, and then the generous vistas of budding marshland and the lacy trim of the sea on the horizon. Nothing was wrong with it, nothing was wounded. The road where I had often walked, content enough, where Bill had driven along so often in his beat-up car, his windows open and his music burgeoning out, a kind of gipsy in this composed world.

I came in my gate. The sea sat out on the beach like a thousand patients at a surgery, still, vexed, worrisome. It was so late in the afternoon that the world, like the shops soon in the village street, was closing. Colours were being picked up from the landscape and the seascape, the brighter blues, the ribbons of inexplicable yellow sitting out on the water, the thousand nesting places of the highlights caused by the sun. But the sun was falling away under the table of the world, like a drinking man. All the plucked colours of the landscape it had gathered into itself, it was a fire for consuming them, it was doing something very violent and terrible, off there in the distance. Now my flowers also burned in their beds, as if reluctant to give up their fantastical plumage. The dark would soon tear that away also, erase maybe for the last time all my tiny victories over soil and salt wind. It would pull away their colours, and then the colours of the struggling lawn, and then my door, my walls, my roof, pull all the colours away, and the colours of my heart with them.

I stepped in the door and stood in the hall, a stranger at last, as if I had never been there before. Indeed it looked bigger and wider, and for the first moments I was taken by confusion. I was staring at things I knew well, and did not know at all. The further door into my kitchen was open, and I could see the sea-light spread like a new plastic paint on the Formica table. There was something beautiful about it, beautiful, vivid, and strange, and I knew in that instant that a person could be truly happy there, all its tinny accoutrements ranged about them, and that I myself had been that privileged person for a long long time. It seemed to me that this new strangeness was the fashion of my dwelling saying goodbye. It knew what I intended and was embroiled in its own necessity for courtesy. I knew, I exulted in the fact that when I was done, there would be something so slight lying there in the dress I wore. That the infinite gap between two points, in this instance being alive and being dead, that the mathematicians tell us cannot be closed, would be closed. I would not have any distance at all to go to nothing.

But still I stood there. This old lady who intended to take her own life with Mr Eugenides's little pills. Something other than the dark was convening beyond the kitchen, marking the darkening window glass, was it even an army of the fog, legions upon legions rising up from the surface of the sea, exhausted soldiers finding again their strength, their fabled lives, and coming onto the beach of Bridgehampton, to take it in a rightful conquest? I did not know. I felt I would never know anything again, I was not in any way dismayed by the feeling. I was absolutely in cahoots with that moment, because contained in it I sensed both my disappearance and my queer victory. I carried Bill in my breast, and now instead of it being a stony weight that would kill me, crush the last breath from me, it was something again entirely, a lightness, a veritable possession, as if I was a little cart for him, to carry his lightest of souls into heaven. I stood there, an utterly old, ruined, finished woman, and the breath was taken out of me, but not by grief or human vengeance. The peaceful darkness filled the kitchen, crept into the kettle to make a nest for darkness, crept into the sugar tin and the baking trays, played in the curves of the ladles and the big mixing spoons, touched everything, peering at everything, even into those cancelled spaces no one sees, the tops of cabinets and the farms and asylums of dust that lie under fridge and cooker. And the darkness was so dark that it looked to me like light, though it wasn't, it was a dark I understood well enough, it was the insides of something, like pips, like kernels, hard poems and items of God that God keeps his own counsel on, keeps secret and marvellous, almost selfishly, greedily, but who can blame Him? The darkness enfolded on itself, like a fog made miniature, it turned and turned and advanced, and framed suddenly in great clarity and lovely simplicity, a creature dancing, dancing slowly, its collar studded with glass jewels, glinting darkly, dancing, dancing, the long, loose-limbed figure of a bear.